Peter Whalley
OLD MURDERS

MACMILLAN

ISBN 0 333 37154 2

First published 1984 by
MACMILLAN LONDON LIMITED
London and Basingstoke
Associated companies in Auckland, Delhi, Dublin,
Hong Kong, Johannesburg, Lagos, Manzini, Melbourne,
Nairobi, New York, Singapore, Tokyo, Washington,
and Zaria

Typeset in Great Britain by
WILMASET
Birkenhead, Merseyside

Printed and Bound in Great Britain by
ANCHOR BRENDON LIMITED
Tiptree, Essex

1

Starting on the top floor, the demolition crew had gone through the block like a swarm of locusts. Bathroom fittings, doors, window-frames, light fittings, copper piping had all been extracted. Oxyacetylene torches had cut away the metal railing that ran down the emergency stairs. The lifts had been dismantled and their mechanism carefully removed.

It was an act of destruction so thorough that it made the vandalism that had plagued the flats for the past seventeen years seem puny by comparison.

Naughton Point, as this particular block was known, was one of four such buildings constructed in Gowling in the mid-sixties. They were to accommodate those displaced by the town's slum-clearance scheme that had cut a swath through the tight terraces surrounding the once prosperous cotton mills. It had been a bold plan promising a brave new world; never mind that a majority of those being moved didn't want to go; or that the four spanking new blocks waiting to receive them were built on a reclaimed refuse tip that, as time would tell, hadn't quite settled.

It was proposed that the blocks be named after the town's first mayors.

'There can be nothing more fitting,' claimed the then leader of the Labour Council, 'than that this town should enter a new age by paying tribute to the men who gave us the old one.'

Thus the flats became Naughton Point, Meynell Point, Crag Point and Fothergill Point. And were notorious within a month of their being occupied, tarnishing for ever the names of the men they had been intended to honour.

Initial problems had been to do with dampness and condensation. Later ones were to do with people. The spirit that had made the humble terraced streets into communities, with codes of behaviour and censure for those who broke them, had evaporated into the air that whipped chillingly along the open balconies of the flats. The grassy surrounds that had been so appealing in conception soon resembled the tip from which they had originated. The concrete walls were stained on the outside and grew mouldy within. Lifts broke down with monotonous regularity. Light-bulbs disappeared. Landings and staircases became no-man's-land into which people were uneasy about venturing after dark.

There were attempts at remedies: tenants' associations, caretakers, community festivals. The rot was slowed for a year or two. Till it was found that the buildings were suffering from differential settlement.

'All new buildings settle to some degree,' explained the county surveyor. 'Which is all right as long as they do so uniformly. The trouble with Naughton Point and Meynell Point in particular is that they're settling in a lopsided manner.'

'No bloody surprise, is it?' was the general opinion. 'They're only held up by a load of old rubbish.'

Cracks appeared in walls and along balconies as the concrete sinews of the buildings shifted imperceptibly. The top two floors of Naughton Point were declared uninhabitable and their lucky inhabitants rehoused.

Vandalism increased and went unchecked. There was no point in trying any more. If the flats were basically unsound then who could point the finger at their inhabitants for being less than immaculate?

It was the beginning of the end for Gowling's brave new world. The single word HELP was spray-painted across the topmost balcony of Fothergill Point. Finally the necessary money was found and a decision taken by the housing committee to go ahead and demolish was put to the full council and passed by a single vote.

Jinx Flats To Come Down was the banner headline in the local paper.

The tenants gave a collective cry of relief and even organised a celebratory party on the asphalt parking area that had long since covered the lawns between the four towers. Something of the missing community spirit came creeping back now it was known that they were getting out.

Naughton Point, being the worst affected, was to be the first to go. By early November, almost seventeen years to the day since the first tenants had moved in, the block was deserted, the area fenced off and demolition under way.

Once the shell had been picked clean, it was a matter of brute force to shake loose the walls and floors and then the reinforced concrete columns that had supported them. One floor at a time was brought crashing to ground level where the huge concrete chunks could be split into manageable segments, loaded up and

6

taken away. What remained of the top three floors was being worked on at ground level by a gang of four men, each wearing protective goggles and wielding a jack-hammer.

Though it was still early enough for there to be a touch of mist in the air, the men wore only singlets, kept warm by their own exertions.

Till one of them stopped and turned off his compressor. He stared, frowning in disbelief, at a fissure that he had made in the concrete on which he was working.

'What the hell . . . ?' he muttered. Then, because he couldn't be heard above the thunder of the other hammers, he went and tapped his colleagues on the arm. One by one they stopped their compressors until there was silence.

'Look at this.'

They looked at him curiously but could see that he was serious, even disturbed, and went to look at what he had to show them.

'There.'

There was a bone encased inside the concrete column. Not tightly held as with a fossil in rock but within its own cavity with room to be moved. Except that, as they could just glimpse, it was held in place by other bones.

'Jesus.'

'What is it?'

One of them took up his jack-hammer again and, with as much care as the clumsy instrument would allow, began to widen the gap.

'It's hollow!' shouted one of the others. 'See if it'll split!'

Obediently he hammered at the concrete in a line above and below where the fissure had appeared. The other men stood back, away from the flying particles, but didn't return to their own work; there was something here not to be missed.

Suddenly there was no more resistance and the head of the hammer had gone through. Its operator pulled back, fearful of damaging whatever might be inside, then began another line some six inches away from the one he had already made and parallel to it.

'It's coming!'

Another fissure appeared, then the whole surface fragmented, revealing the steel rods inside. Now using the hammer in short bursts, the man worked to prise off the lumps of concrete. It was another ten minutes of careful work before the whole of the cavity and what it contained was exposed, but it was clear long before then just what it was going to be.

'Christ,' said one of the men quietly.

'It's a skeleton,' said another.

It was of adult size, seemingly all there though with bones broken and displaced. The four men gazed in at it between the steel rods. Its eyeless sockets looked back, its jaw hanging open as though in protest that it should have been so rudely and unexpectedly disturbed.

2

Christian Lewis was sitting in the kitchen where Diane had left him, drinking coffee and reading the *Daily Telegraph*, when she got back from taking the children to school.

'Still here?' she said tartly.

'Yes . . .' he said, looking round as though in surprise. 'I seem to be.' And gave what he hoped was a disarming smile.

She didn't respond, except to tear yesterday's date off the calendar that was inscribed, 'With compliments, Holroyds Builders.'

'What's the weather like?' he asked.

'Go and find out for yourself.'

He gave a little laugh, knowing that she was right to goad him and that she loved him and that she was only, as usual, trying to keep him out of trouble with his employer. Who, as it happened, was her father and therefore his father-in-law, a situation that made him feel that he could take liberties and her that he should toe the line.

'All right,' he said, folding up the paper and getting to his feet. 'I'm going.'

'And not before time.'

'And it's no use trying to stop me. No use trying to tempt me with another cup of coffee or . . .' – more hopefully – 'by trying to get me back into bed for an hour . . .'

She ignored him and started on the washing-up. He put on his jacket and checked his pockets for wallet and pens and the packet of cigarettes that she didn't like him smoking in the house.

'Give Daddy my love,' she said. 'We don't seem to have seen him for ages.'

8

'I see him every day,' he reminded her.

'I mean socially.'

'He's a busy man,' he muttered, not wanting to hurt her by pointing out the truth: that he resented her father's patronizing attitude towards him and found it hard enough to bear at the office without importing it into his home. She, anyway, knew well enough the faint antagonism between them and strove gallantly to reconcile them.

He came up behind her and put his arms around her waist.

'I thought you were going?' she said.

'I am. Just thought I'd give you another chance to wish me happy birthday.'

'Happy birthday,' she said obediently. Then: 'Are you taking me out tonight?'

'Me taking you out?' he teased. 'I though *I* was the one having the birthday . . . !'

'You're also the one with the money.'

'Not very much,' he said. Then immediately regretted what he knew she would interpret as a sideways swipe at her father. 'Well yes, all right then,' he said lightly. 'Can you get a baby-sitter?'

'I'll try. What time shall I say?'

'Eight o'clock.'

She turned from the sink and, holding her wet hands wide so that they shouldn't mark his suit, gave him a kiss. Her mouth working against his took him by surprise and deflected him from his resolve.

'Why don't I ring the office,' he said. 'Tell them the car's broken down?'

The look she gave him told him that he had overplayed his hand. 'Why?'

'Go back to bed for an hour . . . ?'

'No chance.'

And she turned back to the washing-up. Though with a smile that told him she appreciated the fact that he still fancied her after nine years of marriage.

'Half-an-hour . . . ?' he offered, but now it was a joke without any real hope.

'Go on!'

And he went. Not wanting, in truth, to test his father-in-law's tolerance more than was necessary. He took the car from the garage and drove along the road of red-brick semis.

Thirty-eight. That had been the number on the cards waiting for him that morning, the hand-drawn ones from his children and the tastefully-chosen one from his wife. It wasn't all that old. He wasn't one to yearn for lost youth, having found more happiness in his marriage and his children than in all the uncertain relationships of his adolescence. And yet it nagged at him, knowing that it would be thirty-nine next and then forty. It was the feeling that he was getting older without getting any further.

He had gone to work for Percy Jordan eleven years ago, after university and a spell with a small practice in Bradford and before he had ever met Diane or known her to be Percy's daughter. He had gone brimming with confidence in his own promising future and had even, indeed, admired and been attracted by the pugnacious, entrepreneurial style of his new boss. It was only after his marriage that he had felt himself becoming patronized by Percy: no longer the employee to be judged on his merits but the son-in-law taking the easy route to the top of the family business.

So that he, in turn, had begun to despise Percy Jordan. What, after all, had he to be so self-satisfied about, this unqualified, pushy businessman who had simply been in the right profession at the right time? The right time being the late fifties and then the sixties when the country, and the North in particular, was enjoying a building boom with post-war prosperity demanding the rapid provision of better accommodation and the modernization of town centres. It was a theme on which Christian could wax eloquent for hours, particularly after two or three pints. Never mind the quality, feel the progress. The wartime system of building licences had been abolished in 1954: by the early sixties the whole country was tearing itself apart in a delirious rush for pedestrian precincts, tower blocks and all-weather shopping centres. It had been an architectural Klondike, with Percy Jordan well to the fore in the rush for gold.

From the start he had been quick to see the way the wind was blowing and had assembled a team of architects that could offer a package-deal to those local authorities hell-bent on redevelopment. On the strength of the expertise of the people he employed, Percy himself became regarded as an expert in housing and multi-storey car-parks. When the demand for both slackened with the arrival of the seventies, he went into swimming-pools, squash courts and leisure centres. His practice had continued to prosper as others, less nimble-footed, had floundered around him.

10

'If he ever starts designing fallout shelters,' Christian observed, 'then we've all had it. He can see what's coming two years before anybody else.'

Diane, sensing the change in his manner towards Percy, had taxed him with it.

'I don't know why you've suddenly turned against him. I don't honestly.'

'I haven't turned against him,' explained Christian carefully. 'I'm just saying that he's been lucky.'

'He's worked very hard.'

'Of course he has. But – let's face it – he's not that brilliant an architect.'

'Oh, and you are . . . ?'

'Compared to him, yes!' And then he added quickly, 'If I ever get the chance. I just wish he'd forget that I'm married to you. Just treat me like the rest of the staff.'

'It can't be easy for him though, can it?'

'No,' he had said flatly, wanting to leave it at that lest the matter should become a bone of contention between them.

'And he is successful,' insisted Diane.

'Yes, he is,' agreed Christian with a sigh. 'And if you want me to like him then I will.'

She looked at him, grateful for this but still puzzled by his criticism of a man she had been brought up to admire.

'It's just . . .' Christian had made a last attempt to explain, '. . . just that I sometimes get the impression that he seems to think that I married you . . . well, for the wrong reasons.'

'Well, I'll have a word with him . . .'

'No!' said Christian quickly. Then to his relief, saw that she was joking.

'. . . And I'll tell him that the *only* reason you married me was 'cause you're sex-mad and I wouldn't let you have it unless you made an honest woman out of me.'

'True,' said Christian. 'And d'you think he'll understand that?' So they had laughed it off and he had learned that it was a subject best avoided between them. Only occasionally – like today, his birthday – did he find it difficult to disguise his sense of frustration.

Driving to work, he was stopped by traffic-lights close to the town's new leisure centre on which he had been working for the last two years. It was now near completion, something which on most days gave him a reassuring satisfaction but which today only seemed to reinforce his feeling that time was passing and he was getting older.

From which he was suddenly distracted. He had gone to light a cigarette, then been caught as the amber came up, thrusting the match away in order to put the car into gear. Unfortunately it was not extinguished and flared up on the rubber matting at his feet. He went into a little, frantic dance, trying to stamp out the fire while maintaining control of clutch and brake. The car jerked and stalled. A horn blared out from behind him.

'Get knotted!' he said, knowing that the windows were safely closed. He peered around his feet, traced the thin wisp of smoke to the now spent match and restarted the car.

It was a farce, a small cock-up of his own making, that might have stood as a miniaturized version of the last ten years of his life. For there too he had tried to do two things at once – working for Percy and marrying his daughter – which had seemed reconcilable, even complimentary, but which had trapped him none-the-less.

He was now thirty-eight and several hours old. It was as though he had reached a small peak from which he could see his future stretching as a plateau before him. He would never become a full member of the practice. He would certainly never become senior partner in place of Percy. Even if the old, talentless, boorish despot ever did retire to spend his days tending geraniums and making (ill-designed) models with matchsticks, he would surely appoint Harper or Randall in his stead. Never mind that Christian was – in his own carefully considered opinion – the one best fitted to lead the practice into the nineties. The day that he had married Percy's amazingly lovely daughter had set his career in aspic. He had nothing to worry about in the normal way – he would be kept for life – but also kept in his place.

Coming on to the inner ring road, he caught sight of Naughton Point, now without its top three floors, and with its three doomed sisters, Meynell, Crag and Fothergill, standing forlornly around it.

Part of him – he couldn't help it – took a sneaking pleasure in this public confirmation of the worthlessness of his father-in-law's work. This had been one of Percy's showpieces in the early days, these four gaunt and weather-stained towers with the word 'HELP' still legible on one of them. He had landed the commission against fierce competition, had brought the whole show in on time and within its estimate, and had gone on from it to build a string of equally obnoxious buildings elsewhere. He had even received a small award from an architectural magazine – now deservedly defunct – for the modernity of the design and method of construction.

'I designed those flats for people to live in,' he had told Christian, refusing to consider that the demolition might be any reflection on himself. 'It's not my fault if the council let them to a herd of wild animals.'

Christian drove on towards the office not noticing the empty police-car standing beside the makeshift hoardings that surrounded the site.

The two constables it had brought were staring in through steel rods at the recently discovered skeleton. Around them the demolition men had got over their initial shock and were enjoying the mystery.

'I could take them bones home for my dog if nobody else wants 'em!'

'You probably can if nobody claims 'em within six months.'

The policemen conferred.

'Better let the station know.'

'It's going to have to be cut out of there though, whatever they decide they want to do with it.'

'We'll let somebody else worry about that.'

So there was a further hiatus. The demolition crew drifted reluctantly back to their other tasks. The two policemen radioed in and then mounted guard on the entombed skeleton until higher authority should arrive.

Had Christian been passing the site half-an-hour later, even he could hardly have missed noticing that something untoward was going on. The first police-car had been joined by another and by an ambulance. All work had again stopped except for the sound of a solitary jack-hammer.

More of the concrete was being wrenched carefully away and then the steel rods cut until there was space to extract the skeleton without doing further damage to it. It was eased out on to a stretcher with all the care that might have been afforded to a fully fleshed victim, covered with a blanket and taken away to the ambulance.

'Mortuary?' queried one of the ambulance-men.

The Detective-Inspector who had arrived to take charge of operations nodded. The victim even of an old murder (or accident as this might yet turn out to be) must be subjected to the same procedures as would await a body that was still warm with recent life. There would be a post-mortem, though one that in this case would reveal little about the contents of the stomach or the state of the heart and liver. Nevertheless, there would be hair and teeth and bones to be examined.

And just one other, single, small item of possible evidence that was spotted by one of the policemen as the bones were lifted from their hiding-place. It was an item that was placed in an envelope and then put into the Inspector's pocket.

The concrete sarcophagus would also be needed for forensic examination. It would later be wrapped in heavy-duty polythene and a truck with lifting-gear sent to collect it, but for the time being it remained where it was with a constable for company and a square of red ribbon around it to mark its importance.

The ambulance drove away quietly, without any siren or flashing lights. It would be foolish to pretend urgency with a body that had waited seventeen years to be brought out into the light of day.

3

The Hermitage did most of its business at lunchtime when it was a focal-point for the town's business and professional community. Or at least for that slice of it that couldn't face the afternoon without alcohol. It was a club, whose underground premises had originally been the cellars of Gowling's Victorian Cotton Exchange before that majestic building had been developed out of existence. Now only the cellars remained, offering alcoves and corners that enabled business to go on over the lasagne or Wiener schnitzel.

Christian had mixed feelings about the place but found himself descending its steps every lunchtime and paying its exorbitant prices. It was, he told himself, convenient for the office. Less palatable but probably more truthful was that it represented a world to which he was irresistibly drawn and in which he felt himself to have a rightful place, even if it was one that his father-in-law seemed determined to deny him.

One indisputable attraction was Pat behind the bar, blonde, beautiful and with a figure that went a long way towards justifying

14

the high prices.

'A glass of white wine,' ordered Christian, 'and when are you going to give me that phone number that I keep asking for?'

'What phone number's that?' she said, reaching for glass and bottle.

'Yours of course. How else are we ever going to have that passionate affair we keep talking about?'

He flirted automatically with no hope of success, and not knowing anyway how far he would welcome it if it ever came his way. Down in the bowels of The Hermitage sexual banter was the lingua franca, an alternative to small-talk about the weather.

Simon Neal, a lunchtime acquaintance and marketing manager to a hosiery firm, arrived at the bar beside him as Pat served him with a glass of wine. Simon was tall, prematurely balding and permanently tired.

'And a pint of lager for Simon, love, please,' said Christian.

'Cheers,' said Simon. Then to Pat: 'You look beautiful today.'

'Thanks,' she said, and punched the button on the lager pump.

'She looks beautiful every day,' said Christian. It came out without thinking, a recitation of the next line in a familiar litany.

Simon yawned and turned to Christian. 'Busy morning?' he asked.

'Would have been if I'd got in on time. As it was, they had to send somebody else out.'

Simon gave a little, admiring laugh, which encouraged Christian to go on and give him a full account of the icy reception that he had received from Percy that morning. Though in truth it had been a difficult moment which he could have done without. It had slipped his mind that he and one of the other assistant architects should have gone out first thing to inspect the green field site for the town's new hospice, Percy's latest catch. His late arrival had meant sending someone else in his place and a consequent reallocation of work around the office which had pleased no one. Percy had commented pointedly on Christian's time-keeping and been unmoved by Christian's muttered excuse that it was his birthday.

'So I had to get my head down a bit,' he concluded. 'Last-minute alterations to our wonderful new leisure centre.'

'I thought that that was just about finished?'

'It is. Only you know what these people are like. If they can't mess you about a bit they don't feel they're getting their money's worth.'

A critical view of their superiors was the common bond between Christian and Simon, though their situations were in other respects almost reversed. Where Christian felt his family connection with Percy Jordan to be working against him, Simon had remained unpromoted as his firm had brought in the sons and nephews of its directors over his head.

'The only way I'm ever going to get anywhere,' he told Christian, 'is if I divorce the wife and marry into one of their god-awful families!'

'I wouldn't bother,' had been Christian's reply. 'I tried it and look where it got me!'

They bought bar snacks and another round of drinks from Pat, then stood eyeing the crowd around them. There was a proliferation of suits and brightly patterned shirts. The women, who were in a minority, seemed on average much younger than the men; most were escorted, but there was the odd group that was exclusively female, come from an office and standing tightly together.

'I see the mafia's in,' said Christian.

Simon peered between the standing bodies and the fat stone pillars that supported the floor above.

'Over in their usual corner,' Christian directed him.

'Oh, I see,' said Simon. 'Yes.'

The most distant recesses of The Hermitage held its restaurant area; it was here that the group that Christian had indicated were gathered, half-hidden in one of the alcoves that were a feature of the old cellars. It comprised Percy Jordan and three of his cronies.

'Who's the one who looks as though he's having a permanent heart attack?' asked Simon.

'His name's Rees, Walter Rees,' said Christian, who had made quite a study of his father-in-law's circle. 'He used to be Chairman of Gowling Building Society.'

'Used to be?'

'He's retired now. They say he ended up with more money than the Society so now he's got them working for him!'

Simon laughed. They both continued to gaze at the elderly foursome, finding them, for the moment at least, an interesting alternative to Pat's figure as something on which to rest their eyes. Percy Jordan's near-bald head reflected the lighted candle that stood in the centre of the table. He was, as always, immaculate in

16

dark suit, white shirt and tie; none of his employees, including his son-in-law, had ever seen him in anything else. With Percy and the apoplectic Walter Rees were, Christian knew, Donald Tyson and Councillor Maddox, a man always referred to by his surname and whose first name remained a mystery. He was a Labour Party stalwart, a member of the Council and walked with a stick on account of his arthritis. Donald Tyson had been Chief Executive in the area's planning department prior to his retirement. During his first days with the Percy Jordan practice, Christian had designed an extension for Tyson's house. It had always intrigued him as to whether Tyson had been charged for it.

'Having another one?' asked Christian, pointing to Simon's near-empty glass.

'No thanks. Two's the limit or I'll spend the afternoon asleep.'

'And why not?' said Christian. 'Pat, my love, another glass of white vino when you've a minute.'

Today was his birthday after all. And what would it matter if he did fall asleep over his drawing-board? His father-in-law owned the firm: he would never be out of a job; nor, it seemed, would he ever be in one of the jobs that he wanted.

'Mr Lewis . . . ?'

Christian turned in surprise. A waiter, in waistcoat and bow-tie, had appeared at his elbow.

'Yes?' he said, slightly defensive.

'Mr Jordan says could he possibly have a word with you?'

'Oh. Oh, right, yes, thanks.'

The waiter waved a hand to indicate where Percy was sitting and retreated, leaving Christian to follow when he chose. Which wouldn't be until he had delayed for a few face-saving moments and finished the cigarette that he was smoking.

'Probably wants to buy you a drink for your birthday,' joked Simon.

'I doubt it.'

The cigarette was taking longer to finish than he had anticipated. Whatever disagreements they might have in private, it wouldn't do to appear rude towards Percy in public. Christian stubbed out the cigarette, muttered an apology to Simon and wove his way through the little groups of diners and drinkers towards the table in the alcove.

Was it cowardice or simply commonsense that made him criticize Percy when his back was turned, then act the respectful subordinate the moment that he was summoned before him? Or perhaps it went deeper than that and was a kind of schizophrenia; he despised Percy for his rotten buildings yet desperately wished to emulate his success and be able to afford a table for lunch instead of being stuck at the bar with the other malcontents.

As he approached the table, the four faces around it turned to observe him. Walter Rees did indeed look like a man suffering a permanent heart attack: his face was puce and the veins on his forehead distended. Beside him, Donald Tyson looked bleached white in comparison, a deathmask with the skull all but visible beneath the skin. Maddox, overweight and with hanging jowls, sat awkwardly, a man in the grip of pain. Only Percy seemed to have avoided the ravages of age: his skin was sleek, his moustache clipped and his eyes bright.

A bottle of Beaujolais stood, almost empty, on the table. Beside it was a smaller bottle of Perrier water for Percy.

Tyson was the first to speak to him. 'Good afternoon, young man.'

Christian gave a little nod and waited for Percy to give his instructions. But he seemed in no hurry, content that his dining-companions should have the chance to scrutinize his son-in-law.

'Is it you that's responsible for this sports hall monstrosity that we're all going to have to pay for out of our rates?' asked Walter Rees.

It was a joke and the others cackled in appreciation.

'Not entirely,' muttered Christian.

'A leisure centre,' corrected Maddox, the councillor.

'Not a thing we had a lot of in our day,' said Rees. 'Leisure. We certainly never had to build a centre for it.'

Which brought another chuckle round the table. Rees was evidently the humorist of the bunch. Certainly his fiery complexion betrayed a lifetime of expensive wining and dining.

But it was now Tyson's turn to offer a little badinage for everyone's merriment. He spoke slowly, his false teeth shifting as he did so.

'So how do you like working for your father-in-law, then?'

Percy raised his eyebrows, interested to see how Christian would deal with this one.

'Come on, you can tell us!' urged Tyson, and winked. His eyelids were heavy and lined like those of a lizard.

Christian, irritated at being thus put on show, threw caution to

18

the winds. 'I'd rather he was working for me,' he said.

Which provoked the biggest cackle of laughter yet as the three faces – one blood-red, one bone-white and one jowl-fringed – turned eagerly to see how Percy would respond.

But Percy was betraying nothing. He gave a sad little smile as though in recognition of an attempt at humour that had fallen flat and then said, 'All I wanted to say was that I won't be in the office this afternoon. Neither will Mr Randall or Mr Harper. We have a meeting.'

The practice employed a total of thirty-five people. Beneath Percy came, first, Randall, who was Chief Architect, then Harper, who was Principal Architect. Christian was one of a dozen or so Assistant Architects, though with a nominal title of Senior Assistant, which meant that, with Randall and Harper away as well as Percy himself, he would be in charge of the office.

'Doctor Bellish might be coming in to go over the projected estimates for the hospice,' went on Percy. 'But I'm sure that you can manage that, can't you?'

'I'm sure I can,' said Christian evenly.

It crossed his mind that the four ageing men huddled before him in their self-congratulatory coven might be said to have a vested interest in the building of a hospice, with at least three of them likely candidates for becoming its first customers. He doubted, though, that they would enjoy the observation and carried it with him back to Simon Neal at the bar.

In fact the first visitor with whom he had to deal that afternoon did, indeed, have death on his mind, but it wasn't Doctor Bellish or anyone else connected with the hospice. It was a policeman. He was in plain, even scruffy, clothes, and was in need of a shave.

Christian, summoned by the receptionist, went out to meet him amid the potted palms and chrome furnishings of the foyer.

'Detective-Inspector Charlton,' he announced himself, producing his identification.

'And what can we do for you, Inspector?'

Christian, law-abiding and middle-class, was intrigued rather than alarmed by the arrival of the law. And was in no way disappointed when Detective-Inspector Charlton went on to explain the reason for his visit.

'There's been something rather odd turned up in the middle of that demolition job that they're doing on Naughton Point. A skeleton to be precise. Seems it was sort of built into one of the concrete pillars or whatever you'd call them.'

'A skeleton . . . ?' echoed Christian in surprise.

'Yes. Now, I am right in thinking that you were the firm that designed the block, am I not?'

'Yes . . . oh yes,' he said. Then seeing the receptionist listening open-mouthed, he added, 'Would you like to come through to my office?'

Strictly speaking, it was Percy's office to which Christian led him, but there seemed little point in wasting police time in explaining that. He showed the Inspector to a leather armchair and closed the connecting door on a surprised-looking middle-aged lady, who was Margaret, Percy's private secretary.

'Mind if I smoke one of these?'

One of these was a slim cheroot, which Christian didn't mind in the slightest. He provided an ashtray and lit a cigarette for himself.

'This skeleton,' he asked, 'you think it's been there since the block went up?'

'Well, it certainly looks like it. Though we don't know anything for certain yet. I'm here to ask if you still have copies of the original plans for Naughton Point?'

'I should think so, yes,' said Christian, although it was before his time and therefore not something for which he could vouch. He leaned over to the desk and operated Percy's intercom.

'Margaret?'

'Yes?' He didn't fail to notice the disapproval in her voice.

'Can you see if we've still got copies of the plans we did for the Naughton Point development? And if we have then bring them in here please?'

She didn't reply, which probably meant that she resented being ordered around by him but would go and look in the plan-files all the same.

Christian, intrigued by the thought of a skeleton coming out of a cupboard that was as much Percy's as anybody else's, tried to elicit more from the Inspector but without much success. He sat sucking at his cheroot and would say only that the post-mortem was being carried out at that very moment and that they hadn't yet identified the body or established a cause of death.

'In fact you haven't got very much to go on,' said Christian sympathetically.

'You can say that again,' agreed the Inspector.

Margaret appeared with a set of transparencies on which the

anatomy of Naughton Point was etched in black. She put them on the desk and went out without a word.

'Well done,' said Christian to her departing back.

'It's just that we want to pinpoint exactly where the body was,' said the Inspector. 'I wonder if I could take these away with me? I'd give you a receipt for them of course and make sure you got them back.'

Christian hesitated only a moment, assumed the mantle of authority and said that yes, of course, he could keep them for as long as was necessary.

The Inspector left, taking the plans with him; Christian reluctantly vacated Percy's office and returned to his drawing-board. He did little work, though, unable to concentrate until Percy should return and he would have the pleasure of telling him all about Naughton Point and the discovery of its gruesome inhabitant.

It was a pleasure that was denied him. When Percy did return, his first words cut short Christian's prepared speech at his first mention of their police visitor.

'I know all about it, thank you.'

'You do . . . ?'

'Yes.'

'About what they've found at Naughton Point?'

'The skeleton, yes.'

'Ah,' said Christian, deflated. He was also disappointed that he hadn't been able to witness Percy's first reaction on hearing the news. It might have been revealing.

Now there was nothing to be learned from his sombre visage as he led Christian into his office and pointedly opened a window to let out the lingering aroma of cigarette and cheroot.

'There's a receipt there for the plans. I said they could keep them for as long as necessary.'

'Did you?'

Irritated, Christian asked sharply, 'Well, should I not have done?'

'Oh yes . . . why ever not . . . help the police . . .' said Percy vaguely. Then, as though that matter could now be dismissed as over and done with he asked briskly, 'And what else has been happening in my absence?'

'Not a lot.'

'Then I'm sure you've coped very well.'

Christian drove homewards, slowing down as he passed Naughton Point, which had now taken on a mantle of mystery and even danger. Though there was no visible sign of it. No police-cars or mobile incident rooms. As far as he could make out through the gloom, the demolition had continued and another floor been removed.

His chance to tell the story to Diane didn't come until later. His children, Matthew and Samantha, greeted him on the doorstep with shouts of delight: 'Guess what we've done!' – 'Come and see!' And they ran before him into the kitchen, where there was a birthday cake covered in uneven icing and with 'To Daddy' piped round its edges. Genuinely moved, Christian hugged both the children to him.

'We thought there'd be too many candles so we've put Smarties on instead,' explained Diane.

'Lovely,' said Christian.

It was only after tea and when the children were having their baths that he had the opportunity to tell her his news.

'A skeleton . . . ?'

'Yes. Built-in as you might say.'

She was as astonished and curious as he had expected and he enjoyed sharing the story with her, telling her how and when it had been discovered.

'You don't think though . . .' She hesitated, frowning, and he guessed what she was about to ask.

'What, that it might reflect on Percy?' It was a thought that he had considered and then rejected as unlikely.

'Well, he did design the building . . . ?'

'Yes, but he didn't build it with his own bare hands. There must have been – what? – a hundred people involved in one way or another.'

In truth, it had entertained him earlier to wonder if Percy might have had a hand in the skeleton's being there. But it wouldn't have entertained Diane; it was for her sake that he now pooh-poohed the possibility.

'How will they ever find out anything?' she asked. 'I mean, it's so long ago . . .'

'Seventeen years.'

'So how will they ever find out who he was or how he died or who put him there? Surely it's hopeless after all this time?'

Questions which Christian couldn't answer. He muttered about the police having their methods and then wondered if, in fact, they did have any to meet freak cases of this kind.

'I believe they can tell a lot from the teeth,' he said.

Someone who would know more was Dennis Joiner. Dennis, a friend made through the squash club that Christian patronized, was himself a policeman in the CID. He had at one time, before Christian had known him, been a sergeant, then had been demoted for reasons that Christian had never heard mentioned. So that he wore the faintly cynical air of those who have been passed over and was always willing to pass on any juicy titbits that were going the rounds of the local nick.

Christian was on the point of ringing him when Diane said, 'Oh, and I'm ever so sorry, love, but I haven't been able to get a sitter.'

'You mean we can't go out?'

''Fraid not. And on your birthday as well. I tried everybody but they were all booked.'

He thought for a moment. 'Do you mind if I go out then?'

'No, you do whatever you want.'

Five minutes later he had arranged to meet Dennis and had booked a squash court in both their names. Talking to him, he had mentioned the Naughton Point discovery and been excited to hear him reply that, strictly between the two of them, he could tell Christian one or two things about the affair that were not generally known.

4

The question of the skeleton wasn't raised by either of them until the game was over. Dennis had won with ease. He was fitter and more determined than Christian, who held back from the kind of suicidal commitment that the game demanded. They showered and then went and sat on the bar where Christian bought the first round.

'You'd be surprised,' said Dennis, 'how much they can tell from the bones alone.'

'Like what?'

'Like sex, age, height. Even if there's only a single bone to go on it's sometimes enough.'

Around them other players were coming into the bar or leaving, some of the women still in their eye-catching shorts or tiny white skirts. Christian, although intent on what Dennis was saying, found his eyes following the bare legs as they moved past him. It might have been skeletons that he wanted to hear about; but the well-exercised flesh around him was proving a distraction.

'So what about this Naughton Point business then?' he asked Dennis. 'Have you heard anything about that?'

Dennis gave a little chuckle and nodded. 'I've done more than heard about it,' he said. 'I've seen the PM report.'

'The what?'

'The report on the post-mortem. It arrived before I came off this afternoon. There were a few of us had a look at it. It's not every day you get a turn-up like that.'

Christian had a drink and waited. He didn't want to appear too eager and knew that Dennis would be unable to resist telling him all he knew.

'Wasn't it you lot who designed those flats?' asked Dennis.

Christian nodded. 'Before my time though,' he said, wanting to dissociate himself as far as possible from such an architectural disaster.

'Hmm. Anyway the PM report . . .'

'Yes?'

'Said that it was the skeleton of a male, aged about forty-five. Dark-haired and probably about five-ten or five-eleven tall.'

'I see,' said Christian, doing a little sum. If the body had been in there for seventeen years then, had it survived, it would now have been sixty-two years old. But so what? Well, for one thing, that would make it a close contemporary of Percy Jordan.

'Any idea as to how he died? And how he came to be concreted into that block of flats for that matter?'

'Not a lot,' grunted Dennis. 'Apparently there was damage to the skull and to quite a number of bones but there's no telling how much of that was done after death. I mean the weight of the concrete on top of it must have been at least partly responsible.'

'So you're assuming that the body was taken to the site when the building was half-constructed and they'd got the wooden shutters up for that storey . . .?'

'Well, *they*'re assuming that, yes,' said Dennis, finishing his drink. 'I don't think they're too bothered about *my* opinion.'

'Then the body was forced in among the steel bars,' continued

24

Christian, wanting to have things clear in his own mind. 'Whoever poured the concrete in on top probably didn't even know it was there.'

'Another drink?'

Christian drained his glass and handed it to him. 'And they haven't identified it yet?'

'No. They're going to have their work cut out if you ask me.'

Which no one would, thought Christian, though not unkindly. He had a great affection for Dennis and his continual inference that he alone held the key to most of the country's unsolved crimes if his superiors would only recognize the fact.

'So what happens now?' he asked.

'Everything. The press'll have a field-day, we'll all be on overtime and my chief'll be out to make a name for himself. While yours truly does the donkey work.'

And he strode off towards the bar.

The more he heard, the more Christian was intrigued by this new and crowning infamy which had sprung from Naughton Point's dying moments. His own connection with it was tenuous enough – that he worked for the practice that had designed the building – but it gave him a small vested interest. There hadn't been much melodrama in his life and there was something about investigating an old murder that seemed to promise a bit of fun without anybody getting really hurt at the end of it.

His eyes meanwhile had wandered to a pair of strong, sun-tanned thighs, the backs of which were pressed against a bar-stool. When, to his surprise and embarrassment, their owner spoke to him.

'Hello,' she called.

He recognized her as Janice somebody-or-other whose path he had crossed occasionally in The Hermitage as well as here in the squash club. She was, he guessed, about the same age as himself and for that matter the same height too. Either sun or its manufactured substitute had brought out an appealing rash of freckles on her bare arms. Her blonde hair was drawn back into a pony-tail.

Christian smiled in response to her call and mouthed the word 'Hello' back at her. Then was even more surprised when she left the bar and came towards him across the few yards that separated them.

'Have you been playing?' she asked with a wide smile.

'Yes. Yes, er . . . not very successfully though, I'm afraid.'

Seated as he was, his face was about level with her thighs, which put him at something of a disadvantage. Perhaps he should have stood when she approached but it was too late for that now. For her part she seemed untroubled by her semi-nakedness; or perhaps it was that she realized all too well how much it might trouble others.

'We must have a game some time,' she said.

'Yes,' he said, taken aback. 'Why not.'

He noticed that Dennis had started back from the bar with a full pint of lager in each hand and didn't know whether to be relieved or disappointed.

'See you soon then,' she said, and had disappeared from sight before he had a chance to come up with a suitable response.

Dennis arrived and put their drinks on the table. 'Very nice,' he said, referring to the departed Janice.

'Yes,' agreed Christian, still slightly dazed by the unexpected confrontation.

It was, he remembered, some months ago that he had been introduced to Janice during a lunchtime session in The Hermitage. She had been with a group – were they from the planning department? – whom Percy had known. He had for once been slumming it at the bar before his dining-companions arrived. Christian had thought her attractive and lusted after her in a vague, automatic fashion that meant nothing.

Till now, when she had suddenly made such a point of speaking to him. Though only, of course, to suggest a game of squash. Perhaps she was simply short of partners and her seductive approach had been no more than the preliminary to knocking hell out of him on a squash court.

'The only real chance is the teeth,' said Dennis thoughtfully.

Christian swung his mind back to the matter in hand. 'Yes,' he said, 'they can identify people through dental records, can't they?'

'Well, only if they have any. And if anybody can find them.'

'You don't think it's likely?'

'I wouldn't put any money on it. Not after seventeen years. And, according to the PM, he hadn't had much dental work. Just one filling, I think it said.'

'Oh well,' said Christian, and lit a cigarette.

Why, anyway, should it matter to him whether the skeleton remained anonymous or not? It was absurd that he should feel disappointment at the possibility of police failure.

'There was one thing though,' said Dennis, leaning forward, as if what he was about to say was even more confidential than was most of the information that he casually sprayed around the pubs and clubs of the town.

'What?'

'They found something in there with the skeleton. Only they're not letting on yet. Not until they've searched their little brains to see how it might help them.'

Christian waited patiently.

'A ring,' said Dennis. 'They found a signet ring that the bloke must have been wearing.'

Christian's spirits rose. 'A ring . . . ?' he echoed.

'Yes. I mean he must have been bollock-naked when they dropped him in there because there's no sign of any clothing or anything. But presumably the ring wouldn't come off. Or perhaps nobody noticed it. Anyway, there it was.'

'Is there a name on it, an inscription or anything?' asked Christian.

Dennis shook his head. 'Just a design,' he said.

'What sort of design? Do you know? Have you seen it?'

'I haven't, no,' Dennis reluctantly confessed. 'But I've talked to somebody who has. And he says that it has a lobster design on it. Whatever that means. A lobster design.'

All Christian said was, 'Huh', as though in mild surprise. In fact he was astonished. For he knew for certain that he had seen that ring before. It was a feeling akin to that of *déjà vu*, the sure knowledge of having previously visited a place when commonsense said that it was impossible.

Even as Dennis spoke, he felt a total familiarity with every detail of the lobster-shaped design and could picture it vividly in his mind's eye. But how? If he had indeed seen it before, then when and where? Was it a hand he had once shaken that had worn such a ring? It was, he felt, more familiar than that and yet further away. He stubbed out his cigarette in frustration.

Dennis seemed to have lapsed into one of his black moods and seemed not to notice Christian's preoccupation.

'Well,' Christian cleared his throat. 'Time I was off.'

'I think I'll stay and have another,' said Dennis. 'It's made me thirsty beating you.'

Christian left the remains of his own drink and stood up. He wanted to get away from Dennis, get away from everybody, so that

27

he could concentrate without distraction on pinning down just where and when it was that he had seen such a ring.

'Bye!' someone called as he went out.

He glanced round and saw it was Janice. She had changed out of her squash outfit and was wearing a waistcoat over a white blouse.

'Yes,' answered Christian vaguely.

He knew that, later, he would be intrigued and excited on remembering how she had approached and flirted with him. For the time being, though, he had something of greater urgency to occupy his thoughts.

He sat in the car and allowed his mind to wander, hoping that it might find its own way to a solution. A lobster design. With its claws outspread and open. The head of the ring bearing the design was itself round. This wasn't something that Dennis had said but it was something that Christian felt to be true all the same.

'Sod it,' he muttered, as inspiration failed to come. He started the car and set off for home.

Diane was already in bed. A note on the hall table said, 'Sorry, darling, but must go to bed. Feeling knackered. And on your birthday too. Will make up for it in the morning. Love, Di.'

Which brought a smile to his face.

He got himself a cup of coffee, put on a record of Elkie Brooks and sat in the lounge, his mind returning to the conundrum with which Dennis Joiner had presented him.

Where on earth had he seen such a ring? The longer the answer eluded him, the more he began to mistrust his original sense of conviction. And perhaps if he did ever finally remember the answer would be trivial and disappointing. Had it been in a jeweller's window? Or a photograph in a magazine?

'Christ!' he said aloud as the realization came to him. Of course. By the simple act of returning home, he had unwittingly come close to that for which he was searching.

He remained where he was for a moment, relishing the sense of discovery and the renewed excitement that now flared within him. Then got up and went from the lounge into the dining-room. In the corner stood a bureau which Diane used for her papers and household bills.

He switched on the light and went over to it; then knelt down and pulled open the bottom drawer. It was a drawer in which they kept family photographs. He first lifted out the three bound albums which contained their most cherished pictures and charted the early lives of their children. It wasn't, he was sure, these that he wanted but he flipped quickly through them all the same. He was no longer in a hurry and wanted to be sure that he overlooked nothing.

Next he lifted out their wedding-album, bound in white imitation leather and with a silver cardboard horseshoe now peeling off it.

Even in the midst of his single-minded search, he couldn't help but be moved, as he always was, by these images of their wedding day. There was his wife, looking young and trusting, giving her life over to him as he stood smirking in his three-piece suit.

After the albums there remained in the drawer two old box-files into which were pushed at random all the photographs that hadn't been considered either good enough or important enough to be mounted. He tipped them out on to the table, a jumble of black-and-white and colour – pictures they had brought with them from their separate childhoods, snapshots taken on holidays, pictures of other people whose names they could no longer remember.

It was a debris from the past which Christian found immensely touching and reassuring. There was an achievement here, a compilation of moments that proclaimed that life was after all, worth living.

Applying himself to his task, he started to leaf swiftly through the photographs, placing them one by one back into the box-files. There was a picture of himself on holiday in Blackpool, his hands arrogantly in his trouser pockets (with turn-ups on the trousers); an old woman, her hair in a bun, looking proudly at the camera (one of Diane's grandmothers?); some blurred images of children and trees which was probably their holiday in the West Country three years ago; a picture of a car that they had once owned; a group shot outside a public house that now meant nothing to him at all.

And suddenly there it was. A close-up, black-and-white picture of Diane as a young girl, perhaps ten or eleven years old.

From what bits of the background were visible she appeared to be in a park. And someone – a man – standing beside and slightly behind her, crouched down on his haunches so that their faces were level. His hand rested on her shoulder and on it, clearly visible, was a signet ring.

Its unusual design, a lobster with spread claws, could be seen in tiny but exquisite detail.

5

The following morning Christian waited until the children had been packed off to school before bringing out the photograph and placing it before Diane on the kitchen table.

'You're going to be late again . . . !' she sang out.

'I'm going, I'm going. Just tell me – who's that man, do you know?'

'What have you got that old picture out for?'

'Can't tell you yet,' he said evasively. 'Do you know who he is?'

She took the picture, looked intently at it and then said, 'Oh, that was Uncle Jack.'

'Uncle Jack . . . ?'

'That's what I used to call him. He wasn't my real uncle. His name was Jack . . . Stephenson. Jack Stephenson.'

It was a name that rang a bell with Christian. He had heard mention of a Jack Stephenson having once been in the practice and had even seen the name on some of the older plans. 'Didn't he used to work for your father?'

'Oh yes. In fact I think he was some kind of partner. Until he disappeared.'

Christian all but choked on his coffee. 'Disappeared . . . ?'

Diane shrugged. 'Well, went away. I was only, what . . .' – she looked again at the photograph – '. . . ten or eleven at the time. All I remember is that Uncle Jack was always visiting the house, was always somewhere around, and then suddenly he wasn't any more and I was told that he'd gone away somewhere and wouldn't be coming back.'

It was as promising a tale as Christian could have wished. Not wanting to raise his wife's curiosity, he left it at that, pocketed the photograph and left for the office.

News of the discovery of the skeleton had spread far enough for it to be the main talking-point of the day. There were a few sly jokes about Percy Jordan's probably having had a hand in putting it there, but they were no more than jokes, and certainly weren't made within his hearing. No one, though, seemed to know about the signet ring, and Christian saw no reason to enlighten them.

At eleven o'clock Percy's chauffeur-driven Rover appeared at the front door and Percy marched out to it. He was off to Sunderland where the Council were inviting tenders for a new swimming-pool. It was an area of the country in which the practice already had a foothold so that he had high hopes of landing the commission.

As soon as he had gone, Christian took the opportunity to slip out himself. He was looking for a photographer's and, avoiding the chain stores which did nothing in under a week, he found what he was looking for in an arcade at the back of the High Street. It was a small shop with a window full of cameras and, oddly enough, metal detectors. A sign said, *Developing. Enlarging. Printing.*

'Can you enlarge this for me?' asked Christian, pushing the picture of the youthful Diane and the living Jack Stephenson across the counter.

'Certainly,' said the young man, who wore gold-rimmed glasses. 'How big and when do you want it?'

Going back to the office with everything arranged – it was to be enlarged to 25 cms by 18 cms and he would collect it the following morning – he had to admit to himself that the enlargement would probably serve little practical purpose. He had already examined the picture under a magnifying-glass: it was unlikely that it had any more clues to reveal. However, having it enlarged encouraged him in the feeling that he was making progress. The art of detection was one to which he was a newcomer and in which he needed to proceed one step at a time.

Of his next step he was in no doubt. He had to find out about Jack Stephenson and the whys and wherefores of his sudden disappearance, a disappearance at least from the life of the young Diane if not from everyone else's as well. And he had to be careful about it . . . Suppose that he were, after all, on the right track? The last thing that he would want would be to have gone blundering around asking in a loud voice if anyone knew anything about Jack Stephenson or could suggest a reason why he might have been murdered.

He needed a quiet chat with someone who had been with the practice long enough to tell him what he wanted to know. Bill Croasdale was the obvious candidate, an old-stager who had worked for Percy Jordan from the beginning, even before the heady days of the sixties when most of Jordan's staff had been recruited. Bill, without qualifications or much talent, had found his niche in the building of models and displays, a task usually delegated to more junior personnel. He was one of the office fixtures, treated with much affection but little respect.

Christian waited until lunchtime, then caught up with him as he left the building, deftly steering him away from The Old Ship, his usual haunt and towards The Hermitage, a place that intimidated him and that he seldom entered.

'A glass of red wine, a pint of beer for my friend here, and can I just tell you that you're the loveliest thing that I've set eyes on since I was in here yesterday,' said Christian to Pat.

'Do you want a straight glass or one with a handle?' she asked Bill.

'With a handle please.'

Once they were served, Christian shepherded Bill to a table where they wouldn't be disturbed either by acquaintances or the sight of Pat's figure. While doing so, he looked across to the restaurant area and saw Councillor Maddox lowering himself carefully into a chair. Already at the same table were Walter Rees and Donald Tyson. Rees reached across and poured some wine into Maddox's glass and said something at which all three of them cackled. The fourth place at the table wasn't laid.

'Now then, what is it you want to know?' asked Bill, looking ill-at-ease in the unfamiliar surroundings.

'Oh, it's just an argument that I had with the wife,' said Christian casually. 'And since it involved her father – our eminent employer – I wanted to ask somebody who might know the answer but wouldn't go broadcasting it.'

Bill Croasdale nodded and waited. Christian had judged correctly that he would be flattered at being singled out for his discretion: he saw himself as an old retainer with a special relationship with Percy. Though, as far as Christian could see, Percy simply treated Bill as part of the furniture and ignored him.

'It's about Jack Stephenson,' said Christian. 'We were arguing about when he left the firm and why.'

'Jack Stephenson,' said Bill ruminatively. He glanced round as if to be sure that they weren't overheard. 'Well, it was a bit of a scandal was that, you know.'

'Really?'

'Oh yes. You father-in-law and Jack were partners. Not equal, but partners all the same.' Christian nodded. 'And then there was something went wrong between them. I mean we all knew that. Couldn't help but know it.'

'When was this?'

'Oh . . . some time ago now . . .'

'Seventeen years? About?'

'Must be, yes. 'Sixty-four, 'sixty-five, yes.'

Christian nodded, careful to betray none of the excitement that he felt as yet more pieces of his jigsaw fell into place. 'And what happened then?' he prompted.

'Well, the next thing we knew was that Jack Stephenson'd gone.'

'What, just disappeared?'

'Oh no, I mean gone to Australia.'

Which stopped Christian's racing imagination in its tracks. He had all but convinced himself that Jack Stephenson had departed this life for the hereafter while his body had gone to Naughton Point. Australia was something of an anticlimax.

'You're sure? I mean that it was Australia?' he asked.

'Well, so they said. Only, as I say, we all knew that it wasn't as simple as that and that there'd been trouble between them. I mean for one thing there were no farewell presentations or the like. One day he was there; the next we were told that he'd gone to Australia.'

Christian's spirits revived. Perhaps, after all, Australia and the hereafter were one and the same.

'And then afterwards,' continued Bill, 'there was the embezzle- ment charge.'

'The what?'

'Jack Stephenson was charged with embezzlement. Of course he was in Australia and no one could find him so nothing ever came of it. Except that it made sense of just why he'd hopped it like that. I mean he'd obviously got wind of what was coming. And had decided to get out of the way while the going was good.'

'And the charges were dropped?'

'Well, nothing ever came of them. I mean no one could find hide nor hair of Jack Stephenson so they couldn't do anything about it, could they?'

Christian looked across the club to where Maddox, Tyson and Rees were dining like three ancient warlocks. Did they know the truth behind all of this? It had often suited him to think of his father-in-law as part of a little local mafia, an underground society of mutual backscratchers whose weapons were not guns but planning permission consents and development grants, and it thrilled him now to find that his wild imaginings might have a

33

basis in reality.

He turned back to Bill Croasdale. 'Tell me about these charges. How much was he supposed to have embezzled?'

But Bill shook his head. 'No, I don't know anything about that. I mean we were never told anything officially by Mr Jordan. It was just what we read in the papers and heard on the grapevine.'

That did, indeed, seem to be the extent of his knowledge. Though Christian bought him another drink and tried to coax his memory back into action, there was no more to come. They chatted generally about the discovery of the skeleton – which Bill saw as a shocking slur on the practice – then went back to the office.

'Did you know that Jack Stephenson went to Australia?' he asked Diane that evening.

She had to think for a moment before she recalled their conversation of the morning. 'Oh. No, I didn't.' Then hesitated. 'Although it does ring a bell now that you mention it. Australia.'

'Did you ever get any letters from him?'

'Me?'

'Yes.'

'No.'

'Do you remember your father getting any?'

'No.'

'Any postcards? Christmas cards? Birthday cards?'

Diane shook her head. 'What is this anyway? Why all this interest in Jack Stephenson all of a sudden?'

'Oh . . . nothing. Just . . . . somebody was talking about him at work.'

But she wasn't easily satisfied.

'You're up to something.'

'It's just . . . some silly idea that I want to check out.'

She looked at him. 'You know, I think it's changed you, being thirty-eight.'

'Oh?'

'Made you kinky about old photographs.'

The enlargement was ready as promised when he went to collect it the following morning. There was no problem about his leaving the office. Percy was still holed up in Sunderland, doubtless entertaining on a scale so lavish that it would stop only fractionally short of open corruption.

'I'm sorry that the face isn't too good,' said the young man in the gold-rimmed glasses. 'But you can see that it's poorly defined in the original.'

Christian was only to happy to agree, especially as the area in which he was interested – the man's hand on young Diane's shoulder – was sharp and clear. The design on the ring could now be even more clearly seen for what it was: a lobster with spread claws.

However, as he had now to admit to himself, this told him nothing new, even if it did tell it to him at five times the size. He returned to the office with the now conspicuously large photograph hidden inside his copy of the *Daily Telegraph* and secreted it away in a drawer of his desk. What should be his next step? And how far was he from proving – to himself at least – that the skeleton of Naughton Point was that of Jack Stephenson?

His immediate need was to find out more about the embezzlement charge. If he knew the date on which it was brought then he would also know, to within a few days, just when it was that Jack Stephenson was supposed to have abruptly departed for the land of kangaroos and that architectural monstrosity that was the Sydney Opera House.

'We were never told anything officially by Mr Jordan,' Bill Croasdale had said. 'It was just what we read in the papers and heard on the grapevine.'

The grapevine might well have long since withered but the papers – assuming that that meant the *Gowling Chronicle*, the local weekly – remained to be consulted.

That lunchtime Christian gave The Hermitage a miss and went instead to Victoria House, a bold, stone office block, blackened with age, that stood a mile or so outside the town centre and had thereby escaped redevelopment. The offices of the *Gowling Chronicle* were on the ground floor. Christian went in and found himself in the Classified Ads. department, facing a grey-haired woman across a counter.

'Yes please?' she said. Then, before he could reply, she had turned at the sound of a door opening behind her. 'Oh, hello, Mr Hill,' she cooed at the heavily-built man who had appeared. He was in late middle age and wore a shabby suit. 'I've got those things that you wanted.'

'Wonderful,' he said, and moved to the little pile of photostats that she indicated.

He glanced at Christian and there was a moment when each nearly recognized the other. Then, with both of them unsure, neither spoke and Christian was again faced by the grey-haired lady.

'Sorry . . . ?' she said.

'I wonder if I could look at some back copies of your newspaper?'

'Well . . .' She hesitated and seemed on the verge of turning for advice to the man, who was standing by the photostats while helping himself to a pinch of snuff. Then she asked, 'How long ago?'

'I think I'd like to look through your nineteen sixty-four and nineteen sixty-five editions,' said Christian. If these produced nothing then he would go on to '66.

'Oh no,' she said without further ado. 'No, you want the library for that sort of thing. They have all our back copies on microfilm.'

It was something that he should have anticipated and thereby saved himself the journey. He gave a tut of annoyance but said, 'I see. Thank you,' and was turning to leave when the man spoke.

'It's Percy Jordan's son-in-law, isn't it?'

'Yes,' admitted Christian.

The man came to the counter, brushed the last of the snuff from the back of his hand and held it out. 'I'm Walter Hill, editor of this rag for my sins. We met once when your father-in-law was giving a bit of a do to show off his latest design for something or other.'

'Oh, of course,' said Christian, now remembering. He shook the offered hand and introduced himself.

'Well, since you're here,' said Walter Hill, 'why don't you come through and look at those back copies that you wanted?'

'If that's all right . . .' said Christian with a glance at the woman.

'It is if I say it is,' stated Walter Hill. It sounded like an axiom on which life at the *Gowling Chronicle* was based. He lifted the flap of the counter. The woman moved away and busied herself with other things. 'This way,' he said, and led Christian through into the cluttered newspaper offices which, since it was lunchtime, were empty.

'You don't want to go straining your eyes over bloody microfilm,' he commented as they went. 'Not when we've got what you want here. And when you're the son-in-law of that most famous man.'

They entered a room that had *Library* on the door. Three walls were lined with shelves on which were filed clippings; on the fourth wall much deeper shelves held bound copies of past editions of the newspaper.

'Now,' said Walter Hill, ''sixty-four and 'sixty-five, yes?'

'Yes please.'

And together they lifted down the appropriate tomes.

'Right,' said Walter, breathing heavily after the exertion. 'I'll leave you to it.'

'Thanks.'

'And if I were a betting man – which I am – then I'd bet that what you're after is the name of a skeleton.'

Christian's face must have betrayed the accuracy of the guess, as well as the alarm that he felt, for Walter gave a wheezing laugh.

'Good luck anyway,' he chuckled, and went out. Which at least saved Christian from having to admit or deny the suggestion. Obviously the overweight, snuff-taking editor of the *Gowling Chronicle* was nobody's fool. On the other hand, he was in the business of local news, he knew Christian's occupation and the years in which he was interested. Perhaps it wasn't such a difficult deduction after all.

Christian settled down to what he saw would be a painstaking task. It would, unless he was very fortunate and found what he wanted almost immediately, make him late back at the office. He gave thanks for the fact that Percy was still in Sunderland, destined not to return until that evening.

It wasn't only that there was a great number of pages to be scanned and turned: Christian constantly found himself reading articles that were patently irrelevant to the object of the exercise. Either the headlines were irresistible – 'Butcher Swears That Dog Was Alive' – or the documentation of minutiae of life in the sixties awakened a nostalgic yearning in the thirty-eight-year-old Christian and he had to read on.

It was after two o'clock by the time that he got to the end of the 1964 editions. Should he leave it at that or continue? Common-sense told him to come back later but the thrill of playing detective still held him in its grip. He hoisted '64 back on to its shelf and started on '65.

He had reached February and was beginning to flag. When suddenly there it was. Such an unremarkable, short item with such an understated heading – 'Architect Accused' – that his eyes had flitted ahead to the next column before its significance registered. He gave a little 'Ah!' of pleasure as he realized his success and eagerly scanned the words.

'Gowling architect, Mr J. M. Stephenson, was named by police today as someone they wish to interview in connection with a number of financial irregularities in the affairs of the Gowling firm, Total Plan Building Limited,' the article stated. 'Mr Stephenson, until recently a resident of the town, was rumoured this week to be in Australia, although it is not known exactly where or for how long he intends to remain . . .'

What followed offered little more in the way of hard information. As much as anything, the rest of the article seemed designed to allay readers' fears that this might be the tip of a major scandal. Mr P. Jordan, the firm's senior architect, had made a carefully worded statement, the essence of which was that there was nothing to worry about and it would be business as usual. Then a long paragraph detailing the firm's achievements.

Not, thought Christian, what you would call investigative journalism; rather the anodyne coverage of business misfortune by a newspaper so dependent upon local advertising that it couldn't afford to offend.

Nevertheless, he was flushed with excitement at the discovery and, finding paper and pencil to hand, hurriedly began to copy out the article in longhand. It would go into the drawer of his desk alongside the enlarged photograph.

'Well, and have you found it yet?'

He jerked round in surprise, to find that Walter Hill was standing in the open doorway behind him, tapping out a pinch of snuff on to the back of his hand. There was no telling how long he had been there. Christian quickly closed the newspaper file as Walter took a step towards him. His half-completed copy of the article he folded in half and slipped into his pocket.

'I've had enough for today,' he said, getting to his feet.

'Well, you can come back any time,' said Walter, and busied himself with the snuff and his handkerchief.

Christian made his goodbyes and went out past the grey-haired lady, feeling flustered and in some way threatened by Walter Hill's sudden reappearance.

Only when he was outside, walking quickly back towards the office, was he able to relish the full significance of what he had unearthed. He knew from his perusal of the plans for Naughton Point, while he had been handing them over to Detective-Inspector Charlton, that work had begun on site during the latter half of '64. Although it would be difficult ever to pin down precisely, February of the following year sounded about the right time for the shell of the flats to have been nearing completion. At least for it to have reached the upper floors. If Jack Stephenson hadn't gone to Australia then everything pointed to the fact that he had gone instead into one of the supporting pillars of those floors. The embezzlement story, never put to the test in a court of law, could then surely be seen only as Percy's attempts to cover his own murderous tracks. It was a piece of sheer invention, an ingenious alibi to explain to the world at large why Jack Stephenson should have staged a sudden and total disappearance.

6

It wasn't until that evening that he began to realize the dilemma to which his own success had brought him.

Diane had gone to her keep-fit class, though not before first surprising him by a sudden accusation: 'Something's going on, isn't it?'

'What?'

'I don't know what. Something.'

'One or two . . . problems at work,' he said vaguely.

'With Daddy?'

He shrugged. 'Don't worry.'

'I'm not. You're the one that's doing the worrying.'

And she had gone. Leaving him to babysit and ponder the problem of what he should do with the amazing knowledge that he now possessed.

Sheer curiosity and the excitement of the hunt had led him step-by-step towards uncovering the identity of the Naughton Point skeleton. So that now not only did he have a name – Jack Stephenson – but also a prime suspect for the person responsible for putting him there – none other than Percy Jordan, his employer and father-in-law. And, God knew, relations between them were strained enough as they were. What effect Christian's new-found knowledge might have was nobody's business.

He considered the alternatives.

Number one was to do nothing. Destroy the enlarged photograph. Forget Jack Stephenson. Keep his head down.

Could he, though, really do that? Continue to deal with Percy on a daily basis without ever revealing any part of the hand that he was holding so close to his chest? Wouldn't it only fuel his sense of frustration and resentment that he already harboured where Percy was concerned?

Not that he had any intention of going to the police. Whatever reservations he might have about Percy, he wasn't going to shop his own father-in-law. And there was Diane to be considered. She would be mortified and distressed by any public condemnation of her father. No way was he going to help bring that about.

Of course he had a moral duty to help solve what might well be a case of murder. He might even have acted on it had the victim been found with the flesh still warm and blood flowing. But for a heap of old bones . . . ? It was difficult to feel much of a sense of outrage.

So, if he wasn't going to go to the police – which he wasn't – then he had either to keep *schtum* or to challenge Percy with what he knew. It was a scene which had a certain attraction, not least because it would call into question for ever their present, unequal relationship in which Percy held the whip hand.

He found it impossible to imagine how the other man would react.

'Yes, I admit it. I killed him. Thank God, after all these years I can share the secret with someone.'

Unlikely, to say the least.

'You must help me. Please help me. I'll give you anything so long as you swear never to tell a soul.'

This rang equally untrue. Percy customarily displayed a self-confidence that could amount to a pig-headed arrogance; as long as Christian had known him, he had always gone his own way and seldom sought advice; Percy the supplicant was difficult to picture.

Perhaps more likely was that he would meet challenge with challenge: 'All right, so now you know. So what're you going to do about it?'

Which brought Christian to the heart of the matter.

He must be careful not to allow any move he made to be interpreted as blackmail. That he should face Percy with his discovery in an attempt to screw out of him the respect and recognition of which he had long felt himself deprived was a temptation that he must resist. To hint that he might manage to forget all about Jack Stephenson if Percy were, say, to retire and put the practice into his hands would be contemptible, no better than common blackmail, a demand for used notes in a brown-paper parcel. He would indeed then be Percy's equal, not only in terms of professional status but also in their shared criminality.

He either had to say nothing and thus leave Percy in blissful ignorance that his secret was out or find a way of putting the matter to him that would make it clear that he wasn't looking to profit personally by what he had discovered. It wouldn't be easy.

Diane returned earlier than he had expected. Usually she went for a drink with her girlfriends after keep-fit but tonight had decided otherwise.

'I've been thinking,' she said, and then surprised him for a second time that night, 'do you think you ought to try for another job?'

'You mean . . . with another practice? Leave your father?'

It seemed incredible but, yes, it was what she meant.

'Well, you seem so unhappy there. I don't want you to feel that you have to stay for my sake.'

'Do I seem as bad as all that?' he said, trying to turn things into a joke. The idea of leaving Percy, one which he had in the past flirted with without ever telling Diane, seemed oddly unwelcome at the moment. He had unfinished business there; of all the alternatives open to him, walking away from the firm seemed the least attractive.

He took her in his arms and was taken aback when she gently rejected him, disentangling herself and stepping back as though to say, No, I've thought seriously about this and I want you to do the same.

'Even if I could get another job, it'd mean moving house and going to live somewhere else,' he objected.

'Perhaps we should.'

It was the first time she had ever even recognized the possibility of living elsewhere, of starting life afresh, away from her father and the town that he had helped to shape.

'It'd mean moving school for the children . . .'

'Yes, I know,' she said, stopping him. 'I'm not trying to persuade you. I'm just saying that it's something I think we should think about.'

'All right,' he said sombrely, 'I will think about it. Promise. Now, how was the keep-fit?'

'Boring. And now I'm going to bed.'

'Good idea. I'll come too, shall I?'

She looked at him. 'I mean to sleep.'

She was annoyed – or disappointed, he wasn't sure. Perhaps it was his negative reception of her idea, or that for some reason her evening out had gone wrong. Anyway, she said an abrupt goodnight and disappeared upstairs.

Percy had returned from Sunderland in a black mood. The swimming-pool contract was being offered for open competition. He hadn't succeeded, as he had on so many other occasions, in short-circuiting the system and doing a deal directly with the people who mattered. He had once explained his strategy to Christian. It had been shortly after Christian's marriage to his daughter when there was still some kind of father/son-in-law bonhomie between them.

'On any Council there are only two or three people at the most who matter. Sometimes it's only one. The rest'll follow like sheep. So if you can get that one, or these two or three, eating out of your hand, then you've cracked it.'

Evidently on this occasion the Sunderland councillors had refused to eat out of his hand, or, having eaten, they had failed to come across with their side of the unspoken bargain. That didn't necessarily mean the loss of the contract. The firm could still tender for it along with everyone else; it was the preferential treatment that Percy had expected and failed to get.

His annoyance hung almost tangibly over the practice. Christian, arriving late, felt it the moment that he entered the building. One of the receptionists tipped him off: Sunderland had gone badly and Percy was looking for blood.

It was nearly midday before Christian was sent for. He made his way towards Percy's inner sanctum resolving that this wasn't the moment to raise the question of the Naughton Point skeleton and whether it might have once been called Jack Stephenson.

'What's going on with Bellevue?' snapped Percy without any of the formalities or greetings that a lesser man might have felt obliged to bestow on his son-in-law. 'Why are we a week behind schedule? And why have I had that Fowler character from the planning department on my neck about the landscaping?'

Bellevue was the old name for the acres on which the leisure centre was sited. Until the building was completed and re-christened, it remained the handiest way of referring to it.

Christian began to explain, listing problems that had arisen on site and following the unexpected bankruptcy of one of the subcontractors.

'I don't want to hear about all that,' said Percy icily. 'I've built my reputation on bringing jobs in on time and within budget. I hope you don't see it as part of our relationship that I have to make exceptions where you're involved!'

'Certainly not,' said Christian curtly.

'Then sort it out,' said Percy. 'Sort it out now, today. I don't care how, but do it!' Then, before Christian could respond, he let fly with a second salvo. 'It might help if you could manage to get to this office on time. And stay here once you do arrive!'

Christian sighed. 'I didn't know we had to clock in,' he murmured.

It was a mistake. There were times when Percy seemed to find a perverse pleasure in fencing with his son-in-law. This wasn't one of them.

'I'll have you clocking in if you're not careful!' he exploded. 'I'll have you clocking in and clocking out! And don't think that just because you've married Diane you've got a cushy number for life because you haven't!'

Christian bit his lip. It was Percy whose number was cushy and who was protected by their relationship. It was he, Christian, who suffered from it.

Percy hadn't finished. 'I've heard all about your comings and goings while I've been away. I suppose you think you've got the free run of this place!'

'Oh, I see,' said Christian, stung into a reply. 'I'm supposed to stay here all day, am I? I mean I'm just a bit puzzled as to how the hell I'm supposed to sort out site problems at Bellevue without setting foot outside this office!'

Percy looked at him, then asked quietly, 'So your little jaunts over the past two days have all been on business, have they?'

Having come this far, Christian had little choice. 'Yes,' he said stubbornly.

'Exactly what business, may I ask?'

'Naughton Point,' said Christian, throwing caution to the winds.

It gratified him to see that he had caught Percy unawares. Surprise and perhaps a touch of dismay showed on Percy's face before it was masked by his customary expression of long-suffering patience. He shifted back in his chair. It was as if he were retreating a little, sensing danger but not knowing the nature of it.

'Pardon?' he said almost inaudibly.

He had no other choice but to go on. 'That skeleton they found. I think I know who it was.'

'Oh yes?'

'Yes.'

There was a pause as each waited, daring the other to go a step further. Christian's heart was beating wildly. He had been foolish, he knew, to have let Percy infuriate him so that he had broken his resolve to say nothing about Naughton Point. Too late now though.

'And who was it then?' asked Percy finally.

'Jack Stephenson.'

Another pause. Which went on for so long that Christian, on edge for Percy's response, repeated the name.

'Yes,' said Percy, 'I heard it.' And he smiled.

Whatever Christian had been expecting – rage, confession, outright denial – it hadn't been this. Percy's smile grew to a chuckle.

'They found a ring with the skeleton,' Christian blurted out, affronted by his levity. 'I recognized it from a photograph that Diane has. So I did some checking up.'

'Did you?'

'Yes.'

'And you discovered, I hope, that Jack Stephenson went to Australia?'

'I found out that that was where he was supposed to have gone! Only no one had ever heard a word from him. Or knew where he was.'

Percy had stopped actually chuckling but still seemed to be amused by Christian's story. 'I think I'm beginning to understand,' he said.

'Oh good.'

'You think . . . well, what do you think? You think that I killed him?'

Christian opened his mouth and closed it again, reluctant to accuse the man to his face.

'I think . . . I think somebody killed him,' he said finally.

'Yes, I can see that.' Percy swivelled his chair slightly so that he was looking past Christian and at the far wall on which hung his framed commendations and awards. 'And what about the embezzlement charge?' he said. 'You must have found out about

44

that?'

'Yes,' said Christian. He was about to explain that this didn't prove anything and might simply have been a cover-up when Percy anticipated him.

'Oh, I see. You think that *I* invented that in order to explain his disappearance . . . ?'

And he gave a little laugh, then swung back so that he was again facing Christian across the desk.

'Very clever,' he said, his tone hardening. 'Perhaps you should have been a detective. Or, better still, a writer of fiction.'

Christian gave a sigh, felt in his pockets for his cigarettes, then realized that he had left them on his drawing-board. He was put out by Percy's amusement and didn't know how to take it.

'I wasn't trying to . . . well, to pin anything on you,' he mumbled. 'I mean that wasn't why I started asking around. It was just . . . just curiosity.'

'The same thing that killed the cat,' said Percy.

'I thought we were talking about who killed Jack Stephenson,' retorted Christian.

Percy considered him for a moment. When he spoke it was with the air of a parent who realizes that he has over-indulged a wilful child and must now put his foot down.

'Listen to me, young man,' he said. 'I could be very annoyed, very annoyed indeed, at what you're suggesting. Because it's not every day that people come in here and accuse me of murder. And, just by the way, if you ever breathe one word of this outside of these four walls then I'll skin you alive through every court in this land, son-in-law or no son-in-law.' He paused, letting Christian see that he meant it. Then went on. 'As it is, I'll accept that you've made a genuine mistake. You made your enquiries in good faith and came up with the wrong answer.'

'Oh?' said Christian weakly.

'A very wrong answer. Because Jack Stephenson, who was my partner and, I might say, my friend for many years, wasn't killed by me or by anyone else. He went to Australia and, for all I know, he's still living in Australia. Now that might strike you as being a death of a sort,' said Percy, permitting himself one of his rare jokes, 'but I think that what you had in mind was something a little different.'

'All I'm saying . . .'

But Percy stopped him. 'Yes, I heard what you were saying, thank you, and I've heard enough of it!'

Christian shrugged and gave up. He, anyway, had no more to say. He had played his trump card, had had it forced out on to the table in fact, but had then found that it was valueless.

'Whoever that skeleton was, it had nothing to do with me,' said Percy, spelling it out. 'It was not Jack Stephenson. It was probably some drunken labourer who fell in. God knows who it was. But it wasn't Jack. You do understand that now, I hope?'

Christian remained stubbornly immobile. He might have lost on all counts but he wouldn't give the nod of his head that would admit it.

'Well, let's hope that you do,' said Percy, seeing that he wasn't going to get his submission. 'Because that happens to be the truth. And if you breathe one word to the contrary then you'll be looking for another job. And for a good lawyer.'

This was clearly intended to be his last word on the subject. Christian gave a grunt that might have been acquiescence and got to his feet.

'Oh, and sort out that Bellevue business,' said Percy mildly.

Christian left the office, closing the door carefully behind him. He knew that he had made a fool of himself without quite knowing how. Nor did he know what to make of Percy's attitude. Had he really been amused by Christian's suggestion that the skeleton might have been Jack Stephenson? But then why had he so vehemently sworn Christian to silence on the whole subject?

Thank God it was lunchtime. He went to The Hermitage and met Simon Neal at the bar.

'Do you believe in people selling their souls to the devil?' he said, after Simon had ordered drinks from the curvaceous Pat. 'Only I think my bloody father-in-law's probably done it.'

'What's he been up to now?' chuckled Simon.

'Oh . . .' For a moment Christian was tempted to answer with a full account but restrained himself. 'Nothing special. Just his usual wheeling and dealing.'

'Well, hello there,' said a voice on the other side of him.

Christian turned and found himself almost nose-to-nose with Janice whatever-her-name-was whom he had spoken to at the squash club. Her hair was now free of its pony-tail and hung framing her oval face. Finding her so close was a pleasant shock, though it also made him notice the tiny lines around her eyes that hinted that she was perhaps older than the rest of her appearance was letting on.

46

'Hello,' said Christian, 'can I get you a drink?'

'A campari and soda, please,' she said, and rewarded him with a smile. It brought back the flirtatiousness of their last conversation when she had been in a short skirt and tee-shirt.

'So when're we having that game then?' she said, as though reading his thoughts.

'Oh . . . soon,' he stammered. 'And may the best man win.'

It was a nonsensical comment but she seemed amused by it. He introduced her to Simon and they stood in a threesome at the bar telling one another where they worked. She was a part-time receptionist at the local hospital but spoke of it more as a hobby than a career. She left after the one drink, reminding Christian that she was always at the squash club on Tuesdays and Thursdays and that she would look forward to seeing him there.

She was, he reflected, quite persistent about it. If she were short of partners then it wasn't for lack of trying.

'Another glass of wine, Pat, please,' he called. 'And how's your sex-life these days?'

At least his seeing Janice had distracted him for a while from the business with Percy. His mind returned to it, of course, as soon as he left The Hermitage and followed the well-worn trail back to the office. But he was now calmer. Could see things more objectively. And what he could see most clearly was that things couldn't be allowed to stand as they were. He must tackle Percy again and one way or another resolve the whole business.

He spent the afternoon going over the possibilities while ostensibly studying the landscaping specifications for the Bellevue development. Eventually deciding what his new approach should be, he rehearsed it in his head until he was word-perfect, then went and told Margaret that he wanted a word with Percy.

He was admitted after a wait of some five minutes. But then had a further wait as Percy's bald head obstinately refused to rise until he had finished reading – or pretending to read – what seemed to be an endless document.

When he did look up, it was to fire a question. 'Have you sorted out that Bellevue business yet?'

Christian managed to stop himself replying. He knew this tactic of Percy's of old: take the initiative and throw the other man off-balance.

'I wanted to talk to you about Naughton Point,' he said evenly.

'Well, suppose I don't want to talk about it?'

47

Again he ignored the attempt at deflection and continued along his prepared path.

'It's not that I'm disputing anything you said this morning. Just that I'm now in a bit of a funny position.'

Percy looked at him and waited.

'You see, I don't know what to do for the best. Quite by chance I discovered that the ring that was found with the skeleton is identical to one that Jack Stephenson wore. And then I found that he had disappeared about the time that the block was built. Under what I'm sure you'd agree were rather peculiar circumstances.'

'He disappeared to Australia,' said Percy testily. 'And, quite frankly, I was glad to see him go!'

Christian stuck to his prepared speech. 'Now you tell me this morning that you know nothing about all this. And, of course, I believe you.'

Percy's eyes narrowed, as though suspecting the irony that lay behind that 'of course'.

'So you can see the peculiar situation that I'm in. I've got evidence that may be relevant to the case. And I'm only saying *may* be. Which I feel that I should give to the police. But, on the other hand, the last thing that I want to do is for them to jump to the same conclusions that I mistakenly did and assume that it must involve you in some way.'

He stopped and waited while Percy digested this new view of things. It was the one that Christian had decided was most likely to wrong-foot Percy into a telling response, the only way he could think of that might cut through the bland, polished surface that the man habitually presented to the world: that is, to present Percy with the dilemma and let him attempt to solve it for himself.

'I suppose really,' prompted Christian as the silence lengthened, 'that I'm asking your advice on what I should do.'

'My advice,' said Percy slowly, 'is no different from that I gave you this morning. And that is to forget about the whole thing.'

'Just forget about it . . . ?'

'Yes. And I'll add something else too. Don't come back in here again trying to tie me in knots with your clever tricks because you're nowhere near clever enough.' Christian opened his mouth to protest but Percy continued: 'If you want to go to the police, then go to the police. Though I think you'll find that they'll only be as amused as I was by your deductions. But don't expect me to help you do it!'

'I was only asking your advice,' said Christian, suddenly finding himself on the defensive. Once again things seemed to be spinning out of control. Percy had seen the trap, had sidestepped it, and it was now a repeat of the morning's humiliation.

'You're asking me,' said Percy, 'to help you dig a pit, into which you could then give me the push. Or, if you hadn't the courage to do that, then at least you hoped that somebody else would!'

'Oh, for God's sake . . . !'

'What?' snapped Percy. 'Yes, go on. What?'

'I was asking for your advice . . . !'

'Well, you've got it. Get out of here and keep your mouth shut!'

Christian's anger, fuelled by frustration, overcame all the resolutions he had made to remain calm no matter what.

'You don't seem to realize . . .' he spluttered, '. . . I'm trying to help you! God knows why but I'm trying to help you!'

It wasn't strictly true, but nor was it a lie – he might well have been willing to help a repentant and frightened Percy. All that mattered now was that he should get behind his father-in-law's bland pomposity – try and puncture his gigantic self-confidence.

'Thank you,' said Percy. 'Now you may go.'

'All right!' said Christian, standing with a violence that sent his chair toppling. 'All right! But I'll tell you what I think, shall I? What I honestly think?'

He was almost incoherent with rage, while Percy was in total control, all hatches battened down, content to ride out the storm.

'If you feel you must.'

'I think . . . I think that you were involved with that skeleton. I think that it was Jack Stephenson. And there may not be much that I can do about it but there's nothing that you can do to stop me thinking that either!'

He knew he had gone too far. But he didn't care. He wanted only to go further, to leap over the desk and seize Percy by the throat.

'I can stop you saying it,' said Percy softly. 'Think it all you want but I can stop you saying it!'

Christian, finally rendered inarticulate by his fury, simply stared at him, then turned and left his office. This time he sent the door slamming with a force that reverberated around the building.

The rest of the afternoon he spent quietly cursing himself. Once again he had failed. Failed to shake Percy's overweening arrogance and, even worse, failed to control his own rash temper. His parting shot – that he believed that Percy had been involved in

Jack Stephenson's murder – had been a wild gesture of defiance that Percy wouldn't forget in a hurry. It would tar all their future dealings, ending for ever Christian's faint hopes of promotion within the practice.

He left for home that evening slightly surprised that he hadn't been dismissed. Though, on the other hand, it might suit Percy's interests better to keep him where he was. Should he resign? He had promised Diane that he would think about it and now had all the more reason for doing so.

He gave Naughton Point a baleful glance as he passed. It was now down to its last five floors. The pace of the demolition seemed to be accelerating as the building shrank.

He arrived home to find that news of the day's developments had got there before him.

'Daddy's been on the phone,' Diane said, almost before he had got into the house.

He said nothing but went to get himself a cup of coffee.

'I gather that you've had some kind of disagreement.'

Her note of exasperation told him all too clearly where she considered the blame to lie. So, the old fox had got in first, had he? Making sure that, should Christian start moaning to his wife about his lousy boss, he would receive, not the sympathetic hearing that other men expected, but a sharp reminder that that lousy boss was her father and what was he doing upsetting him?

'What did he say?' asked Christian evenly.

'Oh, he just rang to see how we all were. Only I'd have to be pretty stupid not to realize that there's something going on between you.'

'Well, I'm sorry,' he said shortly. 'And I can't tell you what it's about. But just take it from me, he's even more of a bastard than he usually is!'

And, before she could reply, he left the room and went upstairs to change, so that their antagonism smouldered on over tea – where the presence of the children demanded that truce be observed – then flared up again later in the evening.

'Don't you ever think – just for one moment – don't you ever think that it might be *your* fault?'

'What might?' he asked, though knowing all too well.

'That you and Daddy don't get on.'

'You don't know anything about it.'

'Well then, tell me! I can't know anything if nobody tells

50

me, can I?'

He felt, not for the first time, like a man with right on his side but one hand tied behind his back. His attitude towards Percy had to be tempered by the fact that he was Diane's father; what he could now tell Diane was limited by the same consideration.

'I've found out . . . something that he's been up to.'

'What sort of something?' Then, before he could answer: 'And, anyway, aren't you supposed to be working together? I mean, for God's sake, why are you always trying to catch him out, to prove that he's wrong or he's not a good architect or whatever?'

'I don't want to talk about it.'

'Oh, don't you? Well, believe it or not, neither do I. In fact, I don't want to live with it. I'm just sick to death of it!'

'Then I'm very sorry,' said Christian bitterly. 'It must be terrible for you.'

And, fearing where the escalating argument might take them if he stayed, he flung aside the newspaper that he'd been reading, stood up and left the room

'And where're you going now?' she called after him.

'Out!'

He crashed the gears of the car, reversed out of the drive and sped off in the general direction of the town.

The ring road offered him his first option, between east and west (he chose east), and then the large roundabout offered him other options (he took the second off). Five minutes later he pulled up outside the squash club. He had arrived there – he told himself – by chance. He was doing no more than taking himself out of the way of his wife, as much for her sake as for his, until he had calmed down sufficiently not to be provoked by the mere fact of her being Percy's daughter.

The club was busy, with all its six courts being used. He wandered round then wondering whether a sauna or a stiff drink might be the most suitable antidote to his mood. And still not admitting to himself that he might have further, and greater, expectations.

Until he came to court number five, where Janice was playing. He held his breath for a moment when he saw her. Had he really been seeking her all along? Had even his brutality towards Diane had its ulterior motive, giving him a pretext for storming out and now turning up here? He didn't even know the truth himself. Only that there he was. And there she was, in her natty little outfit that

51

showed off her long legs to best advantage.

She, of course, already had a partner. A heavily-built young man, prematurely balding but with a compensating moustache, who played noisily, panting and grunting as he went for a shot. Janice, beside him, was slim and light, her pony-tail swinging across her face as she swatted at the ball.

Christian stood watching, feeling awkward and in need of a racquet or drink as alibi for his presence. She came to collect the ball from the back of the glass-walled court and must have seen him. However, she gave no sign until, at the end of the next point, she paused to wipe her sweaty forehead, looked in his direction and went through a charming little pantomime of surprise and then pleasure at his presence. It was encouraging that she should have put on such a performance for his benefit. He gave her a wave, turned and wandered off to the bar.

'So. You made it then.'

She arrived beside him half-an-hour later, changed and smelling sweet. He looked instinctively for her partner.

'David's gone home,' she said, seeing his glance. 'I think his wife had his dinner ready.'

Christian shared her smile, though aware that his marital status was no better than that of the luckless David. He bought her a drink and she asked him how his afternoon had been.

'Bloody awful,' he said.

Which seemed to entertain her. He was pleasantly surprised at the readiness with which she laughed at whatever he said.

'What was so bloody awful about it?'

Once started he couldn't stop. He told her about Percy, about what it was like working for him when you were also his son-in-law. He described the rows that they had had. All of which had led to Christian's remaining an Assistant Architect when, on merit, he might well have expected promotion long ago. He paused for breath and noticed that her glass was empty.

'Oh, sorry,' he said. 'Would you like another one?'

She shrugged. 'Why don't we go somewhere else? I'm sick of this place.'

He agreed, kicking himself that the suggestion had had to come from her, so engrossed had he been in his catalogue of woes. They left the squash club, unobserved as far as he could tell. Opening the passenger door of his car for her, it occurred to him that she must have arrived there in somebody else's car, presumably the luckless

David's. And then must have dismissed him, having already decided that she would be leaving with Christian.

They pulled out on to the ring road and he searched his memory for a pub that would be discreet without being down-at-heel. The conversation was about housing; she had asked him where he lived; then offered the information that she herself had a flat in Ramsden House, a recently completed private development.

'I'd like to see those,' muttered Christian without thinking, then, realizing that he was halfway towards making a pass, decided that he might as well complete it and blundered on. 'I mean, er, we could always buy a bottle of wine and, er, take it back to your place . . . ?'

His heart pounded as he waited for a reply. He concentrated on the road and adopted what he hoped was a casual smile but feared was more of a silly smirk.

'All right,' she said lightly. 'I think I've got a corkscrew somewhere.'

'Great,' he said. 'I'll find us an off-licence.'

As he drove, a silence settled between them and became uncomfortable; they weren't yet familiar enough not to have to talk. He racked his brains but she was the first to speak.

'So,' she said, 'and why was this afternoon worse than all the others?'

Grateful for the subject, Christian relaunched himself into an account of the battles between himself and Percy. The one that they had had that afternoon, he explained, had been particularly vicious and had gone beyond the usual professional disagreements on to more personal matters. Though he didn't go into details. They stopped at an off-licence and he bought a bottle of Liebfraumilch which she carried in her lap as they made the last leg of their journey.

Ramsden House was a small development with fitted carpets in the lobbies and subdued lighting. The lift was unmarked and slid noiselessly between floors. A far cry from Naughton Point, reflected Christian.

'Would you like to do the honours?' said Janice, presenting him with the key.

'Glad to,' he said. Although the situation was a novel one to him, he knew that she had already consented to whatever he wished to happen once they were inside.

The flat was newly and even opulently furnished. Everything

matched: carpets, curtains, furnishings. There was a theme of beige and orange that was carried through to the large abstract pictures that dominated the main wall. Christian thought of his own home, with everything improvised and in a permanent state of flux. Though to think about it too long wasn't a good idea.

They sat down and he opened the wine. With everything as good as settled, he now had to admit to the reality of the situation. He was about to commit adultery for the first time in his nine years of marriage. It was a thought that excited him so that his hand trembled as he raised his glass in a toast but didn't please him. He loved his wife dearly and knew that what he was doing was a serious failing in himself.

His only excuse was that it had all really been Percy's fault.

Today had been the culmination of nine years of Christian's suffering as the subordinate to an all-powerful, all-conquering father-in-law. Today he had, on good evidence, all but accused him of murder. And even that had changed nothing. In fact it had left Christian feeling more vulnerable than ever. In despair and frustration he had argued with his wife. Had stormed out of the house and now found himself alone with another woman in her flat.

Well then, so be it. He would avenge himself on Percy through his affair with this woman. Twisted logic no doubt, but it had a force to it that Christian found undeniable.

'Do you think we should go to bed?' he asked after they had had two glasses of the wine each.

'Yes,' agreed Janice. 'Why not?'

She led him to the bedroom. The bedstead was of brass; the remainder of the room was a swirling sea of pinks: pale, blushing, coral, sunset. They embraced briefly then, by mutual consent, decided to undress before taking things further. He glimpsed again the thighs that he had last seen on the squash court. He might blame Percy for placing him between them; but it was a fate to which he would submit with no little enjoyment.

7

'Where did you get to last night?'

'Oh, just . . . you know, went for a drink,' answered Christian evasively.

They were having breakfast. It was the first time in their marriage that he had lied to her about where he had been. The children, Matthew and Samantha, were also at the table, attending with bright eyes to the conversation of their parents.

'Meet anybody?'

He knew that her show of interest was only to demonstrate that last night's row was over and done with as far as she was concerned. But it was a show of interest he could have done without.

'Just, er . . . just one or two from the office.'

He foresaw the ever more complex tangle of lies and deceit with which he would have to learn to live if his newly-begun affair were to continue, and resolved – as he had resolved last night, feeling like an intruder creeping into his own home at midnight – that it wouldn't. He had been foolish, temporarily unbalanced by the treatment that he had received from Percy. Things mustn't be allowed to go any further.

He left for the office on time and kissed his wife and children goodbye with an unusual fervour.

'So what's so different about this morning?' asked Diane, amused.

'Nothing,' said Christian, then added gallantly, 'I love you every morning.'

'I mean setting off for the office at this time.'

'Oh, well . . . I suppose I must secretly love your dear father as well.'

She gave him a warning look: don't let's start all that again.

'Don't worry,' he said. 'It's going to be all right.'

'I hope so.'

He drove off, then, once safely out of sight of the house, stopped the car and looked in his wallet for the piece of paper on which Janice had scribbled her phone number. This he tore up into tiny pieces, put it into the car ashtray and set it alight.

It wasn't that the experience had been so terrible or that he wouldn't have welcomed a repeat of it. The sex had been exciting, made desperately so by the novelty of a new partner and the illicit nature of their coupling. The taking of such forbidden fruit in the air-conditioned luxury of Ramsden House had been an exotic dream-come-true for the monogamous Christian. If that pink room, with the blonde, long-limbed Janice in her brass bed, could have been vacuum-sealed and kept for special occasions then it would have been a wonderful secret vice for which he would have given grateful thanks.

But it couldn't be. He might have been new to the game but he had observed its results for long enough. Mistresses didn't stay locked in their rooms; affairs didn't stay vacuum-sealed. This one would intrude into his marriage, making him adept at lying and subterfuge, dividing his loyalties until the day would come when he would see his wife and children only as obstacles to his being with Janice. Better to stop now before they got properly started.

Percy was again away from the office, though this time no one seemed to know where. It irked Christian that his father-in-law wasn't there to witness his prompt arrival.

It did, though, conveniently shelve the problem of how to face Percy after yesterday's debacle when he had come close to accusing him of murder. On the whole, it was an absence for which he was grateful.

'Doing anything exciting this weekend?' asked Simon Neal when they met at the bar of The Hermitage that lunchtime.

'No chance,' said Christian, and ordered a round of drinks from Pat, foregoing for once the sexual banter so that she gave him a quick, puzzled glance as if suspecting that he was ill.

Councillor Maddox was already at his accustomed table, his stick against his knees, surveying the world with what seemed to Christian to be a proprietorial air. They caught one another's eye for a moment and Maddox gave a stiff little nod to which Christian, before he could stop himself, replied with a smile.

Maddox had for a long time been Chairman of the Housing Committee, responsible for the spending of millions. Of the thirty-eight seats on the Council, thirty-one had been Labour, swamping all opposition and able to rubber-stamp the decisions of such committees, which gave their chairmen enormous power.

Christian wondered whether Percy had told Maddox about their confrontation. If so, had they chortled together about the young man's indiscretions or been worried by the truth in them? Did Maddox know more than Percy? Which would mean that Christian had been barking up the wrong tree. Or, for that matter, was it the whey-faced Tyson or the choleric Rees who was the real villain and who had had Jack Stephenson set in concrete? As Percy's partner, Stephenson would have dealt with all of them. Rees in particular, with his tame Building Society, had had a finger or two in most of the area's redevelopment schemes.

Perhaps Christian had been wrong in seeing his own father-in-law as the leader of the pack. Maddox, Tyson and Rees had all achieved respectability by virtue of being aged and infirm but in their day might have been as capable of murder as the most vicious-looking young thug.

'What's wrong with you today?' asked Pat, seeing him staring thoughtfully into the distance.

'Too much sex,' replied Christian, slipping back into the vernacular.

Percy hadn't returned in the afternoon. Christian felt tired after lunch and even dozed off for a few minutes. The strain of his late night with all its nerve-racking subterfuge was telling.

At four o'clock, as he was wondering about leaving early, the telephonist came through with a telex message for him.

'It's from Mr Jordan,' she said.

He scanned it quickly. MEET ME BELLEVUE SITE SIX O'CLOCK URGENT, it said.

'Oh, Christ!' he moaned. 'Six! What the hell does he want me there then for?'

'No use asking me,' said the telephonist, and clomped away in her mules.

Christian seethed quietly. Six o'clock was an hour after he would have normally left for home. Obviously Percy was playing silly buggers, out to demonstrate that there were ways in which he could force Christian to work the hours he chose. There could be nothing so urgent at this stage about the Bellevue site that it couldn't have waited till Monday morning.

'Damnation!' said Christian, throwing the cover over his drawing-board. He would do no more work that afternoon. He silently withdrew all the reservations that he had felt earlier about Percy's possible villainy: he didn't care whether Percy was pack-leader or merely lieutenant to Rees or whoever – it was enough just now that he was Christian's father-in-law and determined to make things awkward for him. He went to phone Diane to tell her that he would be late home.

'Never mind,' she said. 'Look on the bright side.'

'What bright side?'

'He might want your confidential advice on something.'

Christian gave a hollow laugh.

'Just promise me one thing,' she said.

'What?'

'You won't come home moaning about him.'

He drove to the Bellevue site, allowing himself extra time for the rush-hour traffic. A light drizzle had intensified the early November dusk. By the time he arrived it was almost dark.

The leisure centre, after ten years of Council wrangling, three years of consultation and planning and two years of building, was almost complete. It stood hard-edged in the gloom, its glass-fibre roof rising to a pinnacle, a cheap cathedral built to the worship of man. Only the car-park and surrounding lawns and trees were missing, the land still churned up and covered by builders' rubble.

Christian used the key that he had brought from the office to let himself in. The whole site seemed to be deserted, which was hardly surprising: all the comfortable, inside work had been completed and no one was likely to be working outside in the darkness and drizzle.

'Hello?' called Christian, in case Percy had already arrived and was watching him from the shadows. But there was no response. Only the faint echo of his own voice as it found its way before him along the corridor.

He switched on the foyer lighting. His watch said two minutes past six. It was rare for Percy to be even two minutes late. Christian wondered, not for the first time, if there had been some mix-up in this absurd arrangement. He would wait till half-past and not a minute longer.

He might as well, anyway, have a wander round while he was waiting. He went past the deserted pay-desk and pushed open the door that led on to the balcony of the main sports hall, now a great, dark hole into which the thin light from the foyer didn't reach. He was reluctant to switch on the white arc lights that he knew were set in the ceiling above him. It would seem an unwarranted extravagance to use them to light his solitary path when, anyway, he knew the place like the back of his hand. Had known it even before it had come into existence.

He went along the balcony, feeling for the wooden rail and stepping cautiously in case there had been anything left on the floor on which he might trip. At the end of the balcony there was another door and another stretch of corridor. He switched on the lights here and paused to light himself a cigarette. His watch said six-twelve. It occurred to him that he had left the main door invitingly open. He would return to it but, first, would look in at the main swimming-pool, the tiling and equipping of which had been incomplete on his last visit.

It was another huge, dark hole, but this time with a hard acoustic which sent his every step reverberating around like a bouncing ping-pong ball. Should he switch on the lights so that he could see it completed? (It was, of course, empty. There was no question of a moonlight swim.) He tried to picture whether the lights would be visible from the road. He didn't want to raise false alarms and bring posses of police-cars to investigate reported intruders.

He would risk it. He edged his way along the wall until he came to the office door behind which was the battery of master switches. The door was already partly open. He stepped inside and reached up the wall.

The neons flickered and clicked, then, as each one settled, the pool jumped into view, bright and clean in its blue tiling.

There was a man standing by the diving-board. Christian gave a start and – he couldn't help it – a small cry of alarm. Whoever it was, it wasn't Percy. This was a man in his early fifties, wearing a donkey jacket over what looked like a suit. His hair was greying and his face heavy and pockmarked.

They stood looking at each other until Christian's fright had subsided sufficiently for him to be able to speak.

'Who the hell are you?'

As if released by this from his vigil, the man shifted his stance. He pulled his hands from his pockets and folded his arms.

'Mr Lewis?' he said.

'Never mind who I am.' Christian's voice rose in indignation at the calculated shock to which he had been subjected. 'I said who the hell are you?'

'Got a message for you,' said the man.

'Who from?'

'Never mind that. Just don't go getting yourself involved in Naughton Point, that's all.'

Christian's first reaction was one of disbelief. He was being threatened! He was being warned off in the time-honoured fashion. It was scarcely credible. Outside, the evening rush hour was dwindling away; at home, his wife would be keeping his dinner warm. And here he was being leant on by an ageing heavy.

'All right?' said the man, taking his stunned silence for acquiescence.

'Don't talk so bloody stupid,' muttered Christian. He felt only anger that he had been set up like this, and contempt for the whole cheap charade.

'I'm offering you good advice, that's all. Just stay out.'

'Piss off,' said Christian, red with indignation. He turned to walk out and then saw that another man had appeared in the doorway behind him, a younger, fitter-looking man, whose scruffy dress looked the genuine article, not something assumed for the occasion. He said nothing but stared blankly at Christian.

There was a hiatus as no one seemed sure of the next step.

'Oh, come on,' muttered Christian weakly.

Again it was the man by the diving-board who spoke.

'Just tell us that you're going to forget all about Naughton Point. Just tell us that and there's no reason why anybody should get hurt.'

The prospect of being hurt was a new and sickening one to Christian, who had last been in a fight at the age of nine in his school playground. It was a fight he had lost.

'Oh, come on,' he said again.

His anger and contempt had gone and now it was only fear that he felt, a disabling fear that made him want to cry out in protest against this happening to him.

'We haven't got all night,' said the man by the diving-board. 'We just want to make sure that you've got the message, that's all.'

Christian wanted only to say yes, that he would do as they wished, that he would do anything so long as they didn't touch him or hit him or hurt him. But a deep-seated stubbornness stopped him doing so. It was the same stubbornness that had made him refuse to nod his head to Percy when Percy had made the same demand that he should forget about Naughton Point. In the silence as they waited for his answer, the thought came to him that, if he couldn't oppose them, then at least he might escape them. Risk a mad dash, putting his faith not in his courage or strength but on his architect's knowledge of the building.

He acted before doubt had time to eat away at his resolution. Turning, he made an awkward vault over the small rail that separated the poolside from the spectator seating. Then ran along the front of the seats and, taking steps three at a time, raced up the centre aisle.

'Come back!' called the man by the diving-board.

The other man also shouted something which seemed like a question but by then Christian was at the top of the raked tiers of seating and was praying that the door which he knew to be there wouldn't be locked.

For one heart-stopping moment it refused to budge, but it was only the new wood sticking. He wrenched it open, went through, hesitated, then turned left and ran with his arms out before him down the dark corridor.

He had to risk that there might be something left in his path which could send him flying. He hadn't time to worry about the lights and, anyway, darkness was his ally. It might yet prove an unreliable one but it emphasized the one advantage that he had: that he could from memory find his way through the maze of rooms and corridors.

He reached the end of the corridor, sensing the wall a moment before his fingers touched it. He was already breathless, made so by the sudden exertion but, more than that, by his fear of what might be on the cards for him if he were caught. He turned right, warning himself that there was a flight of steps at the end. It was a thought that increased his caution and slowed his run. And that saved him. He had taken no more than another two strides when his feet betrayed him, sliding away beneath him so that he went down heavily on his back. He gave a cry of pain and there was a clatter of things toppling on to one another. Brushes, he thought, brushes and buckets. He lay frightened, not only by the unaccustomed pain in his own body but also by what was now going to come out of the darkness behind him.

Till he realized that he could hear nothing. No footsteps or cries of pursuit.

'Thank God,' he muttered as he climbed to his feet. 'Thank God.' There was a pain in the bottom of his back where he had fallen and his whole body shook from the shock of it.

He shuffled blindly forward, kicking his way through the tangle of cleaning articles, taking short, safe steps until he reached the top of the stairs. He stopped and listened: still no sound from behind him. His relief was checked, though, by the thought that they might have been going round to cut off his escape; that they were simply being cleverer than he was giving them credit for. He must still hurry. At least there was now a rail to hold; the steps, he knew, numbered twenty-nine; he counted them off as he ran down them.

He reached the bottom, put out a tentative toe to be sure that there were no more, then felt along the wall for five yards and came, as he knew he must, to the emergency exit. He hit both waist-high bars with the flat of his hands and the double door sprang open.

Outside was drizzle, a dark sky, street lights and the sound of traffic. It was like awakening from a nightmare to find that comfortable familiarity had been close all the time. He breathed deeply but still didn't allow himself to relax. His eyes searched the darkness for his adversaries, then, when they were nowhere to be seen, he hurried forward over the rough ground. His car was on the other side of the building. He skirted round the dark shadows that were close to the walls, then made a beeline for it.

He checked quickly to see that it hadn't been tampered with and got in. Twenty yards away the main doors of the centre were open and the foyer lights blazing but Christian hadn't the slightest intention of doing anything about that. He started the car, joined the traffic and began his journey home.

His overriding feeling was one of immense relief that he had escaped in one piece. Further than that he couldn't think. The episode had left him light-headed and he needed time to recover.

He had made an effort of sorts to brush down his hair with his hands and knock the dust off his trousers but didn't realize the dishevelled, rather desperate figure that he presented until he caught sight of himself in the hall mirror.

'Christian . . . !' said Diane, horrified. 'What on earth's happened?'

The two children, alerted by her tone, came hurrying to see.

'Oh, nothing, nothing . . .' he found himself saying. 'Just a bit of a fall. On the site. My own fault. Forgot to take my torch with me.'

It was absurd that he should be laughing it off like that, hurrying away upstairs to wash and change before they could get too close a look at him. Why didn't he cry out: your father has done this! He has been involved in murder! But no. Not, anyway, in front of the children. Or even, for that matter, in front of his wife who insisted on seeing her father as a gentle patriarch rather than a murderer and thug-hirer.

Christian went downstairs, was served his dinner and, when pressed, gave a convincing enough account of how he had tripped in the dark and slid down a small bank. The children lost interest.

'Why did Daddy want you there?' asked Diane.

'Good question.'

'Pardon?' she said. Again there was the implied threat: he criticized her father at his peril.

62

'He wanted to consult me on one or two details. We've been having trouble with one of the subcontractors.'

It seemed he had to lie to her on every subject they touched upon. He felt a gulf widening between them.

'I've just remembered something. I'm going to have to go out again.'

'Already?'

'I think I left one of the doors unlocked at Bellevue. There'll be the devil to pay if some yobbos get in there. I'd better go and check it.'

In fact, when he arrived, staying inside the car until he had convinced himself that there was no one else around, he found that the lights had been switched off and the doors closed. Either the police had called in the contractors or his would-be-assailants had tidied up after themselves. Probably the latter since, when he got out of his car and tried the doors, they weren't locked. He used his office key to lock them, then walked round the building and found that the side doors by which he had made his escape had been pulled closed.

The discovery that the villains had shown a householder's concern for the building helped him to see the whole business in a new perspective. Looking back, it seemed more of a charade, an attempt to frighten him, rather than anything more serious. At least one of the heavies had cut rather an unconvincing figure. The other had done no more than stand and stare. Neither had pursued him. Perhaps they had been as worried by the prospect of a physical confrontation as he had been.

He needed to talk to someone. Someone to whom he could tell the whole story and receive the kind of sympathy and advice for which, under normal circumstances, he would turn to his wife.

Janice's telephone number was Gowling 78142. Even as he had burned the paper in his car ashtray that morning, he had known that the number was lodged in his memory. Just as, when he had made his excuse to Diane that he had to come out again to lock up the doors of the leisure centre, he had known that he would end up in a telephone-kiosk dialling that number and willing that Janice should be there to answer it.

The telephone was picked up. 'Yes?'

'It's me. Christian.'

'Oh, hi. And how're you?'

'Well, it's a bit difficult to explain. I wondered if I might come

63

round.'

'When?'

'Now.'

'Why not?' she said. 'You know the way.'

If only she had been out, he thought sadly as he piloted the car towards Ramsden House. Or if she had had a prior engagement. Then he would have been saved from himself and would have been on his way home to his wife and family, frustrated and moody no doubt but virtuous.

Janice was waiting and kissed him on the mouth as he entered. She was wearing a sort of jogging suit that, with no shape of its own, teasingly moulded itself to her own shape underneath.

'You want to go to bed or talk first?' she said.

'Can't we do both?'

She laughed and pulled him to her. 'We can try!'

But first she produced a bottle of wine and there was a delay as he opened and poured it. He was now glad that he had come and stretched out on the sofa, lighting a cigarette for each of them. Despite what he had said, he was in no hurry to get into the pink bedroom.

She must have seen this for she sat down with him.

'Everything all right last night?'

'Last night?'

'When you got home. I mean your wife wasn't waiting up for you with a rolling-pin or anything?'

'Ah. No. She wasn't, no.'

'So what did you mean on the phone then?' she asked, puzzled. 'You said that it was difficult to explain.'

'Oh, that wasn't to do with my wife . . .'

'I'm glad to hear it.'

'No, it's to do with what I was telling you yesterday. About Percy Jordan, my father-in-law. Only what I didn't tell you yesterday is that I think he's been involved in a murder.'

Her response was gratifying. 'Murder . . . ! Oh, do tell!'

And he did. It was an almost unspeakable relief to have someone to whom he could tell everything. He explained about Naughton Point, Jack Stephenson, Bellevue. She sat wide-eyed and then, when he had finished, slowly shook her head.

'You don't believe me?'

'Oh yes!' she said quickly. 'I'm just amazed, that's all.'

It was a story that amazed him too, not only in its developments but mainly that he should find himself at the centre of it.

'So,' he said, 'what should I do? What can I do?'

She thought before answering. 'You don't *know* that it was your father-in-law who sent those two today.'

'Well, then why wasn't he there to meet me when he said he would be?'

'But wasn't it a telex? You said that a telex arrived . . . ?'

'Yes.'

'Well, that could have been from somebody else. Couldn't it?'

Christian hesitated. He wasn't sure of the mechanics of the telex system but resolved that he would find out.

'I think,' said Janice, now taking the whole matter as seriously as he was, 'I think you should confront him with it.'

'I've tried it!' Christian gestured expansively. 'He just slithers away like a snake!'

'And you *are* sure that you don't want to go to the police?'

'Yes.'

They went backwards and forwards over every detail that he had uncovered and every possible line of action that was now open to him. She questioned him closely and he answered her as carefully as he would have done a barrister in a courtroom. They talked for over an hour, barely touching one another. By the time that the subject had run its course and the bottle of wine was empty, Christian felt he had been brought closer to her than he could ever have been by all their thrashings and couplings of the previous night.

8

The weekend came as an unwanted interruption. Prior to Janice and the Naughton Point mystery, Christian would have welcomed it as the chance to escape from Percy's empire and find solace with his family. Now it was an enforced hiatus in what had rapidly become the twin central obsessions of his life.

Saturday morning began with a leisurely breakfast, then the children watched cartoons on television while Christian read the newspaper.

'Shall I do us lunch or are we eating in town?' asked Diane.

'Up to you.'

'Then we're eating in town.'

'Sure.'

Even while talking to his wife, his thoughts were of his mistress.

They had made love the previous night with a real tenderness and sympathy, the result of their long debate on the subject of Christian's Bellevue encounter. He felt that he had come to know her, not just through their physical intimacy, but through their shared deliberations. He had found someone who was on his side.

Nor was he any longer so repelled by the prospect of an affair, with all its necessary lying and deceit. There was even, he had recognized to his surprise, a certain pleasure to be obtained that went beyond the illicit love-making in the pink bedroom; it was the knowledge that he now had a secret life of his own which gave him a new and flattering identity, additional to those of family man and employee. Even the plotting that would be needed to keep these lives apart and running on separate tracks had its appeal.

It was only when he was with the children that he felt himself to be cheating and underhand. Watching the six-year-old Samantha struggle into her dungarees, his near-moribund conscience came unexpectedly back to life. It was, after all, these young innocents whom he was betraying as well as his wife. With Diane, he could persuade himself that she was allied with the enemy through blood: she was on Percy's side and always would be. Matthew and Samantha were not; they worshipped Christian; their tour around town that morning would be punctuated by their proud references to those buildings that 'Daddy had built'.

What really mattered, Christian attempted to reassure himself, was that they should never know. After all, their mother had worshipped her father despite the fact that he was villainous to the point of murder. What was more, his affair would make him a better father, not a worse one; fulfilled himself, he would be free to lavish all the more love and attention on his children.

His conscience gave a final flutter, lay down and went to sleep.

They went shopping, had lunch at the Co-op and returned home. Christian, his domestic duty done, announced, 'I have to go out. It's business.'

'On a Saturday?'

'I have to see Percy.'

He saw that she didn't know whether to believe him.

'I have to see him,' he insisted. 'It's urgent.'

He wanted to tax him with the Bellevue incident as soon as

possible and not let it fester till they were back in the office on Monday. He wasn't going to telephone but simply turn up on Percy's doorstep, hoping to catch him off-guard.

'Then bring him back here for tea,' said Diane.

He sighed, unable to explain why that would be impossible.

'It wouldn't, er . . . wouldn't be appropriate.'

'Then you'd better go,' she snapped. 'Don't let us detain you.'

Since the death of his wife, Percy had lived alone in a large bungalow called 'Beaumont', which he had designed himself and which was consequently a monument to all the worst features of twentieth-century English architecture. It had been conceived as the unhappy marriage of two styles: European functionalism and English middle-class suburban. The building was long and low with a glass-walled sun-lounge along one side giving the impression of an elongated shop window. The front door was in oak, formidable enough to be the entrance to a mediaeval castle. The red tiles of the pitched roof were surmounted by a weather vane.

Christian drove through the high wrought-iron gates, which were standing open, and pulled up on the broad tarmac drive.

The main gardens were to the rear of the bungalow. These were formal and delightful, having been landscaped by a specialist from outside the practice. A shame that, on Percy's insistence, they were floodlit by night in red, white and blue.

Christian rang the bell on the considerable front door, then, when there was no reply, went exploring around the sides and back of the bungalow.

However, the only figure to be seen there was a statue of Pan playing his pipes. Clearly there was no one at home. Christian lingered for a minute or two, feeling that he had Percy at an advantage, being free to explore his domain during his absence. He even poked around in the garage and potting-shed but came across nothing of interest. Very well then. He would take the opportunity to follow the other nefarious interest currently in his life and give Janice a ring.

He would, anyway, have had to ring her from a public telephone-box. It was out of the question that he should do so from home where any one of his family could wander within earshot.

She picked up the phone before it had completed its second ring.

'Yes?'

'It's me, Christian.'

'Oh, hello. Everything all right?'

She meant, of course, had he been discovered by Diane. He realized that it would probably always be the first question to be asked: not, How are you? but, Has your wife found out?

'Fine. No problems.'

'Good.'

'I've just been trying to see Percy. Thought I'd take your advice and tackle him about that ridiculous business yesterday.'

'What did he say?'

'Well, he's not at home. And I don't know where he is so . . . I'll try again tomorrow, I suppose.'

There was a pause. They as yet knew too little about each other for there to be much that they could chat about.

'Anyway,' he said, 'is there any chance of seeing you tonight? We could go out somewhere if you like.'

'Oh hell,' she said. 'I can't. I am sorry, love, but I've got something else on.'

He waited but she didn't elaborate. He felt a twinge of resentment, even jealousy, then realized how ridiculous this was. How must she feel, knowing that he had a wife and family to whom he returned from her bed? He was hardly in a position to demand that she see no one but himself.

'What about tomorrow night?' she suggested. 'I'm free then.'

He thought of Sunday evening and their usual session of television-watching with the newspapers and supplements cluttering the lounge. It should be easy enough to slip out from that.

'Yes,' he said. 'I'll come round for you at eight, shall I?'

It was this meeting that he first thought of when he opened his eyes the following morning. The prospect of it lifted his spirits. While Diane took a slow bath, he played with the children, making them excited until they ran about the house screaming.

'I'll drive you to church,' said Christian, after Diane had appeared to restore order. 'I want to call on someone anyway.'

'Who?' she asked quietly.

'Dennis Joiner,' he said, and saw her flush slightly, annoyed with herself that she should have so betrayed her suspicions about him. It was a warning that he resolved to heed.

He dropped her and the children off outside the church, which he enjoyed looking at even if he didn't ever actually go in. It was a good example of nineteenth-century Gothic with a fine, pointed arch, slender columns and high-pointed windows. There was a balance and a poise about it that drew Christian's admiration and made him wonder why, if the Victorians could so happily draw on and adopt the traditions of their past, the twentieth century seemed to have lost all awareness of ever having had a past, never mind the ability to learn from it.

Dennis Joiner, who lived only a short distance away, opened the door to Christian looking not long out of bed and with the *News of the World* in one hand.

'Well, come in,' he said, as Christian explained that he was in the vicinity and had thought he would call.

They went into the lounge where Yvonne, Dennis's wife, was half-sitting, half-lying on the sofa, still in her dressing-gown and slippers. The television was on: it was a programme in Punjabi for immigrant viewers.

'Well, and look at the state I'm in!' giggled Yvonne. 'I don't know what you must think!'

Christian apologized for calling unannounced and explained again that he had dropped the family off at church and then thought of calling.

'Church . . . !' said Yvonne with a shake of her head. 'Goodness knows when we were last in one of them!'

And she shuffled off to fetch Christian a coffee.

'So how're you then?' asked Dennis, still glancing over his copy of the *News of the World*.

'Can't complain,' said Christian. 'I'll tell you what I was wondering though.'

'What?'

'You remember that skeleton that they found when they were knocking down Naughton Point?'

'Yes.'

'Was it ever identified?'

Dennis shook his head and gave a little laugh as though to suggest that the entire police service, with all the modern techniques at its disposal, would have trouble identifying its own grandmother.

Yvonne returned with the coffee. Christian thanked her, then asked Dennis, 'What about the ring that they found with it? Hasn't that led to anything?'

'Not a dickeybird. They've produced some posters with a photograph of it but that's a long shot if you ask me. A bloody long shot.'

'So what'll happen?'

'There's a Coroner's Inquest on Monday. That'll be adjourned pending further enquiries. Then that'll be it.'

'Unless they do actually come up with anything.'

'That,' said Dennis, 'is about as likely as me reaching Inspector.'

'I don't know why he doesn't leave the police,' muttered Yvonne. 'I don't honestly.'

The sound of hymn-singing could be heard when Christian returned and parked outside the church. Evidently the service was still in full swing. The sight of a telephone-kiosk further along the road tempted him with the thought of ringing Janice. Not that he had anything specific to say to her. Just that she was on his mind so much that the mere opportunity was enough to make him think of doing so. But he restrained himself – for one thing, he didn't know how much she might welcome such constant attention – and instead passed the time wandering between the gravestones and smoking a cigarette.

Five minutes later the vicar appeared, an antiquarian figure in his cassock, and stationed himself outside his porch to bid farewell to his parishioners. Christian retreated to the car where he was joined by Diane and the children, talkative and impatient after their enforced silence during the service.

Their own telephone was ringing as they returned home. Matthew led the charge into the house and reached it first. For one absurd and awful moment Christian feared that it would be Janice, responding telepathically to his urge to call her. Then, as the boy said, 'Hello, Grandad,' he realized with a different kind of shock that it was Percy at the other end of the line.

Diane took over the conversation while Christian, feigning indifference to his father-in-law, wandered into the kitchen. From where he was summoned by Diane. Percy wanted to speak to him.

'Hello?'

'Good morning,' said Percy. He sounded in a good mood. 'I think we should meet, don't you? Considering all that we have to talk about.'

Christian felt at his customary disadvantage. Did Percy then know about the Bellevue incident? Or was he referring to the accusation that Christian had made when last they crossed swords in Percy's office: that he had been implicated in the death and disposal of Jack Stephenson? It was the wrong moment to seek

70

elucidation, what with Diane and the kids in the house around him.

'Yes, I think we should,' he said, playing a straight bat.

'Good,' said Percy. 'Do you think you could come to the Falcon Hotel at, say, six o'clock this evening?'

The Falcon Hotel was the town's newish and pricey staging-post. It puzzled Christian that Percy should wish to meet him there, but he had no reason for objecting.

'All right.'

'Ask for me at reception,' said Percy, and put the phone down.

Christian grimaced in annoyance as he replaced his own receiver. Once again he had been at the receiving end of a peremptory summons from Percy when all along he had intended to seize the initiative himself. Too late now.

'He wants to see me this evening,' he said to Diane in response to her expectant look.

'So you'll be out again,' she said pointedly.

He gave a gesture of helplessness. 'Sorry.'

The silver lining to Percy's summons was that it allowed him to leave the house early in the evening, announcing in all honesty that he didn't know when he would be back. Assuming that Percy wouldn't detain him for any longer than was absolutely necessary, he would then be free to visit Janice as he had arranged.

If the Falcon Hotel had a busy period then it wasn't six o'clock on a Sunday evening in November. The foyer was deserted as Christian entered. The framed, contemporary prints on the walls were faced only by small groups of empty armchairs. The girl behind the reception desk looked up at him from her paperback novel.

'My name's Lewis,' said Christian. 'I've arranged to meet a Mr Jordan here. Do you know if he's left a message for me?'

She gave him a smile, which was all the more welcome for being unexpected. 'Yes sir,' she said. 'Mr Jordan said could you please go to room 302. The lifts are over there.'

Christian thanked her and followed her directions. Behind him, she returned to her book.

As the lift moved quietly upwards, Christian mentally braced himself for Percy's opening gambit. Whatever it was, it would be designed to put Christian at a disadvantage and allow Percy to dominate the exchange. Trying to stoke up a small sense of outrage, Christian reminded himself of the fright that he had been given two evenings ago and of the skeleton found embedded in the concrete of Naughton Point. He had no cause at all to feel inferior or beholden to his father-in-law, who was not only an inept architect but also a fairly inept gangster.

He knocked on the closed door of 302, believing himself to be prepared for anything. Then found he wasn't. He wasn't prepared for the fact that it wasn't Percy who opened the door at all. It was a stranger, a man he had never set eyes on before. He was older than Christian, considerably older, but also considerably larger. Thick set with a belly that pushed his tie-pin out before him.

'Mr Lewis,' he smiled. 'Come in.'

Christian did. There was little alternative and, besides, he told himself that Percy must be inside the room waiting for him.

But he wasn't. It was a standard hotel room, easily surveyed at a glance: two double beds, wardrobe space, television set. The other man closed the door. Christian, puzzled and uneasy, turned to him.

The man smiled, anticipating his question. 'No, Percy isn't here I'm afraid. Not yet anyway. He asked me to give you his apologies.'

Christian backed away, then the back of his knees bumped into one of the low beds, causing him to sit down on the edge of it. He was suddenly sweating and panicky. He had been cornered again, and this time without any superior knowledge of the premises such as had given him his advantage the last time and allowed him to escape.

The man smiled again. It was a smile of amusement, suggesting pleasure at the prospect of what he was about to do. The gold identity bracelet around his wrist jangled as he put out a thick, pudgy hand.

'Let me introduce myself,' he said. 'The name's Stephenson. Jack Stephenson.'

9

'I was wrong,' said Christian gloomily. 'It's as simple as that. I was wrong all the way down the bloody line.'

He was sitting with Janice in her flat, having gone straight there from the Falcon Hotel. Instead of the romantic encounter that he had foreseen, their meeting had more the air of a wake. They were in the lounge. He was sunk in an armchair, his head in his hands. She was perched on the edge of the sofa, listening carefully and trying to piece his story together.

'You can't be sure,' she urged him. 'It doesn't mean that you were wrong about everything, does it?'

Christian closed his eyes. 'I claimed that Jack Stephenson was dead,' he said, 'and I accused Percy of killing him. More or less. Then there he was, Jack Stephenson, as large as life, telling me I ought to emigrate to Australia.'

There was a pause. Christian lit a cigarette and shook his head sadly. This time he had achieved the all-time cock-up. This time he had fallen all the way and landed very hard, flat on his face.

Janice tried again. 'How do you know that he was who he said he was? I mean he might have been somebody *pretending* to be Jack Stephenson . . . ?'

Christian shook his head again. He had thought of this and rejected it. 'I saw his passport. And, anyway, his story tied up. Everything made sense.'

'Well, not to me it doesn't. I mean him turning up out of the blue like that.'

Christian sighed, then spelled out again carefully what he had told her in a garbled, condensed version when he had first arrived.

'Everything that I'd heard about Jack Stephenson – that he'd been my father-in-law's partner, that things had gone wrong between them, that he'd been accused of embezzlement and that he'd emigrated to Australia – all that was true. Percy had found out that he was helping himself to the firm's money and they'd come to a gentlemen's agreement that if Jack Stephenson left the country –left for good – then nothing more would be said.'

'So why did Percy go to the police afterwards?'

'Because Percy's no gentleman. He didn't believe that Stephenson would stay out of the country as he'd promised and so wanted to make sure. In fact, he always knew where Stephenson was in Australia. Somewhere near Melbourne, I think they said. But, anyway, they kept in some kind of touch. So that when I started shouting my mouth off about Percy having killed him, well, of course, Percy's laughing his socks off. Gets on the telephone and tells jolly Uncle Jack all about it.'

'And arranged for him to fly over?'

'Well, I gather that was Stephenson's idea. He fancied a nostalgic visit and this seemed a good chance to get Percy to foot

73

the bill. Percy didn't mind. I mean, why should he when it makes me look such a fool!'

Janice gave an 'Ahh' of sympathy, reached over and touched his cheek. He shrugged, then stood up and walked about the room.

'I shall resign,' he said, not knowing how much he meant it. 'I can't carry on working for him after this.'

But Janice was still picking at his story, apparently not satisfied that everything was quite so comprehensively sewn up as Christian thought.

'So, why aren't the police arresting this Stephenson character?'

'Why should they?'

'For embezzlement. I mean, I know it was a while ago but the charge will still stand, won't it?'

Christian shook his head. 'Percy had it dropped. Said he wouldn't testify any more and apparently the police were happy enough to let it go so . . . no.'

He stared through the window at the darkness outside but saw only his own reflection: dejected, weary, defeated. Percy, in contrast, had seemed almost the younger man when they had stood facing one another earlier that evening: as neat as a new pin and exuding confidence.

'So it was all kiss-and-make-up,' he said sourly. 'A real old pals' act. And bloody sickening it was too!'

'You saw him then, did you? Your father-in-law?' asked Janice. 'When?'

'Tonight. He was at the hotel, was he?'

'Yes. He was only keeping out of the way till I'd had the pleasure of meeting Jack Stephenson. Then he was into that room like a rabbit out of a hat. And, Jesus . . .' – he stopped for a moment, not welcoming the memory – 'I've never seen him so bloody delighted! Could hardly switch off this bloody silly grin he had all over his face!'

And he leant forward and poured himself another Scotch from the bottle that Janice had opened and placed on the coffee-table before him.

'But listen,' she said. 'What about the other thing? Did you tackle him about that?'

'What other thing?'

'Well, the way that you were nearly attacked – or threatened or whatever it was – at your sports centre place on Friday.'

Christian nodded. 'I mentioned it.'

'Only mentioned it!' She was indignant on his behalf. 'I mean, for God's sake, it sounded serious from what you said before!'

She seemed unable to appreciate the hopeless position in which he had been placed by the sudden appearance of Jack Stephenson, alive and well and with a carrier-bag of duty-free booze.

'All right, I *told* him what had happened. And I asked him what he could tell me about it.'

'And what did he say?'

'Bugger all.'

'He must have said something.'

'Oh, sure. He was as smooth as silk, very concerned for my welfare, and swore that he knew absolutely nothing about it. He didn't know who the men were or what they were doing there or who'd sent them.'

Despite the heavy sarcasm with which he loaded this, Christian had found himself believing Percy. He had, after all, been proved so comprehensively wrong in accusing him of murder that it seemed only fair that he should dismiss the other, less heinous, suspicions that he harboured. And, anyway, if Percy had had nothing to do with the Naughton Point skeleton, which now seemed more than likely, then why should he bother hiring a couple of second-class thugs to try and warn Christian off investigating it?

'So why did he send the telex asking you to meet him there?' persisted Janice.

'He didn't. That is, he says he didn't. Says he knew nothing about it.'

'Oh.'

'So what could I say?' said Christian, draining the Scotch. 'Could hardly call him a liar, could I? I mean I'd done that once and ended up apologizing and grovelling on the carpet in front of him.'

'You did actually apologize?'

Christian opened his arms in a gesture of helplessness. 'Had to, hadn't I? Said that I was extremely sorry, didn't know how I could have made such a mistake, hoped that he could overlook . . . all that crap.'

Percy, in response, had been at his most charming. He had stood with a little smile, letting Christian stumble on with his apology. He had then replied by saying that of course anyone could make a mistake and he was sure that Christian would have learned an important lesson from it for the future. Christian, humiliated, had said that yes, he was sure that he had.

'And what about the ring?' said Janice.

'The signet ring . . . ?'

'Yes.'

She was trying hard – he had to give her that – searching for flaws in Percy's story that might yet help restore Christian's self-esteem.

But without success. 'He had it there,' said Christian. 'Jack Stephenson had it there. He took it out of his pocket and showed it to me.'

'He took the signet ring out of his pocket . . . ?' she echoed in disbelief.

'Yes.'

'So,' she said, working it out, 'the one that he was wearing in the photograph wasn't the one that the police found with the skeleton?'

'No. Then, after I'd seen that ring, Percy puts his hand in his pocket and pulls out another one. They both thought it was bloody hilarious!'

'So that means . . . there are at least *three* identical rings . . . ?'

'There are dozens! Apparently it was a Masonic Lodge ring. This is twenty, twenty-five years ago. A Masonic Lodge here in Gowling had them cut for its members. Only some weren't too keen, what with the secrecy thing and all that, so they stopped wearing them. But they'd all been given one, every member of the Lodge.'

'I see.'

'Never occurred to me though, did it!' Christian bitterly accused himself. 'I'm such a bloody great detective that it never occurred to me that there might be more than just one ring with a bloody silly lobster on it!'

'Never occurred to me either,' she said quietly.

They sat for a while in silence. Christian now felt himself more at home in the flat than he feared he ever would again in his own house, especially when returning to it would entail having to admit his mistake to Diane. She would doubtless make a poor attempt to cover up her satisfaction that her father had been totally exonerated at the small price of her husband's pride and self-esteem.

It was Janice who broke the silence, finding perhaps the only consolation that anyone could offer him in the midst of such a defeat.

'Well, listen,' she said.

'What?'

'Why don't we just forget about it and go to bed?'

Although he knew that he couldn't forget all about it, that seemed no reason for not agreeing. They trooped through to the bedroom and started to undress on what were now their established sides of the brass bed.

'At least,' said Christian as they met in the centre, 'it does mean one thing.'

'What?'

'Well, whoever that skeleton was, he was once a Mason. And in this town.'

'You're a wonderful lover,' she said teasingly. 'If only you wouldn't talk so much about skeletons.'

He left her before midnight, conscious that his alibi had been that he was meeting Percy at the Falcon Hotel. It was a meeting that was hardly likely to have gone on until the early hours of the morning. Despite the cold night air, he drove home with the window down. This partly to help diffuse the aroma of alcohol and Janice's perfume but also that he might the better enjoy the peaceful air that lay over the town at that late hour. Just as a countryman might find solace in the tranquillity of his native hills and fields so Christian, a trained observer of the urban landscape, took pleasure in travelling quietly through it when it was at its most undisturbed.

Tomorrow was Monday. He would be in the office, having to face Percy on even more unequal terms than usual. It might be wise to try and get there on time. He postponed the question of whether he should resign.

He arrived home to find everyone in bed and lingered downstairs, making himself a cup of coffee. The love-making with Janice and his drive through the deserted town had at least pushed the awful revelations at the Falcon Hotel back a little into the past so that he could now contemplate them more equably. Even in the throes of his defeat, he began to espy a couple of minor holes in the jigsaw that hadn't yet been filled.

First and foremost, there was still the matter of what had happened at Bellevue. Had Percy sent the telex? Or had he been speaking the truth in denying all knowledge of it? Although strongly tempted to believe that he had, Christian resolved to try and track down the source of the message.

The other possibility that had occurred to him during his homeward drive was that Jack Stephenson, although imported by Percy for the specific purpose of humiliating him, might yet have a further part to play. After all, he had been around in the town up to the building of Naughton Point seventeen years ago. He had, indeed, been involved in the whole project. It was obvious now that he hadn't himself been the victim; but he might, nevertheless, know more than he was letting on.

It struck Christian, looking back on the evening, that Percy had been careful to steer the conversation away from anything to do with the mid-sixties whenever Stephenson had shown an inclination to wax nostalgical about their time together then. Or had Christian been imagining it? Perhaps Percy simply hadn't wanted Jack to be spilling too many beans about those heady days when the whole of the North of England was furiously developing itself and there were rich pickings for all.

In the event, Jack himself had suddenly tired of the talk.

'I'm whacked,' he had said, lying back on the hotel bed. 'Those flaming aeroplanes. They've nearly killed me.'

His ruddy complexion had ceased to give the impression of seventeen years spent in a sunny climate and suggested instead the unhealthy flush of a man on his last legs.

'Jet lag,' Christian had muttered sympathetically. He had already had an account of Stephenson's journey: a twenty-one-hour marathon with changes of plane at Sydney and Los Angeles.

Percy had jumped at the excuse for ushering Christian out of the room along with himself. Jack Stephenson had to be left to rest. He mustn't be tired by further talk. And, besides, the meeting had already served its purpose to the full. Jet-lagged he may be, but Jack was undeniably alive and in possession of his own skeleton.

But he might still help to throw some light on the Naughton Point discovery. Christian had gathered that he intended staying in the country for a week or so before returning to Australia. Very well then, he would call on him. It would be a natural enough thing for him to do. Perhaps Diane would like to invite 'Uncle Jack' round to the house.

He looked up and switched off the lights before climbing the stairs to bed. His wife moved in her sleep as he entered the bedroom but he didn't wake her.

10

'Good morning,' said Percy with a smile.

'Morning,' said Christian guardedly.

He had been called into Percy's office for a conference on the hospice development and been surprised to find that he was the first there. By design as it transpired.

'I just wanted to say,' said Percy, bringing his hands together on the top of his desk as though in prayer, 'that I hope that our little discussion yesterday has cleared the air a little. Yes?'

This time Christian felt obliged to give the nod of approval for which he was being asked. 'Yes,' he said. 'I, er . . . I'm sure it has, yes.'

'Good. Then let's concentrate on what we're supposed to be here for and forget all about our little misunderstandings.' And he pressed the intercom to tell Margaret that she could now summon the other members of the team who were to work on the hospice.

It surprised Christian, and – he had to admit – pleased him to find his father-in-law behaving so graciously. Perhaps then all wasn't lost and the whole episode, which last night had seemed to have led only to his own ignominious defeat, would rebound oddly in his favour: now that Percy had achieved total victory, he might prove unexpectedly magnanimous and begin to treat his son-in-law with the respect that Christian had all along been seeking. Certainly, as their conference began, Percy seemed to be singling him out, asking his opinion and paying uncharacteristic attention to it when it was given.

Christian vowed, though, that he wouldn't allow himself to be too easily seduced by Percy's flattering attitude. For one thing, he would still like to know who had sent the telex that had set him up for the Bellevue thugs.

Immediately the conference was ended, he went to see the telephonist, who was a girl called Blossom.

She was tall enough to look so even when seated at her switchboard, which she ruled with a lazy efficiency, making and breaking connections while answering Christian's questions.

'You know that telex message that you brought me on Friday?'

'No.'

He reminded her that it had been from Percy and what it had said. She thought for a moment and then changed her mind and said that yes, she did.

'Have you still got a copy of it?'

Again the answer was no. All telex messages were kept until the end of the week, then filed or destroyed according to how important they were. That one had been destroyed.

'So you can't tell me where it was sent from?'

'Not without knowing the code number, no. And, like I say, it's been thrown away. Sorry.'

She gave him a quick smile, then shifted her attention to a voice in her headphone, said, 'Yes, sir. Can you hold?' and flicked the keys of her switchboard.

Christian's reaction was a mixture of disappointment and relief. With perhaps relief having the upper hand in that he now felt that he had gone as far as he could. If the message were destroyed then so was the possibility of his ever linking Percy to it. And, under the circumstances, that might well be for the best. He had attempted once to incriminate Percy in villainous deeds and come badly unstuck; he could hardly afford another such fiasco, especially just when their relationship seemed to have taken a turn for the better.

'Never mind then,' he said. 'Thanks anyway.'

'I do remember one thing about it though,' she said.

'What?'

'Well, it wasn't one of our regular numbers. It wasn't one that I knew. So I checked it.'

'And . . . ?'

'It was a hotel. Not an office or anything. Just a hotel. And I can't remember where either so it's no use asking.' And she returned to the incessantly demanding voices in her ears, not even responding to Christian's muttered 'Thanks' as he left her.

If the telex had come from a hotel then its sender would, anyway, be untraceable. Which was no doubt the intention. That could mean one of two things: either someone had pretended to be Percy; or Percy had sent the telex himself from the no-man's-land of a hotel, knowing that later he would be able to deny it.

Bugger it, thought Christian. He had tried to trace the telex and failed. What more could he do? And, anyway, it was nearly lunchtime.

He was passing through reception on his way out when he saw Percy there scrutinizing a display of mounted photographs. They were of council houses in Middlesborough.

'Look good, don't they?' said Percy, stabbing at one with a well-manicured finger.

Christian hovered between truth and tactfulness. 'They're nicely photographed,' he said.

Percy grunted, still looking from picture to picture, though each as far as Christian could see was near enough identical. The houses – or 'units' as they would have been significantly termed in the contract – were of prefabricated design and looked much like pre-war pebble-dashed semis except that their walls were scored across where the sections met.

'I was thinking of calling on Jack Stephenson,' Christian found himself saying. 'He will still be at the hotel, won't he?'

Percy turned from the photographs to face him. Christian had the sudden and discomforting impression that his own deepest thoughts were fully visible: that Percy would see from his face that he was going to chat up Jack Stephenson in the hope that he might yet give him a lead on the Naughton Point skeleton.

'I think he will,' said Percy evenly. 'I think he intends to stay for the rest of the week at least.'

'You don't mind . . . ?' Christian hesitated, then, when Percy responded by no more than a raising of his eyebrows, he went on: 'You don't mind if I call on him? Do you?'

Percy smiled and said, 'Of course not. Why should I?'

Christian didn't answer. He said instead, 'That's, of course, if I catch him in.'

Percy looked at his watch. 'Oh, I should think there's a good chance that you will.'

Christian left the building, annoyed with himself that he had seemed to be seeking permission from his father-in-law and thus perhaps had reinforced the impression that he was now well and truly under the thumb. Why had he bothered to tell him that he was going to see Jack Stephenson anyway? Perhaps it was a measure of how far the relationship between them had been changed by Christian's abject failure to pin the Naughton Point skeleton on Percy. He was now treading carefully, nervous of any further *faux pas* – even to the extent of clearing in advance this lunchtime visit to jet-lagged Jack.

He shook his head in dismay as he walked along the street. All right, he wasn't going out of his way to provoke further hostilities with Percy; that was only commonsense. But he would not become his lap dog, asking permission to go here and seeking approval for going there. He attempted to think of other things. An advertisement hoarding said, 'Treat Your Wife Like Your Mistress.' He thought of Janice. However, the term 'mistress' struck him as oddly dated and one which she would probably resent. It seemed to bestow proprietory rights upon the man; she was *his* mistress; kept for his exclusive pleasure. Not something that Janice, going her own way in her Ramsden House flat, would be much amused by.

An ambulance, with that absurd reversed lettering across its bonnet and its secrets hidden by smoked windows, was pulling away from the forecourt of the hotel. He stood and watched it for a moment without knowing why. It used its klaxon to force a way into the traffic and was gone. He noticed with the same feeling of detachment that there was a police-car parked beside the hotel entrance and he glanced inside as he passed it, interested to see the crowded dashboard.

The hotel had lost its somnolent Sunday evening air and had a busy, weekday feel to it. Christian stood in line at the reception desk as a man paid his bill and a woman carrying a bunch of flowers collected her keys.

The girl who smiled up at him was a different one from yesterday evening but he noticed that she had been reading the same paperback.

'Can I help you?'

'I'd like to speak to Mr Stephenson,' said Christian. 'I think he's staying in room 302.'

An expression of alarm crossed her face. It puzzled and alerted Christian, who glanced round to see if anything had happened. But no, she was staring at him. She leant forward and spoke quietly.

'Mr Stephenson from Australia . . . ?'

'Yes,' said Christian.

He had a sudden and awful precognition. The ambulance, the police-car and now the strange attitude of this girl: it was like an identikit picture in which each frame was by itself a cipher but which, dropped one upon the other, formed a recognizable image. Jack Stephenson was dead.

'Would you wait just a moment, sir. I think our Assistant Manager would like to have a word with you.'

Christian opened his mouth, didn't know what to say and closed it again. He stepped back away from the desk so that the business of the hotel could go on while he waited to receive the news that he already knew.

The Assistant Manager was a dapper young man in dark suit and black tie, though there was no way of telling whether this was a sign of mourning or his regular working outfit. He took Christian's elbow and steered him into a small office.

'I believe, sir, that you've come to see Mr Stephenson . . . ?'

Christian nodded. He wanted to hurry the young man along; he already knew what was coming: there was no need to break the news gently.

'Can I ask you, sir, are you a relative of Mr Stephenson or a business associate . . . ?'

Christian opted for the latter.

'Only I'm afraid that we've got some rather bad news. Regarding Mr Stephenson . . ' Then, as though feeling that he had done enough to prepare the ground and wanting to get it over with, he ended in a rush: 'I'm afraid he's dead, sir. We found him dead in his room about an hour ago.'

Having already persuaded himself that this was the case, Christian nevertheless felt an acute shock that he had been right. And immediately had to know more.

'How, er . . . I mean what did he die of?'

The Assistant Manager cleared his throat. 'Well, I gather . . . according to the doctor who attended him . . . that it was a heart attack.'

'Heart attack . . . ?'

Why should it come as such a surprise? Had he really been expecting to hear that Jack Stephenson had been beaten about the head with a blunt instrument?

'Can I get you something, sir? A coffee? Or a brandy perhaps?'

The Assistant Manager was staring anxiously at Christian, mistaking his puzzled stare for that of a man struck dumb by grief. He helped him to a chair and hurried off in search of brandy while Christian tried to come to grips with the significance of what he had just been told.

Jack Stephenson had arrived in England. He had been sent for to demonstrate to Christian that it couldn't have been his skeleton in Naughton Point. Having done this, he had promptly died. Death coming from a heart attack.

The Assistant Manager returned with a glass of brandy which

Christian didn't need but for which he was grateful. He must try to find out if anything more were known about this supposed heart attack.

'Well, sir, the chambermaid went into the room late this morning. She saw him in bed and thought that there was perhaps something the matter. So we investigated and, er . . .'

'He was dead,' Christian completed for him.

'Yes,'

'You sent for a doctor?'

'Oh yes. He said that, as far as he could tell, it looked as though the long journey had overtired him and brought on the heart attack.'

'And the police? You called them?'

'Oh yes, sir. We call them immediately in a case of this kind. In fact, I'm sure that the constable would like a word with you, sir. If you wouldn't mind.'

And Christian, who didn't mind at all, was taken up to room 302, which was now under lock and key, and invited to give his name and address to the constable stationed outside the door.

'There were no, er . . . suspicious circumstances . . . ?' asked Christian.

But the constable proved to be of a more reticent school than was Dennis Joiner and replied politely with distaste, 'That's not for me to say, sir. For the Coroner to decide is that.'

Once free to leave, Christian was faced with a lunchtime to fill and made for the familiar territory of The Hermitage.

'Late for you is this,' commented Simon Neal, as Christian arrived at the bar.

'I had somebody to see,' muttered Christian.

'Oh yes, and what was it? Sports centre or hospice?'

'Neither,' said Christian, not keen to gossip. 'Though more hospice than sports centre, I suppose.'

Pat, in stretch trousers that fitted like a second skin, arrived to serve him. 'Hi,' she said. 'We thought you were never coming.'

But Christian was still distracted and it was Simon who had to supply the obligatory punch line: 'He gets complaints from lots of girls about that!'

Over on the other side of the club, Christian had spotted a full house at Percy's table. Tyson, Maddox, Rees and Percy himself: they were all present, and Christian felt an urge to confront them with what he knew. 'Hang on a minute,' he muttered to Simon, and navigated his way through the throng towards them.

Tyson, sucking up his soup, was the first to see him approach.

'Well, well, well,' he said to Percy. 'Isn't this young man one of yours?'

So that they all looked up, presenting Christian with four staring, elderly countenances.

'Yes,' said Percy, taking charge, 'my son-in-law.' Then, to Christian: 'Would you care to join us for a drink?'

The unexpectedly gracious gesture forced a polite response from Christian – 'No. Thank you but no' – before he could say what he had come to say. 'I've just been to see Jack Stephenson.'

'Oh yes . . . ?'

This was Percy while the other three, sensing tension in the air, watched and waited.

'Only I didn't see him. Couldn't. Because he's dead. Died this morning.'

Percy nodded. 'From a heart attack.'

Christian stared at him, taken aback. He had been sure that for once he was going to witness a genuine and spontaneous reaction from the guarded old fox, but no. As usual, Percy was two steps ahead of him.

'You already know . . . ?'

'I have been informed, yes.'

Rees, openly entertained, gave a little chuckle. Tyson's sepulchral visage gave away nothing, while only Maddox had the grace to give a small shake of his head and jowls as a token of respect.

Christian became angry, stung by the all-too-familiar feeling that he was an unwitting actor in a scene stage-managed by the bland master-magician who was his father-in-law.

'Why didn't you tell me?' he said sharply. 'When I said that I was going to see him, why couldn't you have told me then?'

'Because I didn't know then,' said Percy, matching his sharpness. 'I didn't know until I got a phone call. Which was after you'd gone. All right?'

Although not convinced, Christian could only mutter, 'Oh, I see.' He wanted to ask just who had phoned Percy with the news, and why, but he didn't want a public row in which Percy would have everything in his favour.

'The man must have been mad,' declared Tyson suddenly. 'Charging around the world at his age. Asking for it.'

Christian looked at Percy but could tell nothing from his expression. Did this mean that Tyson didn't know why Percy had spirited Jack Stephenson halfway across the world, or was it just another move in the game in which the four of them were allies?

'How old was he?' he muttered.

'Only . . . what? . . . about sixty,' said Maddox, looking to Percy from whom he received a confirmatory nod.

'Carried a lot of weight though, didn't he?' said Tyson. 'Always had a beer gut on him even before he went to . . . wherever it was.'

'Australia,' murmured Percy.

'You'll be planning to live to a hundred and fifty then,' Rees remarked jovially to the emaciated Tyson.

'I am,' said Tyson, unsmiling. 'Outlive you three anyway.'

Christian felt himself excluded by this display of geriatric parrying and sought to bring them all back to Jack Stephenson and the manner of his demise.

'They said it was a heart attack,' he said bluntly.

'So I believe,' said Percy.

'Because of all his flying though,' insisted Tyson. 'That's what did it.'

Percy ignored this and spoke directly to Christian. 'I suppose we'd better make the funeral arrangements and all that kind of thing. Perhaps you can come and see me tomorrow about it. I won't be in this afternoon.'

Christian said that he would and, taking the hint of a dismissal that Percy's tone had contained, absented himself from the table.

'They're a load of callous old sods,' he muttered to Simon Neal when back at the bar.

'Why?' asked Simon.

'An old crony of theirs died this morning. And all they can do is joke about it. None of them gives a damn.'

'Perhaps we won't at their age,' said Simon with a yawn.

At home that evening, Christian told Diane about his visit to the hotel and what he had discovered there. In contrast to the indifference of Percy and his charmed circle, she alone seemed sorry for the man whom she vaguely remembered – and, of course, had photographs of – as 'Uncle Jack'. Did he have any family? she asked. Had they been informed? None of which Christian could answer or had thought about.

It was only later, after she had had time to consider things, that she became puzzled.

'I mean, I don't understand what he was doing in this country. Or why you were going to see him.'

He hesitated, 'Your father wanted to see him.'

'But why?'

'You'd better ask him that.'

'Perhaps I will if I'm allowed to see him,' she retorted.

'I'm not stopping you,' he replied, not wanting another row. 'You can invite him round if you like.'

She didn't pursue it, but asked, 'There'll be a post mortem, won't there? I mean, with him having just arrived in the country and dying suddenly like that?'

Christian nodded. It was a point that he had raised during his brief interview with the police constable at the Falcon Hotel. He had been assured that, yes, in a case such as this a post mortem would be routine. It had made him think of Dennis Joiner – his own local police mole. Would he be able to get a look at the report? It would be interesting to hear what it contained.

Later, when Diane was putting the children to bed, he rang Dennis but found only Yvonne at home. She explained that Dennis was out working.

'When will he be in?' asked Christian.

'God knows. I certainly don't.'

But she agreed that she would get him to ring Christian if his return that evening wasn't too ridiculously late.

In the event it was eleven o'clock. Diane had gone to bed. Christian had been watching television, and wondering what Janice was doing, when the phone finally jumped into life. He hurried to it before it could disturb the rest of the house.

'Hello?'

It was Dennis, sounding jovial, even a little drunk. 'I've got your message,' he said. 'But I'd have rung you anyway.'

'You know about what happened at the Falcon Hotel then.'

'What?'

Apparently he didn't, and Christian had to recount how he had gone to the hotel that lunchtime and found Jack Stephenson dead.

'I just wondered . . .' he said, coming to the point. He found it difficult to offer a reason and hoped that Dennis wouldn't press him. '. . . I mean, if it wouldn't get you into trouble or anything . . .'

'Oh, don't worry about that,' said Dennis airily.

'Well, I'd like to know what the post mortem report said. I

believe it might have been a heart attack but nobody seems very sure.'

'Fear not,' said Dennis. 'With my connections I'll not only tell you what it says but I'll get you a copy of it!'

As Christian had hoped, he seemed interested only in demonstrating that he was a key though much undervalued figure in local policework and wasn't interested in Christian's motives.

But why had he been intending to ring Christian anyway if he hadn't known about Jack Stephenson?

'You don't know?' said Dennis gleefully. 'You haven't heard?'

'Heard what, for God's sake?'

'They've found another skeleton.'

It took Christian a moment to focus his mind back on to Naughton Point and realize what Dennis was saying.

'What . . . ?'

'At Naughton Point! Same as the first, all boxed up inside one of those concrete columns! Only this was on the first floor. Or second, I'm not sure. But anyway, they only came across it today. So what about that, eh!'

'Have they managed to identify it yet?'

'You're joking! They're still working on the first one. Or supposed to be anyway!'

'And was anything found with it? I mean a ring or anything?'

'No. Nothing.'

It was another five minutes before Christian could ring off, so exhilarated was Dennis by what had happened. Christian reminded him about the post mortem report on Jack Stephenson and Dennis said not to worry, he would be in touch.

'And I'll let you know if any more old bones turn up.'

'Thanks,' said Christian.

He put down the phone but remained where he was, sitting in the hallway. He felt marooned, clinging to what little he had left that he could be sure of while events swirled ever more swiftly past him. One minute Jack Stephenson was alive and well. The next he was dead. Now another skeleton had turned up. What next? He tried to tell himself that none of it need concern him but wasn't convinced. Whatever was going on, he felt himself to be central to it.

He stood, moved stiffly back into the lounge and poured himself a whisky. What did he know? What was there that he could be sure of? Naughton Point had been declared uninhabitable and been demolished. As a result, two bundles of old bones and the amply fleshed frame of Jack Stephenson had been trundled through the town's mortuary. Three deaths, two of them seventeen years ago, the third within the last twenty-four hours. Perhaps there was, surrounding all of them, a long-established web of evil and corruption in which they were enmeshed; the bodies, like those of dead flies, were all that was at present visible among the silvery threads.

So what should he do about it? For that matter, what *could* he do, other than go to bed and set his alarm clock for the following morning? Had he been an ancient samurai, he might have ritualistically cleansed himself, prayed to his gods, then, armed and fearless, ridden forth to challenge all comers in the name of truth. As it was . . . well, he would have to wait and see. See what the post mortem of Jack Stephenson said; see if the police could eventually identify either skeleton; see what Percy's reaction would be to the news that yet another embarrassment had popped out of his award-winning building.

Besides, he had arranged to meet Janice tomorrow evening. The mantle of the incorruptible crusader sat oddly on the shoulders of one who was cheating on his wife and whose original investigations had been motivated mainly by a wish to put the boot in on his father-in-law.

11

A week later, Christian was standing with Percy between the trim lawns and well-tended flower beds of the crematorium. They were part of a gathering, no more than a couple of dozen altogether, who had come to pay their last respects to Jack Stephenson.

The results of the post mortem had been straightforward enough: 'Death was consistent with a thrombosis developing in the coronary artery whose insufficiency was responsible for the collapse . . .' And so on, for another page-and-a-half of the pathologist's report. In other words, heart attack brought on by jet lag. No suggestion of foul play.

'He designed this, did Jack, you know,' muttered Percy thoughtfully.

'The crematorium?'

'Yes.'

89

Christian was surprised: he hadn't recognized the building as a product of the early Jordan/Stephenson partnership. Though perhaps he should have done: it was of a strictly functional design and dated from the early sixties when they enjoyed a virtual monopoly of work in the area.

The two men stood, their breath whitening on the cold air. A small hiatus in the process of death was keeping them waiting: something to do with a traffic accident involving the preceding funeral.

For want of something to say, Christian found himself putting into words an idea that he had been uneasily contemplating for the last few days.

'I suppose I'm as much to blame as anybody.'

Percy looked at him. 'For what?'

'For all this.' Meaning the mourners, the hearse, the death itself.

'I fail to see how,' said Percy. His tone implied that he didn't particularly want to be told either.

But Christian stumbled on. 'Well, if I hadn't started playing detective, then I wouldn't have jumped to the wrong conclusions – I mean that that first skeleton was Jack – and so he would never have flown back here. And would be alive today.'

'I shouldn't worry,' said Percy sharply. 'After all, I was the one who invited him here. Even paid his ticket to come over.'

This was true enough. Though falling well short of an absolution, it at least seemed like an offer to share the guilt and Christian was grateful for it.

The crematorium doors had opened.

'Come on,' said Percy. 'Looks like we're going in.'

Diane joined them as they went forward. Her attitude these days puzzled Christian. She should have been pleased by this new harmony between husband and father, yet he sensed that she was still withholding her approval, keeping her distance from him.

It puzzled but didn't unduly worry him. He was sure that she knew nothing about Janice, which was the important thing.

It was a short, non-denominational service. The mourners formed a motley group, summoned by Percy and short on real feeling for the deceased who, after all, was remembered locally either not at all or as an old villain who hopped it to Australia when the going got rough. The Hermitage mafiosa were present: Donald Tyson, looking even whiter and more sepulchral than usual in his black suit and tie; Councillor Maddox, supporting himself on his stick and finding the service hard-going; Walter Rees, scowling at the coffin as though resenting it. Bill Croasdale represented the old lags of the practice who remembered Jack Stephenson as he had been, industrious, ambitious and embezzling. There was also a sun-tanned couple whom no one recognized until they were introduced as Jack's daughter and her husband who had flown from Australia to be there, finding it more appropriate that Jack should be laid to rest in his home town than in his place of exile.

The door opened to admit a late arrival. Christian, glancing round with the rest, saw that it was someone he knew but certainly hadn't expected, Walter Hill, editor-in-chief of the *Gowling Chronicle*. He felt surprise and even a faint alarm but had no time to consider why for the coffin had begun to move, claiming all their attention. It disappeared through the curtains to the tune of *Nearer My God to Thee* and the sound of Jack's daughter sobbing into her handkerchief.

Afterwards they repaired to the Castle Hotel for a drink and buffet lunch where, by common consent, the period of mourning was ended. Walter Rees cracked a joke; Jack's daughter produced photographs of her house which her father had designed and which bore an uncanny resemblance to the crematorium; there was a burst of unrestrained jollity.

Christian, sampling the vol-au-vents, found himself face to face with Walter Hill.

'So,' said the editor, 'we meet again.'

'Yes,' said Christian.

'Did you ever find what you were looking for?'

Christian hesitated. Did this man know that he had mistakenly identified the Naughton Point skeleton as being that of Jack Stephenson? If so, then he must have been chuckling to himself at the irony of their meeting at the skeleton's funeral.

'Not really,' said Christian, playing safe.

Walter Hill took out his snuff-box and arranged a pinch on the back of his hand. 'It's a while ago,' he said vaguely, drawing snuff up each nostril. 'There are some things best left where they are if you ask me.'

'Have you heard anything about the other skeleton? The second one that they found?'

Hill shook his head. 'Nor will do neither, I shouldn't think.'

His manner irritated Christian. This complacent, let-sleeping-dogs-lie attitude was so far from what the free press was supposed to be all about that he couldn't resist a faintly sarcastic reply.

'Surely there's a good story waiting there for somebody? If nothing else.'

Walter Hill shrugged. 'It'll have to wait then. For one thing, nobody's that interested in what happened seventeen years ago, even if they could find out. Most folk find what happened last week boring.'

'So you're not interested?'

'Not a lot. And I'm not the only one.'

'No?'

'You think the police are that bothered? They've enough on their plates without old skeletons popping up here there and everywhere.'

It was an exchange that Percy had observed.

'You know Walter then?' he asked.

'Well . . . not really. Just met him the odd time.'

'Hmm.' Percy's expression was one of disapproval.

'You don't like him?' ventured Christian.

'I don't like journalists. And I don't like old fools who like to pretend that they know a lot more than they do. So I don't like him, no.'

'Oh.'

'I'd steer clear of him if I were you.'

It was advice that came near to being an order, though the hand that was laid briefly on Christian's arm was reassuring rather than threatening. We are both on the same side, it said; let us be united against our enemies.

There was little to keep the mourners together for long now that Jack Stephenson had been reduced to a pile of ashes and the buffet lunch had all but disappeared. Percy shepherded Rees, Maddox and Tyson into the back of his car and instructed his chauffeur to head for The Hermitage. Christian had been interested to observe Percy's farewells to Walter Hill; as cold and formal as he might have expected, knowing Percy's opinion of the man. Hill had remained genial and smiling, as though knowing that he was disliked but not resenting it. Maddox and Tyson seemed to share Percy's views and all but ignored Hill. Rees, however, had spent some time talking animatedly to the newspaper editor. Perhaps it was the two Walters who were in league together. Now that Christian had rid himself of his long-standing obsession that Percy

92

was the *éminence grise* of the bunch, he was able to see any number of alternatives in the relationships and liaisons of these old men.

He took Diane home and, what with the drink, fell asleep in a chair. She roused him in time for him to hurry back to the office to put in at least a token afternoon appearance. There was almost a holiday atmosphere with little work being done. Percy didn't return until after four o'clock, though, of course, stone-cold sober.

Once home again, Christian began to prepare the way for his evening's activities.

'I shall probably pop out for a while later,' he said casually, as though he hadn't yet made up his mind.

The response from Diane was unexpectedly bitter and caught him by surprise.

'I'm sure you will.'

'Pardon?'

'Well, you've been out practically every night for the past two weeks. Why should tonight be any different?'

So that was it. That was the reason he had been getting the cold shoulder.

'Well . . . I'll stay in if you'd rather.'

It was an offer grudgingly made that she had too much spirit to accept.

'No, you go out. Obviously you'd rather be out than stay in with us. I wouldn't want you to feel that you *had* to stay.'

And so he went, promising her that they would have a night out together as soon as she cared to arrange a baby-sitter.

'Thanks,' she said sarcastically. 'I'll see what I can do.'

He picked up his now customary bottle of white wine and let himself into the Ramsden House flat. Janice had left the door off the latch for his entry and was sitting watching television. She kissed him absently, her eyes remaining on the screen.

'Do you mind if I just finish watching this?'

'Of course not.'

How quickly had aspects of his relationships with his wife and his mistress been exchanged one for another. The need to be on guard and to play a part, which he had first felt while in Janice's company, was now there only when he was with Diane. While the freedom to relax, to say whatever he was thinking without having to calculate possible consequences, which he had always enjoyed in his nine-year-old marriage, had now been transposed to these meetings with his mistress.

Yet he still told himself that his marriage was safe. He could cope. There was nothing to worry about on that score.

Once the television programme had ended, he told her about the funeral, how it had gone and what had been said. In particular, he told her about Walter Hill.

'Yes, I think I know him,' she said. 'A fattish man, aged about sixty, wears a toupee . . . ?'

'Does he?' said Christian in surprise, and wondered what else he might have missed. Then he went on. 'I don't know why it should have surprised me, him being there like that. I mean, he's about the right age to have been a friend of Jack Stephenson from way back.'

'Yes.'

'But there was something that seeing him made me wonder about.'

'What?'

'Well, you remember that business that I told you about at the leisure centre, when those two tried to put the frighteners on me . . . ?'

'Yes?'

'Well, you know that Percy's always denied having anything to do with that.'

'Yes. And I thought you said you now believed him?'

'I do,' said Christian. In fact, his one-time distrust of Percy had now been replaced by an almost total faith in the man.

'Anyway,' said Janice, 'what's this got to do with Walter Hill?'

'Well, hang on and I'll tell you.'

She waited with a teasing show of obedience.

Christian began carefully. 'If we're saying that Percy wasn't responsible for setting those thugs loose on me then somebody else must have been.'

'Absolutely.'

He glanced at her to see whether she was taking the mickey but she kept a straight face.

'And whoever that was,' he went on, 'clearly must have known that I was trying to identify the skeleton. Now who, beside Percy, knew that?'

'I've no idea. Who did?'

'Walter Hill.'

And he explained about his visit to the *Chronicle* offices and how Walter Hill had led him to the back copies that he wanted and had then hazarded a remarkably accurate guess as to what he wanted them for.

'And nobody else knew what you were looking for?' asked Janice, now no longer teasing.

'Nobody else knew that I was there.'

'So you think that it was Walter Hill who set you up? That those two thugs were working for him?'

'Might have been. Or at least working for somebody else that Hill had tipped off.'

'Who?'

'Oh, I don't know. He seemed quite pally with Rees today after the funeral. I mean, perhaps he's the one who has something to hide and Hill keeps him informed if there's anything going on.'

'Rees?' queried Janice. 'Is he the one who had the Building Society?'

Christian nodded.

'He looks an evil old devil,' mused Janice. 'Like, you know, one of those medieval paintings of Satan, sharp, red nose and all that.'

But Christian didn't want to be distracted into a discussion about Walter Rees. 'Never mind for the moment who was behind it,' he said. 'Let's just suppose that I'm right and that it was Hill who tipped them off that I was on the trail.'

'Yes.'

He stopped and pondered, wanting to be sure that the new conclusion to which he was about to jump would provide a more secure foothold than had his first.

In fact, Janice anticipated him.

'But you weren't on the trail. I mean you'd got it wrong!'

'Exactly.'

'You were trying to prove that it was Jack Stephenson when all the time it wasn't!'

He kissed her. 'Brilliant.'

'You mean I'm as brilliant as you are,' she joked.

'Yet either Hill or whoever he tipped off,' went on Christian cautiously, 'still thought that I needed stopping. I mean they still sent those two lunatics to threaten me.'

'Yes.'

'So what does that mean?'

They both thought for a moment. It was Janice who spoke first.

'Either they also thought that the skeleton was Jack Stephenson and so they thought you were on the *right* trail . . .'

'Yes.'

She stopped. He waited but she could only giggle and confess, 'Or I've no idea!'

But Christian had. 'Or when Walter Hill saw me searching through the back copies of that paper . . . he thought I was looking for something else.'

And – eureka – that, he was sure, was it. Walter Hill had guessed rightly that Christian was looking for evidence that someone had disappeared around the time that Naughton Point was being built. But mightn't he also have guessed – and this time wrongly – that it was *someone else*, and not Jack Stephenson, that Christian had in mind?

Janice frowned, still doubtful. 'But I thought he knew what you were looking for?'

'No! Well, yes, but only that it was to do with trying to discover the identity of the Naughton Point skeleton. Neither of us mentioned Jack Stephenson.'

'I see,' she said, as the light began to dawn. 'And so you think that there's an article in that paper about somebody else who disappeared about 'sixty-five or whenever it was?'

'Yes.'

'And it was that article, not the one about Jack Stephenson, that Hill thought you were after.'

Christian nodded excitedly. That was indeed what he now thought. He could hardly wait to put his theory to the test.

Janice, seeing this, sounded a note of caution. 'I thought you'd said that you'd given the whole thing up, that you weren't interested any longer . . . ?'

'Oh, I don't think I went that far, did I?' he said weakly, knowing that he had indeed renounced detective work for ever after his fiasco with Percy.

'Not that it's anything to do with me,' she said lightly.

He tried to explain to her – and to explain things for himself. Yes, he had only become obsessed with the mystery of Naughton Point because it had seemed to involve Percy. However, even with that original motivation now gone, he still felt an urge to get at the truth if he could. And, God knew, no one else seemed to be making much progress.

He described to her his conversation with Walter Hill in which Hill had decried the idea of uncovering the truth after so long. Perhaps it wasn't only his toupee that Christian had failed to notice. Perhaps he had also missed the real purpose behind what Hill had been saying: a further, and this time gentler, attempt to dissuade Christian from pursuing the matter.

'You do see what I mean though, don't you?' he urged her. 'A pound to a penny that somewhere in those back numbers – somewhere around 'sixty-four, 'sixty-five where I was looking – there's the clue as to who that skeleton was.'

Janice nodded but seemed unable to share his rekindled enthusiasm for the hunt. No doubt she was concerned that he might end up in even deeper waters than before. It was a concern that touched him.

'Don't worry,' he said gently. 'I'll be careful.'

They went to bed. The sex now was easy and pleasurable with nothing depending upon it. Their relationship was growing other bonds, the strongest being their shared deliberations over Naughton Point and its bony inhabitants. Odd, he thought, how much he owed to that first skeleton. Without it, he might never have found either his mistress, or his new *modus vivendi* with Percy.

He arrived home in high spirits, happy to see that the house was in darkness which meant that Diane was in bed and asleep.

He let himself in, making as little noise as possible, and found a note on the hall table.

DENNIS JOINER RANG, it said. HAS SOMETHING TO REPORT. WILL RING YOU AT WORK TOMORROW. DI.

Clearly he was now involved with Naughton Point whether he liked it or not. First, Walter Hill had turned up to jog his memory and thus lead him to a new interpretation of events and now here was his own police mole with beans to spill. Still, he wasn't complaining. It all served to make life interesting and he eagerly awaited hearing what Dennis had to say. Even if it did help to bring him nearer to the truth, it surely couldn't place him under an obligation to do anything about it.

In fact, by the end of the following day he would know the names of two people who, seventeen years earlier, had come to an untimely end and whose bodies had been disposed of inside the reinforced concrete columns of Naughton Point. He would also be in a position to make a fair guess as to why.

Too late then would he realize that with such knowledge did indeed come both obligations and dangers.

12

Work had never been better. Christian was now one of the small team doing the preliminary work for the hospice. The burden of chivvying along the contractors working on the final stages of the leisure centre had been taken from him. All evidence, if evidence were needed, of his new-found status in the practice.

Odd then that Diane hadn't reacted to this development with the enthusiasm that he might have expected.

'You have noticed,' he said pointedly, 'that Percy and I have settled our differences?'

'Oh yes, I've noticed.'

'You don't seem very pleased.'

'I am, yes,' she said, though in a tone that belied it. 'So everything in the garden's lovely, is it?'

'Well . . . not bad.'

'I'm delighted.'

Christian shrugged and left it at that. He had too much going for him at the moment to lose sleep over her moodiness.

For one thing the practice was riding out the recession remarkably well. Percy's long-established associations had kept the work coming in, particularly from the north-east. There was hope even yet for the Sunderland swimming-pool where he was considering a new initiative. 'There are gentlemen there in my debt,' he confided to Christian. 'Perhaps it's time they were reminded of the fact.' And meanwhile work from abroad had remained steady: a health farm to be constructed in Kuwait, a hospital in the Gambia and, less exotic, a library in the Isle of Man.

Only Percy himself couldn't go on for ever. Jack Stephenson's death might have been a reminder of his own mortality. And, if he were thinking of grooming a successor, then who better than Christian – now that the antagonism between them seemed to have been dispersed – not only was he a capable architect but he was under forty and married to Percy's daughter. Though as yet this could be no more than idle speculation on Christian's part as he drove to work: there was no hard evidence that it was Percy's intention.

Looking for evidence of a different sort, Christian gave The

Hermitage a miss that lunchtime and went to the town library instead.

It was an institution that dated from the 1930s and had been founded by the Carnegie Foundation; a five-year-old annexe had been designed by Percy's firm and funded from the rates. Passing through it, Christian noticed that the toilets were closed. A handwritten sign blamed persistent vandalism. Almost a hallmark of the Jordan style of architecture, he thought wryly.

'I want to look at some back copies of the *Gowling Chronicle*,' he told the woman behind the desk. 'Nineteen-sixty-five to start with.'

This, he had decided, was a more discreet way of conducting his enquiries than returning to the *Chronicle* offices. If he were right about Walter Hill's involvement, then there was no point in alerting him again.

He sat before a viewing machine and fed in one of the three rolls of microfilm with which he was provided. *Gowling Chronicle, May – August 1965*, said the label on the box. It seemed as good a place as any to start.

He settled to his task, inching the film through and scanning the columns of local news that must have once seemed important but that now seemed only to tell of more innocent, optimistic days before things had begun to sour. This time he denied himself any nostalgic self-indulgence. He was interested only in deaths and disappearances and wasn't going to be distracted by anything else.

He plodded on, going from May to June and finding three cases of missing persons though they were none of them promising. They were all elderly citizens who had wandered from their homes and failed to return. It was the fourth case he found that started the adrenalin: this was different, younger, male and a civil servant to boot.

He noted the date – June 20 1965 – and then copied out the article into a notebook which he had had the foresight to bring with him.

'*Local Man Missing*,' was the headline. The single column beneath it was straight to the point.

> Concern is being expressed regarding the whereabouts of Richard Morris Dunmore of 17A, Higher Chapel Street, Gowling. Mr Dunmore, a civil servant, has not been seen since the morning of Saturday June 13th and there are fears for his safety.

A bachelor, living alone, Mr Dunmore is aged 43 and a member of the local fell-walking club. Colleagues at the Planning Department where he works say that he would often go out walking alone at weekends. It is feared that he has met with an accident while on one of his solitary rambles. Local police have been in touch with other forces and with rescue organizations throughout the district.

The Naughton Point skeleton had been that of a male in his mid-forties. Whether Mr Dunmore was also tall with dark hair – the other two characteristics which the post mortem had revealed – there was no way of knowing.

Christian's excitement and sense of triumph at the discovery was tinged with caution. Having made a fool of himself once, he must now proceed tiny step by tiny step. He forced himself to stay at the viewer and plough on to the end of the reel that took him through the summer months of July and August. This produced two more cases of geriatric disappearances – along with the news that one old man who had been reported missing in the first week of May had been found alive and well and living in Harrogate.

There remained October to December. Christian looked at his watch. Bugger October to December, he decided. There was something about Richard Morris Dunmore that told him he had struck gold already.

He returned the rolls of microfilm to the librarian and thanked her.

'Did you find what you wanted?' she asked.

'I think so, yes.'

'Good.'

It was a polite exchange which had none of the sinister implications that had been there when Walter Hill had asked him the same question.

Christian came out into the fresh air. His walk back to the office would allow him to consider his next step.

The article expressing fears for the safety of Richard Dunmore, bachelor, civil servant and fell-walker, had been in a June '65 edition of the newspaper. The one announcing the embezzlement charges that were to be brought against an absent Jack Stephenson was in an edition of February '65. They were thus in the same bound volume of back numbers which Christian had been perusing when Walter Hill was quietly observing him from the doorway. What could have been more natural than that Hill – already knowing the significance of the Richard Dunmore article – should assume that that was what Christian had found? The name of Jack Stephenson had probably never even crossed his mind. The moment that Christian had closed the bound pages and said that, yes, he had got what he wanted, thank you very much, Hill would have thought only of Richard Dunmore.

All of which was assuming that this time Christian really had struck gold and not the fool's gold which his earlier investigations had uncovered and which had so dazzled him. What he now needed was to know whether Richard Dunmore had ever been found or whether he was still missing seventeen years on.

Conveniently, the one man who could provide this information was on the telephone within ten minutes of Christian's return to the office.

'It's Dennis.'

'Oh, hi,' said Christian. 'Diane said you'd rung last night. Sorry I wasn't in.'

'Out chasing crumpet, were you?'

It was a joke, but so uncomfortably accurate that Christian thought it best ignored.

'She said that you'd something to report?'

'Oh yes, yeah. Look, it's a bit difficult to talk now. How about meeting for a jar or two tonight?'

Christian hesitated. He hadn't yet rung Janice to arrange his evening but, anyway, seeing Dennis need take no more than an hour or so. And – two birds with one stone – it would give him the excuse for going out that he needed.

'Love to,' he said. 'Where?'

'How about The Blue Anchor? Say . . . eight o'clock?'

'Blue Anchor. Eight o'clock,' repeated Christian firmly. 'And, Dennis . . . ?'

'Yeah?'

'I wondered if you could do me a favour.'

'Course.'

'Well, it's a bit hush-hush,' said Christian, preparing the ground carefully. 'I wouldn't want anybody else to know about it.'

'Sure,' said Dennis. 'You know me.'

Christian did, but continued anyway. 'Can you find out for me about a missing person? Somebody who was reported missing quite a while ago? I want to know whether he's ever been found or what.'

'For you – anything.'

And Christian, having no alternative if he wanted Dennis's help, related the facts as he knew them about Richard Morris Dunmore.

There was a silence after he had finished.

'Sounds like we've got more to talk about tonight than I thought,' said Dennis finally.

It had, then, been hoping for too much that Dennis wouldn't latch on to Christian's line of thought. He might be a garrulous sceptic but he was no fool. Christian hurried to restrain him from jumping to the kind of conclusions with which he himself was tempted.

'Look, I don't *know* anything! For God's sake, don't start a full-scale investigation or anything like that!'

'Don't worry,' said Dennis. 'Nobody takes any notice of me around here.'

Christian hoped not, but feared that on this occasion they might. He had only to look at himself to see how quickly anybody's star could rise.

'See you tonight then,' he said, and rang off.

The rest of the afternoon was spent working on the preliminary plans for the hospice. Percy was off again to Sunderland in a new attempt to short-circuit the tendering process for the swimming-pool contract.

'I shall be back tomorrow,' he said, looking in on Christian as he left. 'If things look promising then perhaps you might like to come next time. There are some people it'd be useful for you to meet.'

Christian was flattered and encouraged. This was the clearest hint yet that his days as Assistant Architect were numbered.

He was still elated at the way things were going when he arrived at The Blue Anchor that evening. It was an old pub, near the bus-station, seedy and rundown. No doubt Dennis had his own reasons for nominating it as a meeting-place. Christian peered in at the public bar, saw a solitary skinhead tossing darts at a dartboard and withdrew to the lounge, which had a thin carpet over part of the floor and a colour television-set suspended over the bar. He ordered a pint of bitter and took it with him to a corner table.

He had at least been able to leave home with a clearer conscience than usual.

'I said I'd meet Dennis Joiner,' he told Diane, happy that his excuse could be truthful and specific for once.

To his surprise – and relief – she seemed much happier.

'It's all right. And don't worry about me. I'm going out too. Mrs Caton's coming in to sit.'

'Oh. Well. Good,' he said.

At least her sulky spell seemed to be over. God knew, he didn't mind her going out. A pub-crawl with her girlfriends might do her the world of good.

Dennis Joiner finally arrived, looking round and spotting Christian in his corner.

'Ready for another one?' he called across.

Christian shook his head, indicating his glass that was still almost full. Dennis greeted the barman, who was already pulling a pint for him. Obviously he was known here.

'Right then,' said Dennis, sitting across from Christian. 'What do you want to know about first? Your Richard-whatever-he's-called, or the other one?'

'The other what?'

'The other bloody skeleton, of course!'

'What is there to know about it?'

Dennis lit a cigarette and took the top off his pint before answering.

'We know who the second skeleton was. And it sounds as though you might have found out the first.'

'Oh, I'm not saying definitely . . .'

Dennis stopped him. 'Neither am I. Between you and me this, right?'

'Right.'

Another pause as Dennis nodded in the direction of a fat man who had just come into the bar, then glanced round at the worn-out seating and stained tables as though to be sure that they weren't overheard.

'It was the teeth.'

'Pardon?'

'That second skeleton . . .'

'Yes?'

'The teeth. Dental records. Apparently there'd been a lot of work done. Fillings, bridges, all sorts. So they circulated dentists and . . . bingo.'

'You found out who he was?'

Dennis nodded. 'Charles Yates, they called him. Came from this part of the world but had moved to London. Journalist.' Then admitted: 'It'll be in the papers by tomorrow morning so there's no big secret.'

'Any idea as to how he died? Or why?'

'Not a clue.'

They sat in silence for a moment, each toying with his glass. Christian was trying to hide his excitement, even from himself. He had to rein in his eager imagination, to force it to proceed with caution. Certainly the name – Charles Yates – meant nothing to him. But the revelation that he had been a journalist . . . that, taken alongside what he had read that morning, had set his mind racing.

'And as for the other thing,' said Dennis, 'this missing person that you were asking me about . . .'

'Yes?'

'Richard Austin Dunmore . . .'

'Morris,' Christian muttered, correcting him.

'Him anyway. I had a look to see what we had about him.'

'Yes?'

'Lived in Upper Chapel Street. Worked in the town hall,' recited Dennis, telling Christian what he knew anyway. 'That's until June 13th 1965. When he went for walkies and never came back.'

Christian's heart leapt. 'Never?'

'Well, he's still down as missing as far as we're concerned.'

'I see.'

'So,' said Dennis, looking Christian in the eye, 'where does that leave us?'

Christian shrugged, suddenly wary of Dennis, whose customary cynicism seemed absent tonight. It was as if the prospect of real progress on a case had awakened his police instincts. Perhaps he even saw it as a means to glory for himself if he should, aided by Christian's contribution, succeed where his superiors had failed.

'I'll get us another drink, shall I?' said Christian, standing.

'Oh, OK. I'll go and have a pee while you're at it.'

Waiting at the bar, Christian wondered – now that it was too late – about the wisdom of having alerted Dennis to the mystery of Richard Dunmore's disappearance. Any police investigation would surely start by asking how Christian had managed to come up with the name. Would he then have to explain about Walter Hill? God knew where that would lead. He must, he resolved, be on his guard. See if he could discourage Dennis's new-found keenness.

Dennis returned from the Gents and they went back to their corner table. He seemed to have decided to subject Christian to a mild grilling.

'How did you know about Richard Dunmore anyway?'

Christian shook his head. 'Just heard the name mentioned.'

'Who did the mentioning?'

'Can't remember.'

Dennis stared at him. Were it not that they were supposed to be friends and this a social occasion, Christian felt sure he would have been called a liar.

'Looks like it probably was him,' said Dennis slowly.

'Really?'

'Yes.'

There was a long pause, then Dennis gave a sigh and said. 'Sod it. Might as well tell you.' It was as if his normal, indiscreet self had returned; he had done his best to remain the official, responsible policeman and found it too much of a strain.

'Tell me what?'

'You know that ring that was found along with the first skeleton? The one I told you about, with the lobster design on it?'

Christian nodded. He did indeed know the ring and would never forget it.

'Well, it turned out to be something to do with a Masonic Lodge. You know, the rolled-up-trousers brigade. Well, all the members of this Lodge had been issued with one of these rings.'

'Oh,' said Christian, feigning surprise.

'And that was something else that was on this Richard Dunmore's file.' Christian had already guessed but Dennis spelt it out. 'He'd been a member of this Lodge. So he would have had one of the rings.'

It was as if a jigsaw of impossible complexity had suddenly fallen into place. It had been simple all along, had he only been willing to let the picture form itself and not tried so hard to force incompatible pieces together. There was now only one more thing that he needed to know and that, with luck, would lead him to the answer to the next question that must now follow the identifying of the skeletons – *why* had they been killed?

'This journalist . . '

'Charles Yates,' said Dennis. 'What about him?'

'Who did he work for?'

'Nobody specific, I don't think. He was freelance. Quite big

105

time, though. I mean the nationals and that. Nothing local.'

This wasn't the answer that Christian would have wished for.

'You don't know which papers he contributed to?'

Dennis shook his head. 'I gather it was on the heavy side. I mean your posh Sundays, *The Times*, that sort of thing. Nothing that I'd read.'

Christian foresaw that his research this time couldn't be confined to Gowling Public Library or even the shelves in the offices of the *Gowling Chronicle*. It would mean a trip to London.

He finished his second pint quickly. There seemed no more to be got from Dennis and he didn't want Dennis to get any more from him. They came out of the pub together. It was a cold, wintry night that didn't encourage lingering on the pavement but there was a postscript that Dennis had yet to deliver.

'I shall have to mention this,' he said apologetically.

Christian frowned. 'You mean us meeting?'

'Well, not necessarily. I mean about Richard Dunmore.'

Christian nodded. He had foreseen that. But he still felt uncomfortable about being cited as the source of information.

'Will you have to mention me?' he asked directly.

'Dunno,' said Dennis. 'Depends on what it leads to. But I'll try not to, all right?'

Christian believed him. For one thing, Dennis might have a vested interest in letting his superiors think that the name of Richard Dunmore had been produced as a result of his own diligent digging into the files.

They went to their separate cars and Christian let Dennis pull away first. He didn't want him to see that he himself would be driving off in the opposite direction to his home.

He had rung Janice that afternoon and arranged that he would call.

'But not before nine,' she said firmly.

'Why not?' he asked, with a small laugh to show that he didn't really mind.

'Because I say not. I have my own life to lead as well you know.'

And he had to accept it. It hadn't been the first time that she had hinted – indeed, had stated – that there were areas of her life into which he wouldn't be admitted. And why shouldn't she? There were certainly areas of his in which she wouldn't have been exactly welcome. Besides, there was something reassuring in her attitude. It suggested that she knew the size of their affair and was as resolved to keep it in its place as he was.

It was, anyway, almost half-past-nine by the time he reached Ramsden House. He parked in his now familiar spot, then realized as he went in that he had neglected to pick up anything for them to drink.

'I've got a wonderful idea,' he said as they kissed inside the front door.

'And what's that?'

'I think we should go to London.'

She seemed amused. 'Oh yes?'

'Yes! I mean just for a couple of days. And nights.'

She saw that he was serious, took him by the hand and led him through into the lounge.

'Now,' she said with a smile, 'sit down and tell me all about it.'

But first he had to confess. 'I've forgotten to bring a bottle.'

She gave a shriek of laughter. 'You don't have to! It's not like those parties when we were kids and you couldn't get in without one!'

They both laughed at that. Then she fixed the drinks while each said something about the sort of day they had had. He hadn't yet told her about his discoveries: it was a moment that he wanted to savour.

She observed his excited air. 'You're like a cat with two tails!'

'Am I?'

'Yes. So, come on, what's been happening, eh?'

He smiled, happy enough to be able to boast to her of his successes.

'Oh, I've just been solving one or two mysteries, that's all.'

'Mysteries . . . ?' She looked at his face, then realized. 'You've discovered something about those skeletons?'

'Yes.' And he told her about Richard Morris Dunmore and his unexplained disappearance seventeen years ago, and about Charles Yates whose long hours spent in the dentist's chair had finally proved their worth.

'But are you *sure* this time?' asked Janice. In contrast to his triumphant air, she had become more dismayed as his account had continued.

'Well, as sure as anybody can be. Even the ring ties in. Dunmore was a member of the Masons. He would have had a signet ring identical to that one found with the skeleton.'

She nodded, having to accept what he said, though unhappy

about it. 'So what are you going to do?'

'Well, that's why I thought of us going to London.'

'I don't understand.'

'I want to find out what this man Yates was writing about at the time he was killed. He was supposed to be a serious journalist. All right, perhaps that was *why* he was killed. Don't you see? Perhaps he was investigating something and getting so close to the truth that somebody decided he had to be stopped!'

'Somebody in this town?' she said quietly.

Christian shrugged. 'It all points to that. The other man – Dunmore – worked in the Planning Department. So perhaps he was feeding Yates his information.'

'You don't even know that the two deaths were connected,' objected Janice. But she spoke without conviction. It was a forlorn attempt to stop him that only strengthened his resolve.

'Exactly!' he said. 'Which is why I need to know what it was that Yates was investigating. If anything ever can, then that'll be the evidence that ties the two deaths together!'

Janice sighed and then, still unhappy, tried another tack.

'All right,' she said. 'I agree.'

'You do?'

'Of course. Everything you've said, it makes sense and I'm sure you're right. But . . .' – and now she was pleading with him – '. . . why get involved? Why not just leave it? Or go to the police if you must but for God's sake, Christian, you don't know what it might lead to!'

Just a few days ago he would have agreed with her. Now he knew that he couldn't; that he had to take just this one step further to satisfy himself before he could wash his hands of the whole affair.

'Is it that you're still trying to get back at your father-in-law?'

'No!' he insisted. On the contrary, it had already occurred to him that it might be no bad thing if he, Christian, got to the truth before anyone else did in case Percy were implicated in any small way and he could then act as his protector and saviour.

'So why bother?' said Janice. 'Why not leave things alone? Those bones have been lying there for long enough!'

'It's . . . it's all sorts of reasons,' he said, finding it difficult to sort them out for himself, never mind for her. 'It's partly because . . . well, because having come this far, I want to know what really did happen. And partly because, to be honest, I'm fed up of hearing people say that it doesn't matter! That those people were killed seventeen years ago and so we should just forget about it! I'm damn sure that we shouldn't!'

There were more reasons, too, of which he was only half-aware and upon which he was less keen to elaborate. He wanted to find out where the power really did lie among The Hermitage mafiosa, or indeed if it lay elsewhere altogether. He wanted to atone for his earlier, lamentable failure as a detective and get it right this time.

And he very much wanted to take Janice to London with him. To spend at least one full night with her, without hearing the town-hall clock strike midnight and knowing that he must scramble back into his clothes and hurry home before his coach turned into a pumpkin and his whole world came crashing down around his ears.

Perhaps this, after all, was the most important reason of the lot. It was in search of a dirty weekend that he was donning the guise of the disinterested searcher after truth. He was less concerned with the ideals of justice and truth than with screwing the night away in a hotel room.

Well, and so what if he was? He surely could serve both truth and the demands of his mistress without having to make a choice between them.

'Come with me,' he urged her. 'A couple of days in London.'

To his delight, and considerable surprise, she seemed willing to consider the idea.

'When?' she said.

'Day after tomorrow,' he said wildly. 'We'll go for two nights. I'll book a hotel.'

'If I do go,' she said teasingly, 'it'll only be to stop you taking this detective business too seriously.'

'All right,' he said. 'I won't complain if you manage to stop me altogether.'

13

Diane had wanted to see him off, then the children had said they wanted to come too, which was why the four of them were standing together on platform four of Gowling station at seven-forty-five on a wet Thursday morning.

The train, signalled to arrive, wasn't yet in view. It was still dark. A thin drizzle was falling beyond the station canopy, visible only within the halos of the street lights beyond the tracks. Christian and Diane had steaming plastic cups of coffee, from which the children took occasional sips. They all crouched slightly against the cold gusts of wind that came along the platform, shaking the hanging signs.

'When are you coming back?' asked Matthew.

'Day after tomorrow,' said Christian patiently. If they had asked him once then they had asked him half-a-dozen times.

Around them stood a sprinkling of fellow-travellers, mostly either men alone or women in groups of twos and threes. The matter-of-fact air among them made Christian self-conscious about the send-off that he was getting from his family. 'It's not as though I'm going very far or for very long!' he had expostulated to Diane, but she had insisted – 'I'd like to see you off' – and then the children had added their voices and he had had no choice but to submit.

He couldn't, of course, explain to them the real reason that he would have preferred to have gone to the station alone. Thirty yards along the platform, half-hidden by a steel column, stood Janice. She had placed her small suitcase on the ground beside her and was apparently absorbed in a magazine. Absorbed in such a way that Christian knew that she was as painfully aware of him and his entourage as he was of her.

Fortunately, she had foreseen the possibility of such a problem and had insisted that they treat one another as strangers until they were actually on the train and knew that the coast was clear. 'Even if your family don't come,' she had pointed out, 'there might be someone that I know, or someone we both know.' So it was agreed: they were to catch the train as strangers and meet up as lovers in the second carriage from the end.

Suddenly the waiting passengers began to move forward, two porters trundled a row of high-sided mail trucks into position and the long-nosed engine of the 125 Inter-City was moving towards them along the platform, its noise drowning out the announcement of its own arrival. It came past Christian and his family, bigger and more powerful than the children had been able to imagine so that they clung to their parents in fearful delight.

'Can we go on it one day?' shouted Samantha over the din.

'Next time,' promised Christian. 'Next time we'll all go.'

'Look after yourself,' said Diane.

He picked up his bag and, with his family tailing him, joined the movement towards the nearest door. There was a small delay as a woman had to be helped to hoist her two suitcases up and through the doors, then he was aboard. He pressed himself against the corridor wall, letting others pass him, until he could return to the now closed door, lower the window and lean out to Diane and the children.

'Go and find yourself a seat,' she urged him.

'I want to see you go first. It's too cold to be hanging about.'

The children gave a last wave and asked if he would buy them something. Diane reminded him to ring, blew him a kiss and then shepherded them towards the subway. Christian pulled up the window, shutting out the noise and cold air. At last, he thought, watching his family disappear.

The middle carriages were quite full and he made slow progress moving through them, having to wait while people stowed suitcases on racks or behind seats. The train was beginning to move as he reached the less populated end-carriages and saw Janice sitting there, reading her magazine and smoking a cigarette with an unconcerned air that suggested she did this every day of the week.

He wanted to embrace her, so great was his relief that they had pulled it off, but wondered how long they were supposed to continue with their charade.

'Is this seat taken?' he asked, indicating the one opposite her.

She went through a small pantomime of looking up at him and then at the seat before saying, 'I don't think it is, no.'

He sat down and waited, wondering when they would be free to speak. They had left the station and were cutting through the outskirts of the town, heading south.

She put down her magazine and gave him a smile. 'All right?'

He pretended to wipe the sweat from his brow. 'Just about!'

She laughed. 'Oh, it must have been awful for you! I tried not to look. I didn't want to catch your eye or anything!'

It startled and even disappointed him that she should have been amused by the situation. He had feared that she would be upset by the sight of him saying goodbye to his family, that it would be cruel confirmation of her role as the 'other woman'. But no, she seemed even to have been entertained by the spectacle.

Though why shouldn't she? What did he expect? That she should be sharing not only his hotel room but his qualms of

111

conscience too?

'At least we made it,' he said.

'I never thought we would,' she admitted. 'I mean I was sure that something or other would stop us.'

He leaned over and took her hand. 'Two whole days,' he said, 'I can't believe it!'

In fact, the arrangements for the trip had presented remarkably few problems. Diane's wish to come to the station with him had been the only hiccup in an otherwise unbroken run of good fortune.

He had first gone to Percy and asked if he might take a couple of days off. 'I was thinking of tomorrow and the day after,' he said when Percy didn't immediately reply. If asked for a reason, he had little to offer but for a vague reference to 'urgent personal business'. However, Percy asked only that he would be sure to arrange things so that the work on the hospice wasn't delayed and had then given his blessing, showing no interest at all in what Christian might be up to.

Getting Diane to accept that he had to spend two days in London was trickier.

'It's business. All a bit confidential to tell you the truth, but I'd like to go if you don't mind.'

'And suppose I say that I do mind?'

He had hesitated, not knowing how to reply.

'Oh, go on,' she said. 'Why not? You're out so much when you're here that it won't make all that much difference, will it.'

It was her new, strange mood of carefree indifference that he still didn't wholly understand but was glad enough of since it gave him what he wanted.

He took her in his arms. 'Thanks, love,' he said. 'I'll make it up to you.'

'You'd better,' she said, and allowed him to kiss her.

Unable to believe his luck, he had rung Janice, almost resigned to hearing her say that she had changed her mind.

'Do you still want to go?'

'If you do.'

That was good enough. But what about her job? Unimportant though she always made it sound, she surely couldn't just ignore it altogether?

'Oh, that's all right,' she reassured him. 'I've got holidays coming. They won't mind.'

Beginning to believe that the gods were well and truly on his

112

side, he unearthed an old copy of the *Sunday Express* and chose at random from its advertisements for London hotels. The Bertram Hotel, which was near Kensington Gardens, assured him that they had vacancies and, indeed, were offering a special winter rate for double rooms.

So that, amazingly, miraculously, here they were, sitting across from one another, with home, town, friends and family receding into the distance and the bulk of London with its promise of anonymity and freedom all before them.

Of course there were still things that could go wrong. Even in London it was possible to bump into a mutual acquaintance. Or Diane might take it into her head to phone him at the hotel and be put through to Janice. They might be witnesses to a crime and find their pictures on the front page of the national press. The possibilities were infinite but it would be foolish to be deterred by any of them.

Christian returned from the buffet with two cups of coffee.

'Did you ring the newspapers?' asked Janice.

'Not yet,' he said. 'I'll do it when I get there.'

She looked at him, still with reservations about what, after all, was supposed to be the main purpose of their trip: to track down the work that Charles Yates had done immediately prior to his death.

'What are you going to ask them?'

'Oh, whether they ever took articles from a freelance reporter called Charles Yates. And if they can't tell me then . . . well, I'll just ask to look through their back numbers for nineteen-sixty-five.'

'And suppose they won't let you?'

He laughed. 'Why on earth shouldn't they? There's nothing unusual about it. They must have a stream of people making enquiries about all sorts.'

She gave a little shrug and concentrated on stirring her coffee despite the swaying of the train.

In fact, he had intended making the initial telephone contact with the newspapers before leaving Gowling but, in the rush to arrange the trip, he had been unable to find the right moment and the right telephone. He couldn't ring from home, where Diane might have overheard, nor from the office, where Blossom might have been listening in on the switchboard. But he was confident enough that they would allow him to search their files – even if it were unlikely that they would still be aware of the name of Charles

Yates, freelance contributor, seventeen years on.

He had also thought of trying *Private Eye*, the satirical magazine that often carried the kind of no-punches-pulled articles that made other newspapers nervous. If Charles Yates's articles had been such hot stuff that he had been killed for them, they might well have appeared somewhere other than middle-of-the-road Fleet Street. Perhaps he would go to *Private Eye* as a last resort.

He gave way to the motion of the train and slid into a light sleep. His plotting of the last few days had taken its toll: now, able at last to relax, he surprised himself and amused Janice by sleeping for the remainder of the journey so that the next thing he knew was her hand on his arm.

'Wakey, wakey . . . !'

He looked out of the window. 'Where are we?'

'London! Or had you forgotten?'

They were heading into Euston. The flats and terraces of North London were close around the track. They went into a tunnel and came out to find the lines already dividing to serve the different platforms. Christian yawned and shook himself as, along with everybody else, he got to his feet to pull on his coat and take down his bag.

'You were sleeping like a baby!' laughed Janice.

'I must have needed it,' he said, a little shamefaced that he should have neglected her.

Now though, refreshed by his sleep and feeling that they really had escaped together, he felt free to enjoy their adventure to the full. Queuing to leave the train, he hugged her quickly and received a kiss in return. They hurried down the platform, hand-in-hand, careless now as to who might see them.

A taxi took them to the hotel and the business of signing-in. Christian was indifferent as to whether the hotel staff regarded them as married or not, and knew, anyway, that no one in this alien world had the slightest interest.

And then they were in the room. Despite their urgent need for one another, both went through the ritual of exploring, commenting on the bedside controls for the radio and television, the coffee-making facilities and the trouser-press. Only then could they properly come together in an embrace that was interrupted only while they removed their clothes before falling on top of one of the beds.

The strangeness of the setting and the occasion gave a freshness to their love-making that reminded Christian of that first time in Janice's pink bedroom. Further spice was added – if further spice were needed – by the mirrors that covered half of one wall and showed them themselves as a jumble of white limbs on top of the brown bedspread.

The telephone began to ring.

The couple in the mirror stopped what they were doing and looked at one another in surprise and dismay. They were mimicked by the couple on the bed.

'Christ!' moaned Christian.

Janice moved away from him and instinctively pulled up the bedspread to cover part of her nakedness.

'Who can it be?' she asked.

'God knows,' said Christian savagely.

If looks could kill, his scowl would have silenced the telephone forever; as it was, it continued to trill away and couldn't be ignored. Could there be any danger in answering it? They had barely arrived; hadn't even had time to complete the very act for which they might be censured.

He picked up the receiver. 'Hello?'

'Mr Lewis?'

'Yes.'

'I have a call for you. One moment please.'

Christian's fury at being disturbed was suddenly engulfed by fear. A thousand possibilities, each more alarming than the last, went through his head: there had been a fire; Diane had had an accident in the car; his children were dead . . .

'What is it?' whispered Janice.

'Don't know,' said Christian.

A man's voice, which he didn't recognize, came on the line.

'Mr Lewis?'

'Speaking.'

'My name's Bradshaw. Lord Bradshaw. We haven't met but we seem to have some interests in common and I wondered if you could very kindly spare me an hour or so in order that we might get together and discuss them?'

The only thing to register with Christian was that Diane and the children were safe.

'What, er . . . I'm sorry but what's this all about?' he asked.

The voice was confident, authoritative even. 'Well, I'd rather not discuss that over the phone if you don't mind. Like I say, I think it's best that we should meet. I could have my car call for you in . . . what shall we say? . . . ten minutes?'

Janice, who had skipped into the bathroom, came back with a towel wrapped round her. She looked quizzically at him as he asked again: 'I'm sorry, who did you say you were?'

'Bradshaw. Lord Bradshaw.'

Clearly His Lordship was not in the habit of having to explain himself and had no intention of doing so on this occasion. It was a name that rang a distant bell for Christian but from which direction it came he had no idea. Politics perhaps? It struck him as a name that he had probably seen mentioned in the press and, anyway, weren't most lordships political ones?

As though sensing Christian's reluctance, Lord Bradshaw condescended to offer a clue.

'Perhaps if I were to mention a name,' he said.

'Please do,' said the bemused Christian.

'Naughton Point.'

It was a name that offered both too much and too little. It proved that this was far from being a crank call but otherwise left Christian desperate to know why he was being thus summoned. What sort of a morass was he about to be dragged into? Why the hell hadn't he taken Janice's advice and left well alone?

'What is it?' she hissed again, seeing the dismay register on his face.

He held up a hand, meaning that he would tell her in a moment.

'So then,' said Lord Bradshaw, who was beginning to sound impatient, 'you can now understand why I want us to meet, can you?'

'Yes,' mumbled Christian. And then, because he knew that there was no alternative: 'Yes, all right, I'll come then.'

The voice was relieved though not surprised. 'Good. Will ten minutes be all right? My car will pick you up?'

'Can we make it fifteen?' said Christian, looking down at his own nakedness.

Janice, tantalized by having heard only one end of the conversation, was demanding to know what it was all about. When he told her, her alarm at what he might be getting himself into turned to anger with him for the unquestioning way in which he had agreed to go along.

'You could have said no! Why couldn't you have said that you knew nothing about it?'

'Because I do, don't I. And they know that I do!'

He went into the bathroom and turned on the shower, wanting to wash off the stickiness of the journey and of their interrupted love-making. She followed him in and perched on the bidet, her towel wrapped like a bandage around her. The fun was over before it had rightly begun.

'And who is he anyway? You don't even know who he is!'

'He's a politician. At least I think he's a politician.'

'What sort of politician?'

'In the House of Lords, I suppose! How many sorts are there, for God's sake!'

He was irritated by her lack of sympathy: didn't she see that he was as unhappy about this new development as she was?

'I mean, you don't know what this might be about,' she said more quietly. 'You don't know where this car might be taking you.'

He came out of the shower and began to dry himself. His watch told him that he had only another seven minutes before the promised car would arrive to collect him.

'I've seen the name in the newspapers,' he said, softening his tone. 'He's in the House of Lords. He's sending a car to collect me. I mean he's not some sort of gangster or whatever it is that you're thinking!'

'So how does he know about Naughton Point?'

'Search me. But then I don't know *what* he knows about it either, do I? Whatever it is, he might be able to save me a lot of digging through old newspapers to find it.'

In truth, he felt nothing like as confident as he was trying to sound. Determined to proceed with the utmost caution, he seemed to be about to plunge back into the deep-end, this time without even knowing how deep.

'We could go back,' said Janice plaintively. 'Just get on another train and go home.'

She didn't mean it. It was simply a wish that things could be simpler than they were.

'Look,' he said, hurrying to dress himself, 'you were going to do some shopping anyway, weren't you? Well, all right, go ahead and do it. I'll see what this guy has to say and I'll meet you back here at whatever time you like. And don't worry. I'm going to let him do all the talking.'

She made no further attempt to stop him. They agreed that they would meet back at the hotel, either in their room or at the bar, early that evening.

'I've got a feeling that he was better known as something else,' said Christian, thinking aloud as he combed his wet hair.

'You what?'

'Lord Bradshaw. I think the reason I can't place him is that he's only just gone to the Lords. So when he was well-known as a politician it would have been under a different name.'

'Nice for some,' said Janice. 'Changing their name when it suits.' Her spirits seemed to have risen again, for which Christian was grateful. He didn't want to leave her alone in a strange hotel and feeling miserable.

'And have a nice time.' He went and gave her a kiss and she held him for a moment.

'I will,' she said. 'And give my love to old Bradshaw.'

He laughed and left her there, still swaddled in her bath-towel.

Downstairs the large lobby, with its chandeliers fully lit even at midday, held no one who was obviously a chauffeur. Christian sauntered round, then approached reception.

'Has anyone been asking for me? Mr Lewis.'

'I think perhaps it's me you're looking for, sir,' said a voice behind him, even as the girl behind the desk was beginning to shake her head.

Christian turned and found himself facing an eager-looking young woman with frizzy hair and large, round spectacles.

'I've come to take you to see Lord Bradshaw. Sorry if I'm a few minutes late.'

'That's all right,' said Christian, not at all displeased to find that his chauffeur was actually a chauffeuse. His lurking fear that there might be something sinister behind his peremptory invitation receded. This young woman, now leading him out of the hotel, could surely be part of nothing more dangerous than a Brigade of Guides.

The car, too, was reassuring, though in a different way. It was a black Daimler, ageing but dignified, redolent of discretion and respectability. Christian allowed the door to be opened for him and got in. He would enjoy the drive, no matter what might be waiting at the end of it. One small drawback: a glass screen separated him from his driver. A pity – he might have discovered a little more about his host. He settled back into the white leather seat, lit a cigarette and watched London gliding damply past him.

Meanwhile, back in the hotel foyer from which Christian had

just departed in such style, the man who had viewed his departure with more than passing interest returned to his chair and raised again the newspaper which had hidden him when Christian had first appeared. It was a paper that he knew almost by heart since he had had frequent recourse to it as a shield that morning: first on the station platform where he had observed Christian's farewell to his family, then on the train where he had watched Christian's meeting with his ladyfriend, and now in the hotel where he had made a careful note of their room number.

He was a man in his early fifties, of medium height with a pockmarked face and thick, almost Negroid features. Christian, had he seen him at all, would have recognized him as the man who had been standing by the diving-board of the empty swimming-pool at the Bellevue leisure centre. The man who, together with his younger colleague, had scared Christian half to death and sent him fleeing through the darkened building. On that occasion his suit had been covered by a borrowed donkey jacket. He now wore a trench coat, the collar of which he kept turned up as he settled down again to wait.

14

Cocooned inside the Daimler, Christian was transported through central London, a tourist in his own country. The language on the advertisement hoardings was familiar enough but the people seemed alien and the shops full of exotic goods. The railings of a park were hung with oil paintings that were covered by polythene against the drizzle; near them was parked a mini-bus full of policemen. A busker played outside a Mothercare shop; a jeweller's was dignified by a uniformed doorman; while in a tatty square near an underground station there was what looked like a convention of tramps and down-and-outs.

It was as though the steady stream of provincial life had been deflected through the prism of London into its full spectrum of rainbow colours.

The feeling of being on strange territory excited him. Though there was still the apprehension. Where was he going and why? Who was behind the title and the extravagant car and the out-of-the-blue telephone call?

Marble Arch went past, then they were in a tangle of streets to the north of Oxford Street. There were fine Georgian terraces exuding an air of assurance around private gardens. And then came Holborn, where the architecture was increasingly severe and the pedestrians male, white and in a hurry, all signs for those who had eyes for them that they were nearing the City, that financial ghetto that craftily hid its computers behind Romanesque pillars and Byzantine frescoes.

They passed the top of Chancery Lane, then turned into a quieter street of elegant façades that would have been remarkable anywhere but here where such splendour was the rule. The car slowed and stopped.

Christian felt disappointment that the ride was over and a renewed fear of what it might have brought him to. He must be on his guard. Lord Bradshaw, whoever he may be, already knew a good deal too much for Christian's comfort.

'Here we are, then,' said his frizzy-haired chauffeuse who had come round to open the door.

Christian thanked her and even wondered about tipping, but it would have been absurd: she had brought him in a Daimler, not a beaten-up mini-cab.

The building before them was of plain red-brick but endowed with gentle, curving lines and decorative ironwork, every inch cleaned and polished to perfection. It was a building to which Christian gave his full approval.

'It's this way,' said the chauffeuse, and led him away from it, along the street to where, sandwiched between two very passable Victorian Gothic temples of commerce, stood a tall, thin, conrete-and-glass monstrosity. Its nameplate was as imaginative as its architecture and said simply, 'No. 37'. Beneath it, a list of insurance and auditing firms admitted in small letters to having offices within.

Obviously someone couldn't bear the thought of the land standing empty, thought Christian wryly. There must have been, what, twenty yards between the two Victorian blocks so they had to pour in this large-scale concrete telephone-kiosk.

They went in. The young lady said, 'Hi, Joe,' to the man behind the desk who looked up from his newspaper and gave her a wave. The lift was waiting. It was as small as the building suggested it might be, bringing them so close that conversation was essential.

'Lord Bradshaw . . .' began Christian hesitantly.

'Yes?'

'Is he . . . well, *what* is he?'

'Oh, he's lovely,' grinned the chauffeuse unexpectedly. 'Everybody likes him. I mean, I'm sure you'll get on with him wonderfully!'

It would have seemed ungenerous, after such a whole-hearted recommendation, to admit that he was actually wanting to know who the man was.

They stepped out of the lift and went along a short corridor to an unmarked door. Christian tensed in anticipation of what might be awaiting him behind it: violence, interrogation, bribery . . . In fact it was a small reception room. The chauffeuse crossed it to a further door which she pushed open and motioned Christian to enter.

At that moment he knew who Lord Bradshaw was. The first sight that he had of him – behind his desk, in a comfortably furnished room that was more of a study than an office – told him all he needed to know. It was a face as familiar as any in the land, an identity that had been camouflaged by the assumed title.

'Well, hello,' Lord Bradshaw called, coming from behind the desk. 'How nice of you to come.'

'A pleasure . . . sir,' mumbled Christian, taking the soft white hand that was extended to him. It was the hand of the man who had been Home Secretary in the last Government – or had it been the last Government but one? – and, before that, minister of one thing and another in a long parliamentary career that had now brought him his title and, with it, retirement of a kind. Christian had the unnerving feeling that the face, made familiar by a hundred television interviews and a thousand newspaper pictures, couldn't be real, that it was another, cleverer piece of media projection. A hologram that moved and was now gesturing to one of a pair of armchairs that stood together away from the desk.

'Do sit down.' And then to the chauffeuse: 'Margot, love, I wonder what our friend Mr Lewis might like to drink?'

Margo turned to him. 'What would you like?'

'Er, coffee please,' said Christian, not sure what else was being offered and, anyway, having sworn to keep his wits about him.

'For myself,' said Lord Bradshaw, 'a clean glass will suffice.'

'Coming up,' said Margot. She gave Christian a sudden, conspiratorial grin – as if to say, see, I told you he was lovely! – and disappeared into an adjoining room.

Lord Bradshaw sat in the other armchair.

'And how was your journey down?'

'Oh yes,' said Christian, still in a state of shock, 'all right, thanks.'

'British Rail are so much better than they used to be, aren't they? At least over long distances. It's now only the short ones they can't seem to manage.' And he gave a little whinny of delight at his own observation.

They were sitting so close that their knees were almost touching. As his senses calmed and he was able to take a proper look at his host, Christian saw a man whose jutting belly carried on its crest a silk tie of muted colours and around which sat the jacket of a well-cut woollen suit. The trousers draped a pair of thin legs, the ankles now crossed. His shoes were heavy, round-toed lace-ups. He must have been in his early seventies – his life had encompassed so much that he could barely be younger – yet his skin showed few of the ravages of age. Apart from a slackness around the neck, it was sleek and smooth, a testimony to the cosmetic effect of power. There was something slightly and appealingly effeminate about him, a delicacy and alertness, notwithstanding the gross stomach.

As Christian observed him, he knew that he himself was being assessed. He cleared his throat and hitched up the knees of his trousers.

'It takes two-and-a-half hours, the train,' he said weakly.

'And will you be going to the theatre while you're here? Is that one of your interests?'

'I, er . . . I'm not sure,' said Christian, resolving to do so.

'I should advise against it. There's nowhere to leave your coat and you'll be damn lucky to get a drink.'

Margot returned with a cup of coffee in white porcelain which she placed on the small table by Christian's side. He declined sugar. For Lord Bradshaw she carried over the half-empty bottle of white wine that was already standing on the desk and, as requested, a clean glass. His Lordship gave another whinny of laughter as she fussed around them, suggesting that he tolerated her attentiveness for her sake rather than his own. Christian thanked her and she disappeared again.

'Now, what were we saying?'

Christian, not sure, remained silent.

Lord Bradshaw found a new topic but still not the one for which Christian had been summoned.

'And how is the North of England?' he asked, pouring some wine into his new glass.

'The, er . . .' Christian struggled for a reply, then managed: 'Well, it was wet and cold when I left it this morning.' Then, fearing that this sounded stupid and that some thing more considered was called for, he talked a little about unemployment and the recession and likely political trends. The fact that he knew nothing about any of these topics made the going difficult but Lord Bradshaw proved a good listener, nodding encouragingly even in the pauses, of which there were many.

'I see,' he said, when Christian had finally stuttered to a halt. 'Yes, I must say I got a somewhat similar impression when I was there . . . now, let's see, when was it, the day before yesterday.'

Christian coloured with embarrassment and cursed himself for his loquacity. He had spent five minutes being patronizing and boring about life in the Bad Lands beyond Watford for the benefit of a man who probably knew more about it than he did.

And wasn't he, anyway, a northerner himself? He had a seat somewhere in South Yorkshire – that Christian knew for certain – but he couldn't recall whether he had also been a native of that shire. The accent had been adulterated almost beyond recognition but still there were the flat 'a' sounds to point to a birth and breeding that at least wasn't southern. All the more foolish then that Christian should have presumed to lecture him.

'Could you do me a favour?' asked Lord Bradshaw, not seeming to notice Christian's discomfort. 'Could you retrieve the cigarettes from my desk? Save me getting out of this damn chair again.'

Christian eagerly complied and was rewarded by a quite disproportionate expression of gratitude and the offer of a cigarette. He moved again between desk and chairs, bringing the table-lighter for both of them. It was inscribed, referring to some anniversary or other.

The walls of the room, now that he had the chance to take them in, were covered with photographs. Mostly black-and-white and mostly of men, they showed the politician who was now Lord Bradshaw younger and more vigorous and in the midst of things. They were of parliamentary delegations, pausing in their fact-finding tours of the Orkneys or Bangladesh for the benefit of the camera, Cabinets lined up like football teams but without a ball to hold, Shadow Cabinets looking a little less proud of themselves, and innumerable other groups of the still-recognizable and the long-

123

forgotten at ship-launchings, general elections or party political conferences. Each picture was framed in black; they seemed to be in no particular order.

Margot had returned, drawn by the sound of Christian scurrying back and forth.

'You should tell me if you want anything,' she chided Lord Bradshaw. 'That's what I'm here for.'

His Lordship chuckled. 'It's like having a mother again,' he said to Christian. 'Looking after me. Bossing me. I suppose I must be in my second childhood if I've got a second mother.'

'You need looking after,' said Margot tartly. The repartee was probably habitual: she was the court jester with licence to speak out.

'All right, run along,' he urged her. 'We're all right now, thank you.'

She ignored him and spoke to Christian: 'Just give me a shout if you want anything.'

'Thank you,' said Christian.

'You'll be listening anyway,' said Lord Bradshaw to Margot's departing back.

Left alone, they both sucked on their cigarettes. Christian took a sip of his coffee. 'Well now,' said Lord Bradshaw. The words suggested that the moment had arrived when they might properly turn their minds to the one topic that they had so far avoided.

'The reason that I asked you to come and see me was that, as I said, we both seem to have an interest in the same thing.' And, in case Christian were still in any doubt that the polite foreplay was over, he spelled it out: 'Naughton Point. Skeletons. Who were they, and who put the bloody things there and why.'

Christian nodded. 'Yes.'

'I gather that you've been doing a little detective work of your own?'

'I've, er . . . a bit, yes,' said Christian, defensive.

'Very good. However, what I'm going to have to ask you to do now – and I know it's asking a lot – is to trust me.'

Christian nodded again. No other response seemed possible.

'Because it's going to be a bit unfair really. You see, I'm going to ask you to tell me everything you know. But then I can't tell you everything *I* know!'

And he gave a bright smile that sought Christian's compliance. This was a silly world, it said, but they neither of them could alter it so had better go along with it.

124

'You're involved in some sort of . . . investigation?' hazarded Christian.

'Precisely.'

'And it's all rather . . . hush-hush?' he asked, feeling self-conscious about the espionage terminology.

'Absolutely. How nice of you to understand.'

Christian was pleased by the compliment without being sure just what he had done to deserve it.

'You see,' went on His Lordship, 'even though I'm something of a relic and near enough to the knacker's yard, I do come in useful now and again when something odd crops up and they have to find somebody to sort of keep a fatherly eye on things. Especially since we don't know how far the roots of this particular business might stretch. Are we dealing with a piddling little plant that'll come up whole at the first pull or will it prove to have tentacles a mile long that'll lead us to God-knows-who?'

Christian seized on the implication. 'You think that Naughton Point . . . I mean that it might be the tip of an iceberg?'

Lord Bradshaw looked heavenwards and made a gesture that said yes, it could be, anything was possible.

It was a prospect that excited Christian, promising as it did a real-life conspiracy to match the fantasies that he had entertained over the years and featuring The Hermitage mafiosa. It also removed any final doubts about why he had been summoned here. He was wanted as an ally, not as an enemy; the information he had, far from threatening his own safety, had opened doors to that semi-secret world of privilege and power.

Lord Bradshaw spoke. And spoke carefully. 'All I can tell you is this. There has been suspicion for some time – I mean going back to the mid-sixties – suspicion that there might well have been a large-scale conspiracy involving local government, property developers, people of that sort. Individual cases have already come to light and been dealt with, of course.'

Christian nodded, thinking of the corruption trials of the early seventies.

'But some people felt that there was more. That we were only – as you have so aptly put it – dealing with the tip of the iceberg.'

'I see,' said Christian, though what he saw was vague and out of focus. His imagination tried and failed to envisage just what it was at which Lord Bradshaw was hinting. Who was involved? How high did this thing reach? Or was it rather a matter of hundreds and thousands of small-time operators, a conspiracy shocking in its sheer size rather than in the eminence of the individual conspirators?

'Now the discovery of these two skeletons,' went on Lord Bradshaw, 'is important because it's given a new motive – an excuse if you like – for launching an investigation into the possibility of there having been such a conspiracy. An investigation with teeth. I'm sure you'll understand if I don't go into details but it means that agencies who've been reluctant to get involved in the past now have no choice. The destruction of that building uncovered a crime. Now whether it was a simple case of double murder . . .' – and he chuckled at his own description that seemed to relegate double murder to the level of shop-lifting – '. . . or whether those murders are the key that's going to unlock a whole Pandora's box of secrets remains to be seen.'

'But at least it means that something now has to be done,' said Christian to show that he was following.

'It does. And I've got the unenviable job of doing it.'

This was qualified by a chuckle: unenviable job or not, he would take a certain relish in dredging the sediment of the 'sixties. Seeing if the mud would stick.

'I didn't realize,' said Christian. 'I mean, that anything like this was involved.'

'I'm sure you didn't. I very much hope that no one else will either.'

Christian nodded in earnest agreement.

'Would you like a drink now?' asked Lord Bradshaw suddenly. Christian looked at his coffee, which he had barely touched.

'Have a Scotch,' his host urged him. 'I only drink this stuff' – the white wine – 'because my bloody doctor says I have to. Medicinal.'

'Yes, all right, thank you,' said Christian. He had little need now for the caution with which he had approached their meeting and could surely run the risk of a little alcohol loosening his tongue.

Margot appeared as if by magic and did the honours.

'Can you get me a *Herald Tribune*?' Lord Bradshaw asked her.

'I'll try.'

He turned to Christian. 'D'you ever read the *Herald Tribune*?'

'No,' said Christian with a smile: was it anything like the *Gowling Chronicle*?

'Makes you realize how bloody insular and trivial our press is. 'Course you've probably realized that already.'

126

'I hope you're going to eat something and not just booze all day,' said Margot.

'So do I,' he agreed.

She tutted, as though in despair, and left them.

'Cheers,' said Christian, raising his generously-filled glass.

'Your good health.'

Lord Bradshaw emptied his own glass and then, with a remarkably steady hand, refilled it to the brim.

'Now,' he said, 'your turn. Just what have you discovered about this whole business?'

Christian hesitated. It wasn't that he had any reservations about giving a full and honest answer, just that he wondered where to start. He could see little point in explaining about Jack Stephenson; besides, the man was dead. Deciding to give nothing but the truth – but not quite the whole of it – he related everything he knew about Richard Morris Dunmore, who had worked in the local Planning Department before so mysteriously disappearing, and Charles Yates, freelance journalist, whose remains had been positively identified through his teeth. He was gratified to receive a confirmatory nod from Lord Bradshaw at the mention of each name. He told him – without mentioning Janice, who was surely an irrelevance in the matter – of how he had come to London in an attempt to trace the work that Charles Yates was doing immediately prior to his death in the hope that it would both reveal why he was killed and point to his connection with Richard Morris Dunmore. He came to the end of his account, sat back and waited.

'Very good,' said Lord Bradshaw. 'You seem to have made exceptional progress. Considering what you had to start with.'

Christian gave a modest smile, feeling the compliment to be no more than his due.

'Now this is where I have to ask you to trust me.'

'Yes?' He already knew that he would give his consent to whatever he was about to be asked.

'You see, this whole thing is at a very delicate stage. It may be that we've uncovered a mountain. It may be no more than a molehill.'

'I understand,' said Christian.

'We're only going to find out which it is if we can continue to fool certain people into thinking that we aren't really all that interested.'

'Yes.'

'So. Can I ask you not to proceed with these private investigations of yours? To leave everything in our hands? Otherwise there'll always be the risk that you're going to alert the people that we don't want to be alerted. This is no criticism of you or of anything you've done. Just that . . . well, I think that from here on we're probably in a better position to handle things than you are.'

Christian nodded. That much seemed undeniable, even had he wished to deny it. The resources of a small-town architect could hardly be expected to compete with those of Lord Bradshaw, ex-Home Secretary and God-knew-what-else.

'So will you agree to what I'm suggesting?' The voice was gentle, persuasive. 'You'll forget all about the case? Or at least not *do* anything more about it?'

'Yes,' said Christian, 'I will.'

'Splendid.'

Was it such a sacrifice anyway? He could now forget about delving into newspaper archives and concentrate on screwing Janice. He had come this far out of stubbornness and wounded price; what a relief it would be to be able to say to hell with Naughton Point and all those encased within it. His only regret would be if he were never to know the end of the story.

'Will I ever find out what happens?' he asked.

The other man hesitated. 'Possibly. But I can't promise you anything.'

'I'm just curious, that's all.'

'Of course you are. Of course you are. And I'll keep you informed as far as I can.'

'Thank you.'

'But,' added Lord Bradshaw, 'that might not be very far. For one thing, it's still possible that nothing will come out of all this. We could still run up against a brick wall. Or we could still find that all our ideas about a possible conspiracy are sheer fantasy and there isn't a shred of evidence to support them.'

'Of course.'

'On the other hand, if anything does come of it . . . well then, I'm sure that the media will be falling over themselves to tell you and everybody else everything there is to know and doubtless a bit more besides.'

'Yes,' agreed Christian. 'Fair enough.'

He was beginning to see further advantage in his thus contracting out of the whole business. The uncovering of any deep-rooted conspiracy might reveal that one of those roots touched Percy somewhere along the way. Even though his father-in-law no longer figured in his thoughts as the arch-villain he had once appeared, that still left him well short of beatification. His methods of attracting work had always verged on the unethical. His empire had been built through personal contact rather than success in tendering. If Percy ever were to get scooped up in some massive clean-up operation then it would be provident from every point of view that Christian should have played no part in it.

'And don't worry if the local police don't seem very active,' said Lord Bradshaw. 'We aren't relying on them.'

Christian thought of Dennis Joiner, indiscreet and at home in The Blue Anchor.

'They don't seem to have got very far,' he said.

'I doubt they ever shall,' agreed Lord Bradshaw, and they shared a smile.

'There is just one question,' said Christian.

His Lordship beamed. 'You can ask as many questions as you like. What I can't guarantee is that I'll be able to answer them.'

'How did you know what I was up to? How did you know that I was coming to London? And where I was staying?'

'That's three questions.'

'It all amounts to the same thing,' said Christian, now feeling bold enough to fence a little. 'How do you know about me?'

'I'm sorry.' He opened his smooth hands in a gesture of helplessness. 'I can't tell you.' Then added: 'But I can guarantee you complete confidentiality. No one will ever know anything about your visit here or . . . anything else that you don't wish them to know.'

A nod being as good as a wink, Christian interpreted clearly that the main thing that no one would ever know was that he was in London with his mistress. He was grateful for the reassurance. It had concerned him that an organization that could trace him so effortlessly would doubtless know all about Janice, left behind in the hotel room and wrapped in a bath-towel.

'Thank you,' he said.

Lord Bradshaw leaned forward in his chair. 'So I have your word that you'll proceed no further in this business but that you'll leave all the dirty work to us?'

'I'll be glad to,' said Christian, and they shook hands.

'Now, I mustn't keep you any longer,' said Lord Bradshaw

abruptly. He hoisted himself to his feet. 'I'm sure you've plenty of more interesting things to do than sit chatting to an old so-and-so like me.'

It was a genial dismissal with which Christian reluctantly complied. He had been enjoying the interview and was sorry that it should end. Margot appeared, car-keys at the ready, but he assured them that he would prefer to walk. His glimpses of London had intrigued him and he wanted to see more. Besides, he wouldn't be meeting Janice until the early evening: what had he to rush back for?

They shook hands again. Lord Bradshaw went back to his desk and Christian was shown to the door by the attentive Margot.

'You can find your own way . . . ?' she said, indicating the lift. He said that he could and thanked her.

'A pleasure,' she said, gave him a departing grin and went back to minister to His Lordship.

Christian's high spirits survived even having to jam into the small lift with four other people and finding himself up against a fur coat that smelt of moth-balls. Hadn't he spent the previous eight years or so of his life – or anyway the lunchtimes of it – leaning on the bar at The Hermitage, bemoaning his lack of progress towards his own little room at the top? And now here he was, emerging from a tête-à-tête with one of the country's leading politicians – retired from the centre of the fray perhaps but evidently still with free access to the corridors of power. And not only that: he had been taken into the man's confidence and asked to assist in a cloak-and-dagger operation that could have unspecified but spectacular repercussions. It was heady stuff. And Christian was intoxicated by it.

He came out of the lift. Joe was still behind the desk and called, 'Goodbye, sir,' as he went past.

Outside it was raining steadily and Christian paused within the final set of glass doors to pull up the zip of his anorak and lift its big collar around his ears. It was while doing so that he noticed a small brass plaque that was set into the wall beside the doors.

PAWLEY HOUSE, it said. OPENED 10TH SEPTEMBER 1967. PAWLEY DEVELOPMENTS LIMITED. ARCHITECTS: TOTAL PLAN BUILDING LIMITED.

It was the kind of plaque common enough in the entrance of modern office blocks. Nothing remarkable about it, except that the name 'Total Plan Building' had been the original trading name of the architectural practice which Percy had founded and in which Christian was now employed.

The coincidence at first amused him. He must tell Percy that he had seen it. Though he wouldn't, of course, be able to admit what he had been doing there.

Then, about to step out and brave the weather, another thought struck him and he paused again, this time to re-read the name of the development company: 'Pawley Developments Limited'.

It was a name that he had seen before. More than once. It had, he remembered, featured on several of the old plans that were kept in the archives of the practice back in Gowling.

He finally left the shelter of the building and set off towards Chancery Lane, his head down against the squalls of wind and the rain they carried with them. His sense of elation, punctured by what he had just seen, was beginning to ebb. A new, disquieting possibility had occurred to him.

15

He tried persuading himself that it didn't matter anyway. He had washed his hands of the whole business, and done so under what he had believed to be honourable circumstances. At the behest of an ex-government minister no less.

For a while it almost worked. He meandered through the rain as far as the Covent Garden redevelopment, which proved a temporary distraction. Then he felt hungry: he hadn't eaten since an early and hurried breakfast. He went into a McDonald's and had a cheeseburger, hot cherry pie and a raspberry milkshake. Not a happy combination. He came out with his stomach as unsettled as his mind already was.

He had to admit that he was no longer interested in sightseeing. Not until he had resolved the nagging doubts that that brass plaque had awakened. Up to that moment he had taken every word that Lord Bradshaw had uttered for gospel. And why not indeed? The man was eminent, well-known, had appeared on 'Any Questions'. Was it his fault that he happened to have an office in a building designed by Percy Jordan and financed by Pawley Developments?

Well, maybe. That telltale plaque linked that ugly office block, however tenuously, with Naughton Point. It might still be an innocent coincidence. But it might be something more.

Christian found himself on the Embankment, looking across the sluggish, grey waters of the Thames at the arts complex of the South Bank. More concrete. The bloody stuff was everywhere.

An idea came to him. A way in which he could test his suspicions. But did he want to? Having once extracted himself from the whole messy affair, did he want to run the risk of being plunged back in again?

He made a telephone call.

'Bertram Hotel. Can I help you?'

'Room 305 please.'

He would arrange to meet Janice and let her talk him out of it. She had always feared for where his curiosity might be leading him. She would be sure to argue that he should let sleeping dogs lie. With her help he might persuade himself.

But the only voice on the line was that of the operator again: 'I'm sorry. There doesn't seem to be any answer.'

Christian put down the receiver and stepped out of the kiosk. He couldn't be surprised – she had intended to spend the afternoon shopping – and it was a decision of a sort. If she had been there then he would have gone to meet her and allowed himself to be – reluctantly – talked out of his suspicions. She wasn't there and the scales tipped the other way, leaving victory to the nagging voice in his head that told him that he couldn't stop now. He had to follow up the one lead that remained to him. It could still prove a blank (pray God that it should); but then at least he would be contented.

He went into a post office along the Strand, found their set of London directories and looked up the name that he was seeking. He then telephoned and was given instructions on how to get there, and a warning that they closed at four-thirty.

He hurried to the Underground, bought his ticket and then, as the escalator carried him downwards, worked out his route from the small map in the back of his diary. It looked straightforward. Up the Northern Line to Euston and then change.

At least down there it was warm and he could unfasten his sodden anorak. He walked along the platform reading the advertisements that were for nylon stockings, Russian restaurants and Life Assurance. The train came. He got on and realized too late that it was a no-smoking compartment.

'Do you know where your life is heading?' asked an advert for an employment agency. No, thought Christian, no, he didn't. Had he known that, he would never have started tracking down those accursed skeletons. Having started and got this far, would he ever be allowed to stop?

He changed trains, this time making sure that the compartment allowed him to smoke, and was finally at Old Street station. Following the directions given him, he went out through Exit 4 and found himself going up City Road. Companies' House was ahead of him, no more than fifty yards away. He looked at his watch. Ten-to-three. Plenty of time.

It was an institution that took itself seriously with security guards on the door. Their presence confirmed Christian's recent discovery that information was precious and could be dangerous. The clerk to whom he was directed was shielded by a glass screen.

'Yes, please?'

'I want to look at the records of a company called Pawley Developments . . .'

Before he could go further, she had slid a form under the glass at him.

'Could you fill this in? Then bring it back to me.'

Christian took it and moved away to one of the long tables at which other seekers after truth were filling in similar forms. Probably journalists, he thought. Or tax inspectors. They couldn't all be involved in double murders.

He looked through the index of companies and found the number of Pawley Developments. Then, with the form completed and his one pound search fee at the ready, he returned to the woman behind the glass screen. He had found only one problem in the rules and regulations to which the form had introduced him.

'It says here that I can see the company records for any or all of the past three years . . .'

'Yes?'

'Can't I go back further than that?'

'Not here, no. If you want records before that then we have to send away to Cardiff.'

'And how long does that take?'

'Oh . . . about a week.'

Well, that was out then. He would take the last three years and see what they told him. Whatever secrets Cardiff held, Cardiff could keep.

'Just the last three years then, please.'

He was asked to wait. A vending-machine provided him with a cup of coffee while an abandoned copy of the *Daily Mail* helped to pass the time. Meanwhile the woman behind the glass screen was kept busy by a steady stream of enquirers, some of whom seemed to be regulars and to know the ropes, others who were obviously there for the first time. They were all fishing in the same great sea of information, in Christian's case blindly; he wouldn't know what he had hooked until the catch was landed.

It finally arrived – a short roll of microfilm in a protective container – and he took it to a vacant viewing-machine. There must have been fifty of them in the room, each with its own absorbed user. Putting in the film, Christian applied himself to his own screen. The image flickered nervously, exaggerating his slightest touch on the control. He sharpened the focus and the 1980 company records for Pawley Development Limited jumped into view.

After the long wait, it was over in an instant. There were columns of figures to do with trading and profit-and-loss but he ignored them. He wanted only the list of company directors; it was a short one and he took it in at a glance.

There were six names: Donald Amos Tyson; George Crawley; Walter James Rees; Gerald Maddox; Neil Harvey Bond; John Knightly Renbourne.

George Crawley and Neil Harvey Bond were the only two unfamiliar names on the list and could be dispensed with.

Tyson, Rees and Maddox were familiar enough. Percy's three dining-companions from The Hermitage. Not surprising then that Percy had been commissioned to design the building which they had financed and which Christian had visited only hours earlier.

But it was the sixth name on the list that held his attention even beyond these. It was this for which he had been looking and fearing that he would find. William Knightly Renbourne. More simply Bill Renbourne. It had been as familiar a name as almost any in the land until his recent elevation to the peerage had given him the title of Lord Bradshaw behind which to shelter.

The bastard, thought Christian. The clever old bastard.

He savagely unwound the film from its spool and pushed it back into the box. He needed to look no further. The microfilmed company records had removed all his doubts and left him depressingly certain: he had been conned, bamboozled, taken for a ride. It was all so clear that he felt like laughing aloud at the farce in which he had played such a willing part.

How delighted Lord Bradshaw, the benign old sod, must have been at the success of his ploy. He had sent his pally chauffeuse and his reassuring Daimler to collect the all-too-gullible Christian. He had first humbled him with a display of urbane civility, then buttered him up with hints of top-level intrigues. And then finally moved in for the kill, persuading him to forget everything he knew and leave the whole business in His Lordship's soft, pale hands. He had been conned rotten from first to last. And how? By subtle flattery, by being induced to consider himself as privileged, as one who was being given a glimpse of that secret world of power and influence. It was his Achilles heel of old. The wish to be sitting at the table with the mighty and not left standing at the bar with the other malcontents.

Inevitably it was Janice who took the brunt of his bitterness. He went back to the hotel and hung around in the bar until she appeared. The more he thought about it, the more his anger wasn't so much with the insidious Lord Bradshaw but with himself for proving such a willing dupe.

'Oh, you're here,' she cried, finding him hunched over a pint of bitter. She had returned from her shopping and been up to their room to wash and dress for the evening.

'Yes,' he said shortly.

'What's the matter? What's happened?' she said, as his mood communicated itself to her.

'They set me up.'

'What?'

'Oh, sit down. What do you want to drink?'

And despite her protestations that she first wanted to hear his story, he made her wait while he got her a gin-and-tonic and himself another half-pint.

'What's happened?' she asked him again when he got back. 'What did that Lord-whatever-he-was-called want you for?'

'Bradshaw.'

'Yes. What did he want?'

'He wanted to shut me up.'

'Oh God . . . !' she said, alarmed.

'Oh, no, nothing violent, no threats. They're a lot cleverer than that down here!'

And he told her about Margot and his journey to Pawley House, his recognition of Lord Bradshaw as one of the country's senior politicians and his own gracious welcome. He gave her, just as he had been given it, the account of the hush-hush investigations with which his own puny efforts had become entangled. And told her how he had finally agreed to the request that he should abandon his own personal crusade in the wider public interest.

'Well,' she said, puzzled, 'and what's wrong with that?'

'What's wrong is that Lord Bradshaw – or Bill Renbourne, or whatever you want to call him – is in league with Tyson, Rees and Maddox!'

'Who?'

He reminded her of the unwholesome trio that regularly lunched with Percy. And then explained about the brass plaque that he had happened to see as he left the building and the journey that he had then made to Companies' House.

'And there it was. Black-and-white. The four of them directors of the same bloody development company!'

She sat and looked at him for a moment. Then shook her head, still puzzled.

'And that's it, is it?'

'Isn't it enough!'

It evidently wasn't. 'I don't see that it proves anything.'

Christian gave a short laugh and put down his glass with a force that turned several heads towards them.

'I mean, all right,' she said, trying to calm him, 'all right he does know them. But why shouldn't he? That isn't a crime, is it?'

'No. But it might mean that he was involved in one once.'

She thought for a moment. 'The Naughton Point skeletons?'

'Yes.'

She shook her head. 'Why? Why on earth should it mean that?'

'Because there's too much bloody coincidence,' he said, becoming annoyed with her stubborn refusal to see things his way. 'There's so much bloody coincidence that they just *have* to be involved, that's all!'

Then, seeing that she was still unpersuaded, he forced himself to spell things out quietly and as simply as he could. He had, anyway, had time to mull the situation over and grasp its implications. It was perhaps unfair to expect her to have an instant grasp of what had taken him a whole afternoon and a journey to Old Street to understand.

'That old sod that I saw this lunchtime tried to put me off the scent.' Then quickly, before she could protest: 'Never mind *why* for the time being. He tried to put me off the scent. To get me to forget all about Naughton Point and the rest and go home and keep quiet like a good boy. Right?'

She nodded. 'All right, yes.'

'He acted as though he'd never had anything to do with property development . . . or even the North of England, come to that! And he certainly never mentioned knowing Rees and his gang.'

'But why should he?'

'Because, since he knows so much, he must know that I know them. So wouldn't the normal thing have been to have at least mentioned them?'

'He didn't *have* to,' she insisted.

'No,' he said, seeing that she wasn't going to be shifted. 'He didn't *have* to, no.'

'Well then.'

'He wanted to impress me – to intimidate me if you like – with the idea that he's Lord Bradshaw. That he's still got the ear of the Government. That he's a big shot. Too big to be involved in anything like this.'

'Well, he is. I mean he is a Lord and a big shot and all that.'

'Yes, but he's also been a northern MP. He's also been a director of at least one development company. And he's also got strong links with Gowling. Via Rees, Tyson and Maddox. And Gowling, as I'm sure I don't have to remind you, is where those bloody skeletons were found!'

'All right,' she said. 'Keep your voice down.'

'But you do see what I'm getting at?' he insisted, though more quietly.

She shrugged. 'Yes. But I still don't think that it proves anything.'

He sighed. She was, he had to recognize, a very persistent lady. Not to say mule-like.

'No,' he said, 'perhaps it doesn't prove anything in a legal sense. It just makes it highly unlikely that he's been entrusted with any sort of investigation into anything and a damn sight more likely that he's simply trying to shut me up!'

'It's possible.'

'Thank you,' he said, a touch sarcastic.

'But if you're right . . .'

'Yes?'

'Then that means he knows a lot more about that Naughton

Point business than he should.'

'Exactly!'

'So hadn't you better shut up anyway?'

He looked at her, startled by her abrupt warning. She met his stare: yes, she meant it. It reinforced his not altogether comfortable feeling that this was a lady with a will and opinion very much of her own. And, while it had been flattering to feel that she was concerned for his safety, it was less so to be more or less accused of being pig-headed.

'You think I should just . . . give up?'

She placed a reassuring hand on his arm. This time her tone was more sympathetic.

'I just don't want to see you getting into something . . . well, something that might turn nasty. I mean they threatened you once already, didn't they? When those two came after you at the leisure centre?'

He didn't need the reminder.

'That was phase one,' he said. 'This was phase two. Same idea – to persuade me to keep my mouth shut – but being a bit cleverer about it!'

'So what are you going to do?'

'Oh . . . God knows!'

It was the old story. He had been unable to resist going one step further – just one more look at one more set of microfilms – and had thus set himself a new dilemma: what to do next? He hadn't the slightest idea but, with Janice clearly against him doing anything, he didn't want it to seem that he was giving way to her.

'God knows,' he said again.

They sat in silence. The bar around them had filled with early evening customers. It was Happy Hour and drinks were half-price.

'Well,' said Janice brightly, 'and what about tonight then? I don't know about you but I'm starving!'

He told her about his unwise choice of lunch at McDonald's and they laughed about it. He brought her a dish of canapés from the bar – 'to keep you going' – while he went up to their room to wash and change before they decided on where to eat. He had also remembered his promise to call Diane. It would be tactful to do so while away from his mistress.

'You're sure you're all right here?'

'Oh yes, fine. Don't hurry. I'll read my book.'

And she settled down with her paperback as he took the key and

never found a single bone!'

She couldn't resist the opportunity. 'Then just forget about it,' she urged him. 'Just take that Lord Bradshaw at his word!'

'I don't believe his word.'

'So what? You've done as much as you could. As much as anybody could!'

He knew that they would never agree and that their only chance for a peaceful evening was to drop the subject.

'Look, let's talk about something else, eh?'

'You were the one . . .'

He stopped her. 'I know. It's my fault, I know it is. And I promise not to say another word about it, OK?'

'OK.'

But there was still a distance between them so that conversation was hard to come by. At least, though, the food was good. Christian went on to moussaka while Janice had lamb kebab and salad. She ate ravenously while he picked at his food, leaving half of it.

Although he had made a conscious attempt to slow the pace of his drinking, he had started too early and too eagerly for it not to have affected him. They had each had a glass of retsina to acompany their Turkish coffee. He now found himself stumbling as they left the restaurant and began the short walk back to the hotel.

'Sorry,' he said, bumping into her; they were again arm-in-arm. 'I'm sorry.'

'You're drunk,' she said, but seemed not to mind.

'Not really drunk,' he said, but then rather spoiled things by stepping heavily off the edge of the pavement.

She laughed and pulled him more tightly to her.

'Come on,' she said, 'before the police pick us both up.'

'It's this cold air,' he mumbled. Which made her laugh all the more.

They reached the hotel.

'I'll make coffee,' she said, steering him away from the bar.

Going up in the lift, he felt sick, but managed to hide the small groan that he gave by turning it into a cough. They got into the room and he sat on the edge of the bed.

It was hardly the romantic, passionate evening that he had envisaged. First that phone call and now this, he thought, remembering their spoiled love-making earlier. But he was beyond doing much about it. At least Janice didn't seem too disappointed. She switched on the television and watched *Newsnight* while making the coffee. Then, despite his protestations, she helped him to undress and climb into his side of the double bed.

'Goodnight,' she said, and kissed him chastely on the forehead.

'You come in,' he mumbled.

She gave a little laugh. 'Go to sleep,' she instructed.

To his surprise, he did.

For a long time he lay comatose, hardly moving. The only sound in the room was his heavy breathing, so heavy as to be almost a groan, and the occasional clicking of the radiators. Then, in the early hours, his body began to shift uneasily, triggered by a dream in which he found himself lost in a giant maze and being pursued by distant, unseen figures. The walls of the maze were of concrete, grey and stained and unbroken. He hurried this way and that, unable to shake off his unseen pursuers or find a way of escape.

Suddenly the maze betrayed him, its zigzagging path reaching a dead end. He tried to climb but could find no foot- or handhold and, looking up, he saw that the wall went up to what looked like infinity.

With a sob of despair he turned to face his pursuers whose snarls and yells were growing ever nearer. They came into view, down on all-fours and moving like giant dogs. Their leader had a soft, white face and his paws, when he raised them, were manicured and fine. Behind him crowded three differing visages, all aged yet none alike. One had hanging jowls and dribbled, another was illuminated by a thin fire coming from its lips while the third had no skin at all but was a skull, its jawbone snapping emptily.

Christian awoke with a gasp of relief. He was sweating. His mouth was dry and his head throbbing, though he welcomed all these discomforts for the end to his nightmare that they signalled.

The unfamiliar, darkened room baffled him for a moment. Then he realized that the body turned away from him on the other side of the bed was Janice, not Diane, and remembered that he was in a hotel. A hot, airless hotel room. He pushed aside the covers that were damp with sweat and, cautiously so as not to disturb Janice, swung his feet to the floor and found the switch for the bedside light. He could then move to the window, ease off the catch and open it a couple of inches. A draught of cold air sliced into the room.

His head still beating, he shuffled to the bathroom and was able

142

to relieve both his thirst and his full bladder. Then back to the window for some more of the fresh air.

Tomorrow, he thought. Tomorrow he would be wiser and better. He would drink less – perhaps he would stop drinking altogether. He would smoke less. He would be less of a fool. It was the middle of the night, the time for such resolutions and changes of heart.

He felt better and knew that he would now sleep. Janice, he was glad to see, hadn't stirred. Their day had begun early with the train journey: she must have been exhausted. He looked forward to the morning when they would awake together.

He would have looked forward to it with less confidence had he been able to see her face. The eyes were wide open, though unseeing. Her lips, from which the tip of her tongue protruded, were suffused with blood and purplish in colour. There was a thin, cruel line around her neck.

Christian climbed back into bed, turned out the light and snuggled into her back.

16

He would have slept longer but for the sound of the traffic that followed the cold air in through the open window.

He opened his eyes, saw that it was still dark and closed them again. He was aware that he again needed to visit the bathroom and that he was going to have a medium-sized hangover, both discomforts that could be ignored for a while longer. He slipped back into a light sleep, still hearing the traffic moving below him as it shunted towards central London.

Half-an-hour later he opened his eyes again and saw that dawn was beginning. He fumbled for his watch on the bedside table. Five-to-eight. Breakfast was served until nine-thirty. Loads of time. He closed his eyes again but this time couldn't get off. Like it or not, he was awake. No use pretending otherwise. He yawned, stretched, counted to five then pushed himself out of the bed. Ignoring his body's protests, he crossed to the window, lifted it still further and stuck out his head.

Below him were two lanes of cars, taxis and buses. As he watched, the lights at the end of the road changed, there was a concerted revving of engines, the first cars drew away and then, as though joined by an elastic band, those behind were drawn after them until the surge forward had passed along the line and they were all in motion together. Christian shivered and became aware that he was getting wet. He pulled in his head and closed the window.

Janice, he saw, hadn't moved. Indeed, she hardly seemed to have moved all night. She was still lying facing the opposite wall so that all he could see of her was a bunch of tousled, blonde hair.

'Morning,' he muttered experimentally, but it had no effect.

He left her and went into the bathroom. The prospect of the day ahead lay ominously upon him. Had he really resolved to go through with his plan to search the archives of the national press until he came upon the name of Charles Yates? Shouldn't he first consider where such a move might end up?

Well, yes, he should, but not until after breakfast. And until after he had had the novel and, hopefully, delightful experience of awakening Janice from her slumbers.

In anticipation of this, he swilled his face in cold water, cleaned his teeth and gave himself a generous application of Givenchy after-shave.

'And why not?' he muttered, eyeing himself in the mirror.

Their experiences of the previous day had stopped well short of sexual bliss. It was fortunate that they had another full day and night in front of them in which to put that right.

He brushed his hair flat, noticing the way in which it was beginning to recede from his forehead. A few strands of white cotton where the towel had caught on his unshaven chin delayed him further. Checking that the bathroom door was firmly closed, he quickly plugged in his electric razor and began to shave. Might as well do things properly.

'I'm in the mood for love . . .' he hummed softly.

She still hadn't moved when he came out of the bathroom and he stood for a moment, uncertain how best to proceed. This wasn't Diane, on whose early morning moves and moods he was an expert; this sleeping woman was a comparative stranger to be approached with caution.

He got back into bed, careless now about disturbing her. In fact, wanting to disturb her. He put off his bedside light and waited. Nothing happened. He put it on again, coughed, then went through a small pantomime of awakening with plenty of sighs and

144

shufflings, ending by giving the headboard a sharp blow with his elbow. Still nothing happened.

Perhaps she had taken sleeping-tablets. He had known Diane be like this – and then remain half-drugged for the rest of the morning – on the few occasions that she had had recourse to them. It annoyed him to think that that might be the case. Were they to be cheated out of their love-making yet again? He looked at his watch. It was nearly ten-past-eight.

He would make some tea, he thought. That was the kind of noisy activity that could normally be guaranteed to disturb anyone.

He got out of bed as clumsily as he could, pulling some of the bedclothes back. He took the electric kettle into the bathroom, this time leaving the door open. The water drummed noisily into it but, returning, he saw that Janice still hadn't stirred.

'Oh, come on,' he muttered irritably.

He plugged in the kettle, sorry to see that it wasn't of the whistling variety.

The cups had in them the dregs of the coffee from the night before and would have to be washed. He went first to retrieve Janice's from where it stood on her bedside table. and so for the first time had cause to go round to her side of the bed.

Catching sight through the tangle of hair of a blue eye wide open, his first thought was that his ploy had worked and that she was awake.

'Morning . . .' he started to say. And then stopped. His open mouth mimicking hers, he dropped slowly to his knees and peered into her face, half-hidden as it was by the bedding and the silky strands of her hair.

What he saw was so unexpected that his cry of horror was delayed while he looked again. The swollen face, the protruding tongue, the staring eyes; it was all so dreadful and inexplicable. He put out a finger and, wincing at the touch, lowered the sheet an inch or two until her throat became visible. There was a deep, red welt around it, as well as other, more random, bruising and grazes. She had been strangled. Savagely killed and then tucked up beside him for the night.

He gave a cry of revulsion, tried to stand but fell back against the wall.

'Oh my God,' he said. 'Oh my God.'

He struggled to his feet and stared wildly round the room. It had to be a dream, a hoax, an illusion . . . But the evidence was all to

145

the contrary: the room was real enough; he was awake; the body – he looked again – was as dead as a doornail.

Averting his eyes from the bed, he went to the window and looked out. There was an office block opposite in whose lighted windows he could see people silently talking, greeting one another, joking even. He yearned to join them.

He looked back at the body (as he already thought of it: the name Janice didn't relate easily to this obscenity) and then edged round the bottom of the bed, craning forward as if to catch it by surprise. No good. It remained as he had seen it the first time, its face bloated as though in rage at the way that life had been throttled out of it.

'Jesus,' he said. 'Oh please. Oh no.'

It was a plea to anyone to come and take this off his hands; that something – anything – might happen to save him.

He went into the bathroom, wanting to be as far as possible from the bed. This time the face that he saw in the mirror was white and dismayed, an unlikely lover.

Approaching the body for a third time, he wondered if he could bring himself to touch it, to feel for a pulse or make some other gesture towards confirming that all life was gone. Not that he had any doubts. Just that there was some kind of ritual to be gone through here.

Trying not to look at that blown-out face, he thrust a hand under the bedclothes and touched the top of a thigh, something that ten minutes earlier he would have regarded as a happy accident but which now caused him to jerk his hand away. The arms had to be somewhere. He felt further up, nearer to a shoulder, and followed the arm down to where a hand hung limply. It was cold: there was no pulse or life or possibility of either.

The kettle began to boil and Christian hurried to turn it off. It was an unwelcome reminder of the designs that he had had on the body. He shuddered afresh to think of how he had slept beside it.

A sense of his own desperate situation began to intrude through the shock. Janice was dead and out of it, leaving him to face the music and with the responsibility of setting in motion those wheels that would bring officialdom to the hotel room to clear up the mess. They would come and find him and his dead mistress and want to know what had happened.

'Oh, Christ,' he muttered. 'Oh no . . . !'

He sank on to a chair, careless of the clothes that were already piled on it. It was all too awful to contemplate. He though of Diane and the children and of their learning about all this: that he, Christian, had been found in a hotel room with a woman who had been strangled. He groaned aloud and a few tears of self-pity dropped on to his pyjama jacket. He would do anything to avoid that. He would give anything, promise anything . . . He drummed his bare feet on the floor in anguished frustration.

There were voices in the corridor outside. He hurried to the door to check that it was locked and found that it was. The voices went away, a family on their way down to breakfast.

For a moment his body was flooded with a new alarm. If the door were locked then was the murderer still inside the room? He pushed back the sliding doors of the wardrobe to be met by some empty hangers and Janice's dress. Of course, he told himself, the door would lock automatically. That it was locked now meant nothing.

Though his panic didn't subside. Rather it was recharged by the realization of how close he himself might have been to such a gruesome death. Had Janice been killed right there in the room as he had snored on, anaesthetized by drink? Or had she been killed elsewhere and then dragged back to her bed? What might have happened had he been roused? Could he have saved her or might her killer – or killers – have done for him as well?

'Oh shit,' he said.

It was all he could manage, these short curses and pleas and cries of help or despair.

'Oh, God, no, please . . . !'

None of them, he knew, would be answered. This was a nightmare from which he wasn't going to awaken but which was already growing larger with past horrors to be remembered and horrors to come that were beyond even these. The finding of Janice's dreadful body had sent his mind reeling. Now, as it fought to recover, it could only focus on consequences and repercussions that were even more dreadful than that poor, mottled face.

He would be arrested. Not only would he be found out in his adultery, he must surely be the main suspect for the murder. His mind leapt ingeniously to supply the motive: he was a sexual pervert; they had been indulging in sadistic practices when things had got out of hand and he had accidentally garrotted his partner.

So strongly did he feel the accusation that he glanced down at his own hands. Could they indeed have done this? In his sleep? No, he told himself. For God's sake. It wouldn't help him or the truth to indulge in such wild fantasies.

'The old bastard,' he muttered, and then realized that he was thinking of Lord Bradshaw.

Could he be behind this? Christian's mind hesitated at the scale of the assumption and then sidestepped it. What did it matter anyway? His present predicament was enough to worry about without all the whys and wherefores that could wait till later.

He was still in his pyjamas. Now there was something he could put right, a purposeful activity that would stop his frantic pacings about the room. He threw them off and looked round for last night's discarded clothes. Doing so, he glimpsed himself in the mirror: thickening around the waist, sloping shoulders, reddening hands and face against a white body. He instinctively pulled in his stomach, then let it sag again. This was no time for vanity.

He must escape.

It came to him as a revelation as he pulled on his shirt. His first reactions had all been instinctive, conditioned by terror. Law-abiding by nature, he had thought only of what would happen when he reported the body, of what the police would say and do. It was only now, as he became capable of less instinctive and more considered reactions, that it came to him. He wouldn't call the police or anybody else. He would get out of there. And fast.

He pulled on his shoes and socks. His ideas became more ambitious. Was there even some way of dissociating himself from all this? Was there some clever trick, some device, by which he could cover his tracks, return home and expect to hear no more about it? Putting on his jacket he felt less vulnerable. Why should he stay here and quietly submit to accusation and degradation? There must be a solution, even if it involved acting more like the murderer that others might think him to be.

He remembered a story in which a man in a similar situation to his own – hotel room; dead woman; need to escape – had pushed the body out of the window, making it seem that she had jumped of her own accord. The verdict had been suicide; they hadn't even been able to establish from which room she had jumped.

But it was surely nonsense. The idea of lugging Janice's body to the window and then heaving it over the sill repulsed him. And anyway, knowing what near-miraculous deductions could be made from seventeen-year-old skeletons, he felt sure that any competent pathologist would have no difficulty in uncovering such a ruse.

Suppose he could get her into another room and let her be discovered there?

But they had been seen together, had signed in together. Even could he achieve such a feat, she would soon be traced back to room 305 with all the telltale traces of her occupancy.

Suppose . . . suppose he were to undress, climb back into bed beside her and then mutilate himself? Then they could both be discovered as the joint victims of an attack which only he had survived.

Worse than ever. He doubted that he had the nerve even to get back in the bed beside her, never mind the rest of it.

'No chance,' he groaned, viewing himself in the mirror. 'Stupid.' He meant his wild plans, none of which would work in a thousand years.

Besides, if there was one thing that he had learnt from his years of draughtsmanship, it was that the simplest design was usually also the most elegant and effective. Why try and move Janice and go through all kinds of dangerous and nerve-racking performances when she would probably remain undiscovered for longest simply by being left where she was?

'Yes.' He nodded encouragingly to his image. 'Yes.' That was surely best. Just leave her where she was and get the hell out of here.

He gathered his belongings – razor, hairbrush, deodorant – into his bag, zipped it closed and took a last look round to see that he had left nothing.

'Right,' he said aloud. 'I'm going.'

No one contradicted him.

There was first, though, something important that he had to do. He approached the side of the bed where the body was lying and forced himself to go down on his knees and look into the poor, swollen face that stared unblinkingly out from its veil of wispy, blonde hair. He had to say his goodbyes.

'Sorry,' he said. Then cleared his throat and tried again. 'I mean if I hadn't persuaded you to come . . . I suppose it's my fault really.'

Again no one contradicted him.

His hand trembling, he reached out and gently stroked her cheek. He would, he vowed, think more about her when he had the time to do so.

149

'Sorry,' he said again. This time it was an apology for the way in which he was abandoning her and rushing off with his bag packed. It was an apology for the fact that he no longer thought of her as his lover. She had become a dreadful thing that he could barely bring himself to touch.

He stood up, then, in a final benediction, bowed and kissed the top of her cold head.

''Bye, love,' he said.

There was a plastic 'Do not disturb' sign hanging on the inside of the door. How powerful a charm it was against the visitations of chambermaids and others Christian didn't know but at least it seemed a better bet than had any of his other more weird and wonderful notions. The room key he left where it was: there was no point in taking it with him.

He listened but could hear nothing from the corridor and so opened the door and peered out.

There was no one in sight. He stepped outside, pulled the door closed, checked that it had locked and hung the 'Do not disturb' sign over the handle.

It was an enormous step, one that made him a fugitive. It had been bad enough picturing himself trying to explain how he had woken to find his mistress dead beside him; how much worse having to say why, having done so, he had informed no one but left the body and fled.

No going back now. He hastened along the corridor, wondered about the lift but then chose the staircase. Still no one in sight. He tiptoed down, counted six short flights and saw the foyer through glass doors ahead of him.

He wished – too late – that he had left his bag in the room. It seemed a conspicuous sign of a man making his getaway. Admittedly the bill had been paid on arrival but it would be ironic if they should now suspect him of trying to avoid it.

He took a deep breath and pushed through the glass doors. A cleaner was hoovering the carpet; there was a small queue of people at reception; a porter was replacing a light bulb. None of them took any notice as Christian went past. He let the revolving doors carry him through them and was finally outside, in the cold, damp air and amid the noise of the traffic.

Taxis were waiting. Why not, he thought. Speed was of the essence; concealment hardly mattered. He went to the taxi at the head of the line, not daring to look back in case someone were calling him from the hotel.

'Euston Station, please,' he said.

Only when he was out of London would he be able to consider what on earth he was going to do. And even where, precisely, he was going to go. All that he knew at the moment was an overwhelming urge to escape, to get out of the hell that London had become. It passed by him now, outside the windows of the taxi, garish and bloated, corrupt and poisoned. Its architecture, once dominated by graceful churches and inspired cathedrals that had lifted the eyes to heaven, was now intimidated by the ugly perpendiculars of office and tower blocks. The old gods had been eclipsed; these monuments to human greed cast long shadows, turning streets into ravines and men into monsters. Was it only yesterday that he had revelled in the anonymity and freedom that London had seemed to offer? It seemed an age ago.

'What time's your train?' shouted the taxi-driver without turning his head.

'Er . . . don't know,' admitted Christian.

'Oh well,' said the man and laughed. 'Can't miss it anyway!'

Christian felt in his pockets for a timetable but couldn't find one. He would anyway catch the first train that would take him northwards, towards home. Beyond that he couldn't think. He was responding to a basic instinct, that of of the frightened animal seeking only to get back to its lair.

Again the face of Lord Bradshaw appeared before his overcharged imagination and again Christian refused to contemplate it. He was a man on the run, without the time to indulge in speculation as to who had put him there. All that would come later once – touch wood – he had reached the temporary safety of the train.

They came at last to Euston and he left the taxi and hurried through the tiled tunnels, following the signs that said, '*Main-Line Station*'. He wouldn't feel safe until he was on the train and not even then until the train was moving and it was physically impossible for the dreadful thing that he had left behind him at the hotel to reach him.

The forecourt was busy and crowded even at that early hour. He welcomed its mild chaos. People were preoccupied with their own journeys and had eyes only for the departure and arrival boards, none for him. Though, even now, Fate had a cruel trick to play.

'WE APOLOGIZE FOR THE DELAYS TO INTER-CITY TRAINS,' announ-

151

ced the board in white lettering. 'THIS HAS BEEN CAUSED BY A DERAILMENT.'

Christian gave a small, hopeless laugh. He wasn't surprised. His nightmare of the previous night came back to him. He was in a maze from which there was no escape.

'Excuse me.' He accosted a porter, a short, black man with greying hair. 'When are there likely to be any trains going north?'

The man shrugged. 'Should be soon.'

'You don't know when?'

He shrugged again. No, he didn't.

Christian stood and let the tide of frustrated travellers ebb and flow around him. It was almost a relief to feel powerless. There was nothing more he could do – so he would do nothing. He lit a cigarette and nearly retched on it. He was hungry and thirsty, but so what? He persisted with the cigarette, welcoming the light-headed feeling that it gave him. Around him the din grew. He wondered, with a detatched interest, if he were going to faint.

He thought of Percy, immaculate and fastidious. How would he take to a son-in-law soiled with the disgrace of such a sordid affair? He thought of Diane, blissfully ignorant of the turn that her life was about to take.

He would tell her himself. That was the least he could do. Get to her first and try and explain everything and apologize. He could expect no more than a couple of days of freedom before the body was discovered and a hue-and-cry raised. That is, if he was ever released from this antechamber to hell.

He shook his head and tried to focus again, alerted by a new murmur and bustle around him to the fact that something was happening. The departure board had come to life, its slots flickering through all the possibilities and then settling into lines of place names. The derailment had been dealt with and the trains were running again.

It took him a moment to persuade himself that escape was still possible. Part of him had already given up and thrown in the towel, wanting to stay where he was and feel the hand of the law on his shoulder.

His train was platform nine. He picked up his bag, hesitated, then wandered towards it.

There was a disorderly queue, swelled by those left waiting when earlier trains hadn't run. He joined it, still detached and indifferent as to whether he would make the barrier. The pushing

152

and jostling around him edged him forward.

'Ticket please?'

'Oh, sorry . . . !'

He fumbled for it, brought to life by the sudden embarrassment at holding up the queue. Someone behind his back commented on his stupidity. He found the ticket and presented it for clipping. And was through to the platform where the train was standing, all of its doors wide open.

It mattered little this time which compartment he chose. The first ones that he came to were all full. He pushed his way along until a few vacant seats began to appear. He took one at random, careless as to who else was at the table – barely seeing them – and dropped into it, his bag on his lap. In a few minutes they would be moving and he could then perhaps begin the painful business of facing up to his predicament. In the meantime he preferred to keep the world at bay.

He closed his eyes and, what with fear and hunger and thirst and perhaps because it was what he most dearly wished, he lost consciousness.

17

They had left London well behind them before Christian regained consciousness and opened his eyes. For one blissful moment he was aware only that he was on a train and wondered where he could be going. Another moment and he had remembered everything and yearned only to return to unconsciousness.

He also became aware of the middle-aged woman opposite who had lowered her newspaper and was regarding him over her reading-glasses.

'Nothing like a train for putting you to sleep, is there?' she said, with a smile that sought his confidence.

'Pardon?' Then, as his wits returned, he managed to stammer, 'Oh no, er . . . late night, I'm afraid.'

'Really?' she said, inviting him to go on. Then she stared and her expression changed to one of concern. 'Excuse me, but are you feeling all right?'

He wasn't. The crowded train was hot and stuffy. He felt the colour drain from his face and the hand that he raised to his brow was damp with sweat.

'You've gone all white,' observed his travelling-companion. Beside her, a young woman in a shawl was eyeing him indifferently while at his side a man about his own age looked up from his book.

'I think I need something to eat,' said Christian, though even as he spoke the idea revolted him and he knew that he was going to be sick.

He lifted his overnight bag from his lap and on to the tabletop, then stood up and edged sideways into the centre aisle. The train swayed and he clutched at the top of the seat.

'Are you sure you're going to be all right?' asked the woman.

'Yes,' said Christian faintly. 'Got to get some . . . something.'

He couldn't bring himself to mention food again but lurched quickly forward down the aisle. He was carried along by the rhythm of the train until he came to the end of the carriage, the door slid back before him and he stumbled against the toilet door. Mercifully its sign said 'Vacant'. A moment's fumbling with the handle then the lock on the inside and he was vomiting into the bowl, finding the oblivion that he had been earlier seeking.

Finally it was over and he opened his tear-filled eyes to confront a stretch of formica wall. He was half-kneeling, half-crouching on the tiny floor. He was on a train. He had just been violently sick. There were, he knew, other disasters looming larger and more distantly that he preferred to ignore for the time being.

Important first to do the simple things. To stand up. To pump water from the tap. To swill out his mouth and nose and dab his heated face.

Doing so, he realized with surprise that he felt better. In fact, a lot better. Last night's Greek meal, so violently rejected by his stomach, seemed to have carried away with it much of the shock and suicidal depression which had followed the discovery of Janice's body. He went out of the toilet and opened a window. The cold air swirled in and around him, making him shiver. He breathed deeply. The feeling of being emptied was a not unpleasant one and sharpened his senses.

He set off down the aisle again, this time away from his own seat and towards the buffet car. He walked briskly, riding the lurching of the train, almost swinging between the hand-holds that were on the tops of the seats. The tables he passed were covered in newspapers, plastic cups and the other paraphernalia of travel; children were squashed on to parents' knees and luggage spilled

154

into the aisle.

There was a queue for the buffet and he joined it. He would have some coffee, and perhaps something to eat. His guts gurgled quietly but he ignored their protest. It would do him good to eat. A line ran through his head: 'The condemned man ate a hearty breakfast.'

Was he then condemned? Wasn't he, for all that he might have absconded from the scene of the crime, innocent of the charge as read? However much it might look like it, he hadn't murdered Janice. He had done nothing worse than to love her. It was a truth that he mustn't lose sight of.

There were now perhaps a dozen people ahead of him in the queue. The person at the front had turned to speak as his turn had come to be served so that, from glimpsing the back of his head, Christian was now presented with a profile. It was a distinctive face – pockmarked and heavy-featured – that he had seen before. It was the man who had stood by the diving-board in the Bellevue leisure centre, the older of the two thugs, the one who had worn the donkey jacket over his suit.

Recognizing him, he felt fear, a residue of their Bellevue encounter. Then something else. Seeing him there now, he knew that this was the man who had strangled Janice.

The evidence was hardly overwhelming – amounting as yet to little more than the fact that they were on the same train coming back from London – nevertheless he knew it as surely as if he had seen the man with his hands around her throat. It had to be. The conviction came even before he could assemble the reasons that had fed it. Which were what? Well, starting from the obvious, he *was* on the same train as Christian and he was, presumably, returning to the same town.

More tellingly, he had been involved in an earlier attempt to dissuade Christian from his interest in the Naughton Point skeletons. Of course. Suddenly the reason for poor Janice's death was blindingly clear. It was to stop Christian pursuing his one-man crusade; to stop him finding out about those piles of old bones incarcerated inside Naughton Point. He hadn't taken the heavy hint when it had been given him at the Bellevue leisure centre. He had resisted the more genteel attempts of Lord Bradshaw to charm him into submission. Janice's murder had, then, been a third, infinitely more brutal method of stopping him. After the threats and the blandishments had come the violence,

155

intended to discredit him forever.

The moment of insight was almost his undoing for the man with the pockmarked face had now been served and was coming back towards him, edging past the waiting queue. There was only one line of escape. Christian ducked his head and turned, left the queue and hurried away back down the train.

Even then he couldn't be sure that he had moved quickly enough to prevent Poxy-Face seeing and recognizing him. He went through two carriages before daring to stop and look back. Poxy-Face was coming slowly after him, concentrating on the coffee he was holding. It reassured Christian that he hadn't seen him.

Nor did he need to flee any further. Poxy had reached his seat, sat down and disappeared from view.

Christian stayed where he was at the end of the carriage, grateful for the respite. He lit a cigarette and, keeping an eye on where the man was sitting in case he should begin to move again, considered as calmly as he could where this new development left him.

If he were right – and Poxy-Face had killed Janice – then what the hell could he do about it? He knew what he would like to do: avenge Janice by killing the other man with his own bare hands. But he also knew that he never would. So here he was, hopelessly compromised by his flight from the hotel room and its macabre contents, and now finding himself on the same train as his mistress's murderer. Not a situation for which his training as an architect had prepared him.

It did, though, offer the first, faint glimmer of hope that there might be a way for him out of this mess and it raised his battered spirits. If only he could prove that Poxy were the murderer, he might yet save his own skin. He lowered the window and threw out his cigarette. At least he felt capable of action again.

And he now had time to plan, more than two hours in fact before the train was due to arrive in Gowling. He set off back to his own seat. Poxy-Face could safely be left where he was for a while.

'Feeling better now?' enquired the woman opposite as he sat down.

'Yes,' said Christian, and meant it.

'They get very stuffy, don't they, these trains.'

She had finished her newspaper and seemed intent on conversation.

Christian, with weightier matters on his mind, parried a series of further observations on trains and the weather; then, at the first opportunity that a lengthening silence between them gave him, closed his eyes as though he were slipping off again into sleep. The woman gave up and directed her attentions instead at the younger woman by her side.

Keeping his eyes closed, Christian considered his options. If Poxy-Face had killed Janice then it was surely a safe assumption that he had done so to discredit Christian because of what Christian knew – or was on the point of discovering – about the skeletons. If Poxy-Face hadn't killed her then Christian was still well and truly in the mire.

Ergo. Assume that Poxy-Face had done it. If it turned out to be wrong, it could hardly make matters worse. If turned out to be right, it offered his one and only chance of salvation.

So then. Poxy-Face was working for whoever had been responsible for the original Naughton Point murders. He had been instructed to put the frighteners on Christian when – via Walter Hill? – it had first been learnt that Christian was showing a dangerous interest in the case. This had failed and so Lord Bradshaw, political heavyweight, had been wheeled out of retirement in the hope that gentle persuasion and flattery would do the trick. And, finally, when Christian had proved resistant to that too, Poxy-Face had been sent in again with instructions that this time there had to be no messing.

It was possible, of course, that Lord Bradshaw was himself the power-behind-the-scenes, but Christian wasn't convinced. Lord Bradshaw was based in the heart of London where they surely had thugs of their own. Christian had first come across Poxy in Gowling; and now here he was again returning there by train. It suggested that the rotten core of this conspiracy was in Gowling and not London. Christian remembered the list of Pawley Development directors which had featured that familiar threesome: Rees, Maddox and Tyson. There, he felt sure, was a more likely short list of candidates for the role of Mr Big.

A problem occurred to him, a gap in his scenario. Whoever he was, how had Mr Big known that he, Christian, hadn't fallen for Lord Bradshaw's soft-soap approach? After all he had given every sign of having done so, leaving the Pawley House office with no intention of pursuing things further. And yet he had awoken the following morning to find Janice dead beside him.

The answer had to be that he was followed. Either Poxy or some other hired thug had followed him to Companies' House and

157

observed his researches into Pawley Developments. It would have been easy enough: his fury at being taken for a ride had made him oblivious to most of the world around him. It would then have been a matter of a simple phone call to report what had happened and for Phase Three to be put into operation.

So what should he now do? What *could* he do?

Well, he could follow Poxy. See where he went. Find out where he lived and who he was. At least then Christian would have a name to give to the police when Janice's body was eventually discovered and they came hot-foot to his front door to arrest him.

Wouldn't Poxy sooner or later have to report to his boss? And mightn't Christian be able to follow him? Observe from the shadows which member of the aged trio it was who would hobble forward to identify himself as the arch-patron of murder and mayhem? Commonsense warned him that such a report might have already been made by telephone. If so, then he could do nothing about it. There still remained the strong chance that Poxy would have to be paid and that, for that reason alone, a face-to-face meeting would be needed.

His stomach rumbled. He was hungry. He was also desperately thirsty after his vomiting, but he couldn't risk the walk along the train to the buffet-car which would take him past where his enemy was sitting. Keeping his eyes closed, he stuck it out.

It seemed an age before an announcement from the guard alerted him to the fact that release was near.

'The next station will be Gowling,' it said. 'And we apologize for any inconvenience caused by the cancellation of earlier trains. Thank you.'

Thank *you*, thought Christian. The probability was that Poxy had been intending to catch one of those earlier trains. He would have had little reason for hanging about in London once he had completed his dirty work.

Christian opened his eyes.

'Nearly there,' the woman across the table informed him brightly. 'You have had a good sleep.'

'I needed it,' said Christian, and stood up.

Now came the dodgy part. He had to get himself into position so that he could observe Poxy leaving the train without himself being observed. And then manage to follow him, not knowing whether he would have a car waiting, take a taxi or whatever.

He took his bag and went along to the end of the carriage, made

158

his choice of which door would be the correct side for the platform and established himself at it. He would be first off. Poxy was two carriages along. It was to be hoped that he didn't have a similar plan for a quick getaway.

As the train came into the station, Christian saw, firstly, that he had made the right choice of door and, secondly, that Poxy's carriage would come to rest nearer to the exit than his own. He opened the door as the train slowed and, as soon as he dared, made an awkward jump on to the platform. A porter gave him a disapproving look.

All the way along the now-stopping train other doors were opening but he had gained the precious seconds that he needed. A truckful of mail gave him cover from behind which he scanned the alighting passengers. He didn't, of course, know from which door Poxy would come; it was even possible that he had walked along the train to another carriage, which wouldn't help matters.

In fact he was one of the last off. Christian was beginning to think he had missed him and was debating whether to make a run for the ticket-barrier when he saw him. He was wearing a trench coat and carried a small holdall.

Christian hurried after him as he crossed the platform and disappeared into the 'Exit' subway. He couldn't afford to let him get far ahead since he had no idea what he would do once out of the station. He stuck almost to his heels, praying that he wouldn't suddenly turn as they came out of the subway and up to the barrier.

It was on the station forecourt that Christian's plan looked as if it had come unstuck. If Poxy had had his own car waiting then at least he could have taken the number. If he went for a taxi – as he was now doing – Christian's only chance was to grab another one and give chase. Unfortunately, there wasn't another one.

He stood cursing and too far away to overhear as Poxy gave his instructions to the driver of the taxi in view, then opened a rear door, threw in his bag and climbed in after it. Christian shrank behind a pillar, desperate and helpless.

Mercifully the taxi's departure was delayed as it was hemmed in by another car depositing its passengers. The cab-driver leaned out of his window and shouted something. The driver of the offending vehicle grew flustered and stalled his motor. Further delay. And, finally, at the station entrance another cab appeared, approached and stopped some distance from the first.

Taking a chance of being seen, Christian ran across to it. There was already someone waving and calling 'Taxi!' – it was his travelling companion, the loquacious, middle-aged lady – but he ignored her and took possession by opening the passenger-side door and getting in. As he did so, the other taxi had begun to move so that Christian was able to gasp, 'Could you follow that other taxi, please?' as it came past them.

'OK,' muttered the driver, and pulled out behind it.

They came to a roundabout and were delayed, only just moving forward in time to spot the exit chosen by Poxy's taxi.

'Do you know where he's going?' asked the driver, foreseeing problems.

'No idea,' admitted Christian.

The man grunted, but seemed willing enough to apply himself to the task, taking liberties with a set of traffic-lights that threatened to separate them.

'Well done,' muttered Christian encouragingly.

They were on the ring road, among familiar landmarks. Ramsden House went past and Christian felt a touch of nostalgia and sorrow but had to ignore it: his attention was all on the car in front and its occupant. He gave a small sigh of relief when it turned on to the Sunningdale Estate, which was a large estate of council houses, a maze to trap the unwary, but at least without roundabouts or traffic-lights to hinder them.

'When they stop,' said Christian to the driver, 'don't stop behind them, will you.'

'No?'

'I don't want them to know they're being followed.'

The driver gave a quick, sideways glance but said nothing. He was clearly a man accustomed to indulging the lunatic whims of his passengers.

The other taxi pulled up before one of a line of council houses.

'Stop here,' said Christian quickly.

The driver obediently did so and then sat back with arms folded as though to say: What next? They were some fifty yards away from Poxy, who got out of his taxi, put his bag on the pavement and then paid his driver.

'Who is he then?' asked Christian's driver suddenly.

'I, er . . . sorry, I can't tell you that.'

'Are you the cops?'

'Can't tell you that either,' said Christian.

It was a silly enough reply but seemed to satisfy him. He sat watching with Christian as Poxy went into the house and the other taxi drove off.

'Let's drive past the house,' instructed Christian, wanting to see what number it was.

It was number twenty-eight and had a neglected look about it that went with the overgrown garden.

'Now, can you take me home, please,' said Christian, and gave the driver his address.

It was his own car that he needed. Inventing a pack of lies for Diane to explain his early return was something he could have done without, but his own car was essential if he was to track Poxy to his master.

'What're you doing here?' she asked in surprise, seeing him enter the house. It was as much an accusation as a question.

'Back early. We got through everything a lot quicker than we expected.'

He gave her a perfunctory peck on the cheek. Despite her faint air of resentment, he was moved by the familiar domesticity, the kids' comics on the kitchen table and some new drawings of theirs tacked up on the wall-board. If only he could settle back into this and forget the terror that was following him.

'You might have told me. I could have collected you from the station.'

'I took a taxi.'

He didn't want her to see how desperate he was for something to eat and drink. With trembling fingers he took a bottle of milk from the fridge, poured himself a cup and downed it in one.

'Are you all right?' she asked, suddenly doubtful.

'Yes, just . . . there wasn't any buffet or anything on the train.'

'I suppose you'll want something to eat then?'

He admitted that he might perhaps be able to manage something, and drank another cup of milk.

'So how was London? Did you enjoy it?' she asked, pushing some sausages under the grill.

'Yes . . . sort of.'

It was a feeble answer but seemed enough. She didn't ask him any more but busied herself getting him some sort of meal together.

'And how're you?' he said to fill the silence.

'All right.'

For a moment he wanted to tell her everything, to lay his head upon her lap and beg forgiveness. But he knew that he mustn't, not while there was the slimmest chance of escape. Even lingering there in the kitchen while she prepared his meal was a luxury that might cost him dear if Poxy were already on his way to a rendezvous with his master.

'I've got to go out again,' he said.

'What, straightaway?'

'Yes. I'm sorry but . . . well, I've got to go and see Percy.' He knew that this was the lie that she would most easily accept. 'You don't mind if I take the car, do you?'

'No.'

She sounded resigned to everything, to his coming or going, taking or leaving the car when it suited him.

He went to wash and unpack while his meal was cooking. As he came from the bathroom there was a knock at the front door and he froze, terrified lest it should be the police come for him already. But it was the milkman, calling to collect his money. It was, though, a reminder that he was on borrowed time and that perhaps the worst thing of all would be for him to be arrested right there in the house before Diane's horrified gaze. He stayed in the bedroom, from where he could watch the avenue, until she called him down to his meal, which he wolfed quickly.

'Right,' he said. 'Got to rush.'

'I don't suppose you know when you'll be back?' she said with an edge of bitterness.

'No, not, er . . . not for sure.'

He felt again the temptation to blurt out everything, to say that he might never again return to her and the children. But he again resisted it. Not while there was still a chance.

''Bye then.'

And he went out, feeling freer once he was outside the front door and on the move. At least in his own car, in a town that he knew, he was unlikely to be surprised by a police hand on his shoulder. Even so, every hour that passed brought nearer that inevitable moment. It would be ironic if Dennis Joiner should be the one to take him in: without his willingness to tell tales out of school, he might never have got involved in the whole bloody business in the first place.

He drove to the Sunningdale Estate and found Poxy's road again. Going down it, he slowed outside number twenty-eight and peered across the tangle of garden, hoping for a sign that Poxy was

162

still inside. But he could see nothing – only dirty lace curtains – and had to drive on, circle the block, then come back again. This time he parked some way down the road in as inconspicuous a spot as he could find which still offered him a view of the house. He would wait. It might be a total waste of time but it was all he could do.

He switched on the radio, lit a cigarette and wished he had a newspaper for cover should he need it. A boy cycled down the road. A woman, slovenly and unkempt, walked past pushing a pram, then looked back at him suspiciously. He didn't resent the look, feeling himself an undesirable alien in his own world. He wound down the car window a fraction to let out the smoke from his cigarette.

He remembered the day of Jack Stephenson's funeral and the earnest conversation between Walter Rees and the snuff-taking Walter Hill, editor of the *Gowling Chronicle*. Was it Rees then, he thought idly. Rees with his choleric complexion and his building society and his fingers in financial pies? Was he the demon godfather of the bunch?

Or was it the cadaverous Tyson, rich beyond the expectations of retired planning officers? Seventeen years ago Richard Morris Dunmore had been employed in the Planning Department; Rees had probably been his boss. Had he also been the man who had had him encased in concrete to stop him spilling the beans to Charles Yates? It was an interesting thought.

Maddox was the least likely. A councillor could be bribed, could dish out contracts worth millions but was seldom himself in a position to take the initiative. Chairmen of housing committees didn't build their own houses; they merely accepted back-handers from those who did.

Perhaps then it should be: Rees – 2-to-1 (Favourite); Tyson – Evens; Maddox – 4-to-1 Against; 10-to-1 the field.

The radio distracted him, making his pulse quicken.

'The time is four o'clock and here are the news headlines . . . '

He listened fearfully to the summary of events which followed, then gave a sigh of relief and permitted himself another cigarette: there was no mention of a body found in a London hotel. Not yet.

Poor Janice, he thought, remembering her playing squash and full of randy life. She would now be stone cold, a thing of terror to whoever would eventually find her.

It was already growing dark. They were close to the shortest day in the year and the small ration of daylight was all but spent. It was a darkness that offered a further freedom to Christian, who left his car for a walk along the road, keeping on the opposite side to Poxy's house. He had grown cold and stiff and was glad of the chance to stretch his legs.

A thin chink of light raised his hopes. It showed through the curtains of an upstairs room in number twenty-eight and suggested that Poxy might be still in residence. A paperboy came along the row, pushing evening papers through most of the letter-boxes. But he ignored number twenty-eight and Christian, disappointed, returned to his car.

When things finally started to happen they did so in such an abrupt and unexpected fashion that Christian was caught flat-footed. He was lost in wandering thoughts – half-dozing even – when there was the sound of a motor being kicked into life and then Poxy appeared from the back of his house on a large, elderly-looking motorbike. It was Poxy disguised in helmet and goggles, gloves and donkey jacket, but unmistakable all the same. He hesitated for a second at the edge of the pavement, glanced right and left, and was away up the road before Christian had reached for the ignition key.

Christian cursed his own inattention, got the car going and accelerated after him. The darkness was now his enemy: he strained to pick out the single rear light of the motorcycle.

His worst moments were among the tight, twisting roads and crescents of the council estate. Once out of it and on to the ring road, he could draw up closer to his adversary. After all, Poxy wasn't expecting to be followed and there was no reason to think that he would recognize the car.

Christian caught up to within ten yards of him and settled down to follow. It excited him to be so close and yet unseen.

There was a fair amount of traffic as the rush hour was still under way. They passed the Bellevue leisure centre. The contractors had at last begun to clear and landscape the site. The though crossed Christian's mind that Percy would be pleased: another building brought in on time.

They were now climbing out of town again on the other side. Three tall blocks rose before them out of the gloom and Christian knew, even before the motorbike turned, where they were heading – Meynell Point, Fothergill Point and Crag Point, the doomed sisters of Naughton Point, itself now razed to the ground.

Of course. Where could be more appropriate for such a meeting than here where the skeletons had first appeared? It was confirmation that Christian's gamble was about to pay off and that Poxy was indeed on his way to meet his master. There surely could be no other reason for his coming to this now desolate spot.

For the evacuation of all three remaining towers was now complete. The area around them was littered with rubbish of all kinds and ringed by a Berlin Wall of contractors' hoardings, topped by barbed-wire.

Poxy had left the road and was slowly crossing the churned-up turf towards the three towers and their perimeter fence. Christian, unable to follow in the car, pulled up at the side of the road, killed his lights and engine and sat watching to see what the other man would do now.

Poxy drove his bike up to the hoarding, got off it and then, quite suddenly, had disappeared.

There must be a door, thought Christian, scrambling from his car and hurrying to follow. A door in the fence through which Poxy and his bike had gone.

An abandoned, wheel-less bicycle nearly proved his undoing as it caught at his feet. He must be careful. So much depended on his now managing to remain silent and unobserved. The darkness was his ally again, but would only remain so if treated with respect.

He came to the fencing and searched for the door. In fact he found seven of them and could doubtless have found more had he gone further in either direction. They were old ones, nailed together to form part of the barrier. Feeling slightly foolish, he tried them one by one. It was the fifth whose handle turned and which swung open to admit him to the grim landscape within.

He realized immediately that there was something beside him and flinched away in alarm. But it was only the motorbike, ticking and groaning quietly as its engine cooled. So Poxy had left it there and gone on foot towards the buildings. But to which? Meynell Point was the nearest and Christian headed for it.

Promisingly, its door was open. He stepped gingerly inside into the blackness. He was – he knew from earlier visits – in the small, mean hallway; there was a lift door somewhere ahead of him and stairs to one side of it; all around was concrete, stained and unlovely, and liable to echo and amplify the slightest sound. He stood, holding his breath.

Far, far above him came the distant whine of a motor slowing. It stopped and there was the slide and clang of lift doors opening.

165

Poxy had gone up then. And where Poxy had gone Christian had to follow. He went forward with his hands held out until they found the metal of the lift doors. He moved along them and found the beginning of the staircase, the cold air swirling down to meet him.

It was a long, slow climb, made dangerous by the darkness and doubly so by the littered steps. And still there was the need for silence. Somewhere above him was waiting a cruel, ruthless man who had already murdered at least once. Christian would be an easy target if he let his presence be known.

His eyes ached from the strain of trying to make out the different shades of black objects and corners. His legs ached even more from the slow, deliberate climb, one cautious step after another, always having to test that he had chosen a spot clear of litter before trusting his weight to it.

On one landing a squealing gang of mice scattered at his approach. On another the shape of a body terrified him until it turned into a roll of old carpet and some other junk. He had to stop and rest, not only from the strain of the exercise but also so that he could control his breathing and keep it shallow and quiet.

It was like climbing a mountain blindfold. Knowing that the slightest sound might bring down an avalanche.

At last he was at the summit. The top floor. He froze and listened but could hear nothing. For five eternal minutes he didn't move. Until he heard a footfall. It was from above him, on the roof.

He began again the slow, painful business of edging forward, locating the service stairs and then taking them one delicate, slow-motion step at a time till suddenly there was a door facing him. On the other side of it he could hear the faint whispering of the wind.

After all his care and agonizing caution there had to be a moment of risk. He could stand there behind the door forever and nothing would help him to know what was beyond it. He pushed gently. It creaked and opened. He looked round it.

After the pitch darkness inside the tower, the darkness outside was a relief, allowing things at least the silhouettes of what they were. He could see across the whole, wide, flat top of the tower block with its thin edging of metal fence. There were ventilator shafts and a small block of buildings for services and storage. And there was Poxy.

He was some distance away, near the edge and looking out over the town. There was a constant sound up here, the thin wailing of the wind and the town noises climbing up from below, that had masked the sounds of Christian's ascent and the creaking door.

Now – another risk – he slipped out on to the roof and made a little, crouching run to the oasis of the building. He got there, waited, then peeped out. Poxy hadn't turned and was still staring out over the town.

Christian still couldn't relax. He had to keep an eye on Poxy so that he would be able to move as the other man did, keeping the small rectangle of building between them. Still, it was a chance to breathe freely again and take a rest after that agonizing climb. He looked up at the stars. The height gave him an unnerving feeling that he was nearer to them than he was to the town.

'Please,' he found himself praying, 'get me out of this. Just get me out of this and I'll . . . well, anything.'

What he meant was that he would be better, he would be honest, he wouldn't deceive his wife, he would devote his life to great architecture . . . anything.

He heard before Poxy the whine of the lift motor and so was prepared and ready to move when the other man, finally hearing it, came walking back across the roof to the door. Christian scuttled round to the other side of the outcrop of building.

There was still a wait for both of them as the lift had to descend the length of its shaft before beginning to climb again and finally coming to rest below them on the top landing. There was a repeat of the slide and clang of the lift doors and then another wait as the newcomer negotiated that last, treacherous, dark climb that would bring him on to the roof.

Poxy had opened the door and stood holding it, respectfully. There was a shuffling of uncertain footsteps on the concrete steps and he muttered something that sounded like a greeting.

Christian, watching from some twenty yards away, had a sudden awful premonition. Even before the figure appeared, he knew who it was. Perhaps he had known all along but refused to accept it.

His adversary, with whom he had fenced in the dark for so long, came forward out of the doorway. The moonlight caught on the bald dome of his forehead.

The old fox, thought Christian, not surprised in the least. The cunning old fox.

18

'You all right then, Mr Jordan?'

Poxy's polite enquiry carried to where Christian stood, too stunned to react to what he was seeing.

'Yes, thank you,' replied Percy, immaculate in black overcoat with fur collar, then added sharply, 'Despite you making an unholy mess of everything.'

Poxy's manner was apologetic and self-effacing before his master.

'Like I told you on the phone, Mr Jordan . . .' As his voice became a whine, there were parts of what he said that Christian couldn't catch so that only incomplete phrases reached him. 'Was doing all like you said but then . . . Stupid tart . . . Nobody saw me, I mean you need have no fears on that score . . .'

What did the sense of it matter anyway? He had come to identify his enemy and had done so. It was neither Rees nor Maddox nor Tyson, nor some other little-fancied outsider. It was Percy Jordan, his adversary of old, his employer, the father of his wife, the grandfather of his children. The only surprise was that he could have blinded himself to it for so long.

He had been right in the first place when, way back, he had suspected Percy of the Naughton Point murders. Then, when he had made such a mess of bringing Percy to book, he had so far abandoned his first reactions as to begin to see the old fox as his mentor and benefactor. He had been wrong in identifying the first skeleton as that of Jack Stephenson. But his major mistake had been to assume that he was therefore also wrong in identifying Percy as the man who had caused that skeleton to reside where it did.

Something else occurred to him. Of course, Percy's name hadn't appeared on that list of Pawley Development directors – the list which had provided Christian with his short list of suspects. The Royal Institute of British Architects had a code of professional conduct, a code which forbade its members from acting as contractors and thus being in a position to employ themselves. Percy, wanting to have his cake and eat it, might well have been the *éminence grise* behind Pawley Developments and God-knew-what-other companies but he couldn't have allowed his name to appear among those of their directors.

A silence had fallen between the two men. Percy, his hands in his pockets, was looking thoughtful; Poxy was waiting for him to speak.

'And I suppose you'll still want paying?'

'Well . . .' Poxy obviously did. 'It was what we agreed.'

'I don't remember agreeing to murder.'

He strode across the roof, away from Poxy, who followed him. Christian had to move swiftly round to the other side of the brick outcrop that was covering him.

'Here then,' said Percy contemptuously, and pulled a handful of notes from his pocket.

'Thanks,' said Poxy, taking them.

'And I don't want to hear any more about this. Just make sure you keep your hands clean for a while. Otherwise you might find yourself in a bigger mess than I or anybody else can get you out of!'

'Yes, sure. And thanks, Mr Jordan,' said Poxy, shuffling the notes through his fingers.

'Go on then.'

It was an abrupt dismissal that sent Poxy scuttling back towards the doorway and caught Christian on the hop. He stepped back hurriedly and felt something strike the back of his ankle. There was a crash and then a dying rumble as the dustbin lid that he had caught struck the wall and then rolled around its own handle.

Christian closed his eyes and waited until the undulations had come to a stop. There was no sound from the other two men until Percy spoke.

'Who's there?'

Christian hesitated, thought about making a run for the doorway, and then decided against it. He would have had to confront Percy sooner or later and he might as well go along with Fate that had decided it should be sooner. For a moment his legs wouldn't move. Then he managed to step forward and saw them both waiting, turned towards him, Percy expressionless, Poxy crouched as if ready for action.

'Jesus, it's him,' said Poxy.

Christian ignored him and stared at Percy, who took a deep breath, then forced a chuckle.

'Well,' he said, 'Fancy meeting you here.'

A click made Christian look at Poxy, who had drawn a flick-knife from his pocket and sent the blade springing forward. Percy, too, had been distracted by it.

'Go on,' he said to Poxy. 'Leave us.'

But the hired man, now that he had been paid and saw a threat here to his own safety, had stopped taking orders and stayed where he was.

'What, and have him going to the cops?' he objected.

'I said leave us!' insisted Percy.

'I'm not leaving him! I'm not leaving him knowing what he knows!'

Christian felt rooted to the spot on which he stood, absurdly dependent upon Percy for protection. He thought about the dustbin lid and using it as a shield. Poxy took a step towards him and held out the knife, ready for attack.

'He won't say anything,' said Percy, now more persuasive.

His change of tone frightened Christian, suggesting as it did that he wasn't fully in control of his murderous subordinate.

'He won't when I've done with him!'

'I'll look after him,' said Percy smoothly. 'But if you touch him then I'll tell you one thing. I'll see that you're looked after as well.'

Poxy looked at him and the knife wavered.

'Go on,' said Percy gently, nodding towards the doorway. 'You've got what you came for.'

Though still clearly unhappy, Poxy finally obeyed, closing the blade of the knife and dropping it back into his pocket.

'I hope you know what you're doing, that's all,' he muttered and then, without a backward glance, went to the door and disappeared through it.

By mutual consent neither Christian nor Percy spoke until they heard the lift doors close and the motor start. Even then, Christian waited for the other man to speak. The little confrontation with Poxy had placed him obscurely on the defensive. Without Percy's intervention he might well have ended up skewered on the end of Poxy's switch-blade, a fact which now made it difficult to launch upon the tirade of accusations that he wanted to hurl at his enemy.

'So now you know,' said Percy.

'I know that it's you who had those two killed,' said Christian, finding his tongue at last. 'Richard Dunmore and that journalist. It was you who put them inside that bloody building of yours!'

'Not personally.'

'No,' relented Christian. 'Probably not. But you had them put

170

there all the same. Who did you get to do it? That murderous ape, was it?' He waved towards the door, below which the lift could now barely be heard as it reached the bottom of its shaft and slowed.

'Yes, it was, as a matter of fact. Only he was younger and a bit cleverer in those days. Before the alcohol had rotted his brains.'

'You're a cool bastard,' muttered Christian. He approached Percy, who still didn't move. He wanted to insult and abuse him, to strike him even. 'And now you've paid him for killing again!'

Percy shook his head. 'No.'

'But that's what he's done!'

'So I believe. But that's not what he was meant to do.'

Christian gave a groan of fury and frustration. Why was he again swopping words with this villainous old fox? Why, after all that he now knew, was he still having to fence with him, finding his thrusts parried and deflected?

'And so what was he meant to do?' he asked quietly.

Percy shrugged. 'Frame you.'

'Yes! By killing her, killing Janice!'

Naming her felt like an admission but he would now let nothing deter him. He was standing face to face with Percy, the two of them suspended on their square raft of concrete in a sky of infinite darkness.

'He wasn't supposed to kill her,' said Percy patiently. 'Just leave something there in the room. For the police to find.'

'What?' said Christian in disbelief.

'Drugs.'

It was beginning to make sense of a kind so that Christian hesitated. Percy, sensing that he had his attention, went on.

'Then he would have tipped off the police and that would have been that. Even if you'd finally not been charged – and I think we might have been able to arrange that – it would at least have put paid to your obsession for delving through old newspapers.'

Christian nodded slowly. 'And I'd have been eternally grateful to you for helping me out of the jam and letting me keep my job.'

'You might have been.'

'So what happened?'

Percy made a little gesture – who could say for sure? – then admitted, 'I gather your ladyfriend woke up when she shouldn't have done. And made a brave attempt to defend your honour.'

Christian gave a groan of dismay, thinking again of poor Janice and the nightmare of her death. He wished that Poxy hadn't been

171

allowed to leave. Knife or no knife, he would at that moment have gone for him and tried with his bare hands to avenge her.

'All very unfortunate,' said Percy smoothly.

'Not for you,' said Christian.

Percy moved away and walked to the edge of the platform. He began to speak quietly so that Christian had to move towards him in order to hear.

'I know what I must seem like to you,' he said. 'But I was no worse than the others. I've worked hard – you don't know how hard – to build up this practice and keep it together. And I'm not letting it all go now because of a load of old bones that nobody except you gives a damn about anyway?'

'They were people that you had killed,' said Christian evenly.

'They were people that would have seen me killed,' retorted Percy. 'A bloody journalist and some pipsqueak in the Planning Department who'd be making sure he got his fair share out of it.'

'So Charles Yates – the journalist – he was going to write articles that would have exposed you?' asked Christian, feeling that he might as well have all the details now that he had come this far.

'I suppose you might say that,' allowed Percy.

'And Richard Morris Dunmore was the source of his information?'

Percy nodded.

'What was it that he knew?'

'Nothing much. Nothing out of the ordinary. It was going on all over the place. It was the only way you could get any work, keeping the right people happy, greasing a few palms here and there.' He made it sound harmless, like an appealing local custom. 'I had no choice. If I wanted to stay in business then I had to swim with the tide.'

'And kill anybody that tried to stop you.'

Percy shrugged. 'They gave us no choice.'

'Us . . . ?'

'Oh, I wasn't the only one who had good reason for not wanting such publicity.'

'Bill Renbourne . . . ?' ventured Christian.

Percy nodded. 'And the rest. Like I say, it was the way things were done. And the way that got things done. Almost everything that got built in this country of ours – I'm talking about the sixties and early seventies – there was somebody on the make somewhere down the line.' He turned to face Christian. 'So what was I to do?

172

Go out of business? Lay people off? Or play the game along with everybody else?'

It seemed like an honest question from a simple man, who had wanted only to do well and to prosper and had found himself competing with the sharks. Listening to him, it seemed that kill or be killed, the law of the jungle, had also been the law for local government and its architects and builders.

'There was no choice,' he repeated softly, insidiously. 'It was the way business was done.'

Christian resisted – just – the invitation that he should agree and thereby declare a truce between them. We're not in a jungle, he areminded himself. Life isn't that simple or that brutal. Even councillors had their standards and architects their principles. Nor was Percy the naive beginner, drawn into a vicious power-struggle not of his own making. Christian knew better than anyone the man's capacity for deviousness and cunning, his arrogance and selfishness. He thought of poor Janice's bloated face: there had been nothing inevitable about that.

'You didn't have to kill people,' he muttered.

Percy spread his hands in a polite gesture of apology. 'As I said, that was unfortunate . . .'

'I mean the other ones as well!'

'They were a long time ago. We all have things in our past that we're not proud of . . .' And another gesture, as though drawing a curtain. 'That's all over. Forgotten.'

'It won't be forgotten when the police discover that body,' Christian retaliated. Then felt, too late, that he was committing a slight betrayal in referring to Janice as 'that body'.

'We might be able to take care of that,' said Percy quickly. 'I say might because it's not going to be easy. And it'll need your co-operation.'

It was an offer. Come on to my side and I'll look after you.

Christian hesitated.

'I'm sure that we would both do anything to save Diane from having to learn about what's gone on,' Percy continued seductively. 'I assume that she doesn't know anything yet?'

Christian, unable to meet the other man's look, shook his head and remained silent.

'Well then. Let me see what I can do. There's no sense in making things worse than they already are. What do you say?'

Still Christian remained mute, wanting to agree, indeed

173

wanting more than anything what Percy was now offering: that Diane should never know. All he had to do was to say yes, and yet he knew that he couldn't.

Sensing that things hung in the balance, Percy stepped to the very edge of the building and gestured Christian to follow him.

Below them were the lights of the town, sharp and clear. It was as if they were looking down from a high mountain upon a kingdom whose valleys and peaks were mapped by tiny, iridescent pinpricks. Highways were bright, glittering strings, coming together in a concentrated blaze that was the town's centre and its glowing heart.

'You see all this?' said Percy. 'I've helped create it, make it what it is. And it can be yours. You know that. You stand to inherit it. All you have to do is to let me help you. Let me do what's necessary to protect both of us.'

Christian felt the temptation as a tangible grasp on his arm, pulling him into submission. It would be so easy, and such a relief, to accept Percy's offer of an unholy alliance and be able to fall back upon the other man's strength and resources. It was the offer of a world which he had actively sought to inherit. He had been long in the wilderness and had surely earned the right to such a reward. So why not accept now and with gratitude?

Perhaps it was the feeble stirrings of his comatose conscience; more likely it was his old obstinacy that wouldn't let him give in. Almost to his own surprise, he found himself slowly shaking his head. No, it wouldn't do. It was the soft option, the cop-out, the greatest sin of all.

Percy, skilled in the arts of persuasion and blackmail, looked hard at him, as if seeking to recognize what more he needed to throw into the balance to tip the scales in his favour.

'Is it Janice?' he asked.

'What?'

'You feel guilty about Janice? About what happened to her?'

Christian shrugged. That might be part of it. Everything was part of it.

'You blame yourself for her death?' Percy went on probing. 'You feel that you ought to be punished for it?'

'I think somebody should,' blurted out Christian bitterly.

'No,' said Percy, sounding quite firm about it. 'She knew the game that she was playing. She just lost, that's all.'

Christian looked at him, wondering just what game it was to

which Percy was referring. The old one of adultery or something else?

Interpreting the look, Percy explained.

'How do you think I always knew what you were doing . . . what you were thinking even . . and what you were going to do next?'

Christian stared at him dumbly. It surely couldn't be . . . ? His mind baulked at the inference and wouldn't accept it. Until Percy spelled it out and there could be no further room for doubt.

'I'm afraid that the lady was working for me. She was what I believe is nowadays referred to as a mole. A spy in the enemy camp.'

He gave a sad smile that was almost one of sympathy.

'What, right . . . right from the beginning?' mumbled Christian.

'Yes,' said Percy, with a shake of his head that said – see what I mean? No one is to be trusted. 'I asked her to keep an eye on you. Well, I had no choice. It was for your own sake. For all our sakes.'

'That was why she . . . picked me up at the squash club?'

'Yes.'

It certainly provided the missing link to the chain of the previous day's events.

'And that was how you knew that I'd found out about Pawley Developments and that I didn't trust Bradshaw any more?'

Percy nodded. 'She rang me from the hotel.'

Christian, now knowing himself to have been duped from start to finish, stared out into the black sky.

'So why kill her?' he asked in a small voice.

Percy made another of those gestures that suggested that such small tragedies took place far away and beyond his control.

'She'd apparently grown quite fond of you. Felt protective towards you. And so when our friend made his visit to your room late last night, instead of just letting him in as she should have done, she tried to stop him. At which point he took it upon himself to dispose of her. All very unfortunate.'

'Yes,' said Christian.

'But she was hardly the innocent victim. You understand that now, I hope? You have nothing to blame yourself for.'

But you have, said Christian to himself. You're to be blamed for everything.

The news that Janice had been acting under orders had hurt and stunned him but he wouldn't turn his back upon her memory all the same. Hadn't she been used by Percy even more ruthlessly than he'd been? And they had had their moments of love together. Even Percy admitted that she had grown fond of him and had tried at the end to protect him. He remembered now – and understood when it was all too late – her anguished pleas that he should leave well alone.

'So,' said Percy persuasively. 'I think it's best if we let sleeping dogs lie, don't you?'

The fury that had been growing inside Christian now swept over him.

'You bastard!' he shouted, his voice made high and thin with rage. 'You rotten, lying bastard!'

Taken by surprise, Percy flinched away and took a step backwards. His unguarded expression was one of annoyance that his strategy should have so misfired.

'You don't care who dies, do you!' screamed Christian. 'You don't care about anybody!'

And he swung an arm up to that pale forehead. It was as much a slap as a blow and caught Percy across his ear. He gave a little cry of pain and shock, ducking away towards the edge of the platform and grabbing for the rail to save himself from falling.

Eighteen years earlier, when the construction of the tower blocks was being planned and sites surveyed, the County Surveyor had had serious misgivings about the wisdom of building on a reclaimed refuse-tip which hadn't been given long enough to settle properly. Percy had removed the Surveyor's reservations by arranging for the man and his wife to go on a two-week cruise of the Caribbean and then, as a surprise going-away present, had given them a brown envelope inside which was one thousand pounds in fivers. On his return, bronzed and compromised, the Surveyor had passed the site as suitable and Percy had submitted his designs to the Council. The flats had been built and the rubbish had settled, setting up stresses and sending cracks and fissures, some six inches wide, up the sides of the buildings.

Meynell Point was as badly affected as any. One crack in particular had shot like a bolt of forked lightning from the base of the block to the very top, touching even the concrete platform in which the safety railing was anchored.

Percy, flung sideways by Christian's blow, grabbed the railing at the spot where the concrete had split. The supporting strut, with nothing beneath it, dropped away, the metal rail buckled and Percy, a look of amazed terror on his face, toppled over and disappeared.

Christian made an instinctive, hopeless attempt to clutch at him. There was a wait of a second or two and then a soft thump as the body reached the ground fifteen floors below.

19

No one, not even Percy, could have survived such a fall. Christian knew it; nevertheless, as he waited on the dark landing for the recalled lift to reach him, he was still haunted by the notion that his father-in-law would prove indestructible and would be standing there, dapper and spruce as ever, to meet him at the foot of the building.

'You weren't trying to kill me, were you?' he would say with a thin smile.

And Christian would grovel and beg for forgiveness.

A crazy idea of course, the wild imaginings of an over-taxed brain. And hardly surprising. He had awoken that morning to discover his mistress dead in bed beside him and was now travelling downwards through a deserted, desecrated and pitch-black tower block to where his father-in-law was lying just as dead and even more grievously mutilated. When the lift came to a stop and the doors opened, Christian had a strong urge to stay where he was. Simply to slide to the floor and fold himself up into a ball. Anything to keep out the world and its horrors.

It was only the lift doors starting to close again that prompted him to move. He skipped forward between them, crossed the dingy foyer and emerged into the night. His first reaction was to stare at the ground around him. What with the darkness and the littered rubbish, it was difficult to know which of those shapes might be Percy's crumpled body. He tried to think back and work out which side of the building Percy had fallen from. Probably the back. He walked carefully around, bending to inspect each potentially human shape that he came to. It wouldn't do to step on him.

It had, indeed, been the back of the building. Percy lay there amid the discarded furniture and the other rubbish, easier to spot than Christian had feared. He went to him and stood looking down, grateful for the darkness that masked most of the details.

Percy had landed on his face. All that Christian could see was his

177

spread overcoat, his hands and feet and the back of his head. It was enough, though, and drove away forever his wild fantasies in which Percy had miraculously survived. The man was as dead as a doornail and, as the light of morning would doubtless show, a good deal messier.

'So,' said Christian – to himself, to the building, to the sky – 'what now?'

It all seemed monstrously unfair. He had pursued Poxy to that wretched place in the faint hope that there might yet be a way of dodging the consequences that would surely and swiftly follow once Janice's body was discovered in their hotel room. And what had happened? Not only had he failed to find a way of avoiding the blame for one death – he now found himself liable to be blamed for another. It was so unjust and cruel that he wanted to cry. Had there been any way of simply surrendering on the spot, anyone to whom he could have said yes, all right, you win, then he would have done so.

It was this feeling of self-pity and hopelessness that dominated all else. Even the thought of how grief-stricken Diane would be seemed an idle one beside the overwhelming problem of the moment. Which was – what the hell was he going to do now? He'd no intention of keeping a night-long vigil beside Percy's body; he couldn't go home; he didn't want to go to the police – there would be time enough for them to come to him.

Something of what Percy had said came back to him.

'We might be able to take care of that. I say might because it's not going to be easy. And it'll need your co-operation.'

He'd never, of course, learned just what it was that Percy had in mind. His father-in-law had inadvertently launched himself into space before he could explain. But the inference surely was that *someone else* would be roped in to help; whatever needed to be done, Percy wouldn't have been doing it alone. 'We might be able . . .' Who else was it then to whom he would have been turning for help in saving Christian?

Although he hadn't been told, Christian reckoned that he could make a good guess.

Perhaps then there was a chance after all. It wasn't a realization that was wholly welcome to him. The effort of that day – which had led only to this tragic finale – had drained his capacity for action. He was tired and frightened. Even his sense of self-preservation seemed to have all but deserted him.

178

Nevertheless, he bent over the prostrate body and patted the pockets of the coat. One gave out a faint metallic jangle. He put a hand into it and fished out a heavy bunch of keys, glad that he hadn't had to move the body in order to find them. In fact, doubting that he would have had the nerve to do so.

The keys seemed a comprehensive bunch, all shapes and sizes, covering office, home and possibly car, though that didn't matter. He had his own car: it was the office and possibly the home to which he wished to gain entry. It meant adding burglary to his list of crimes but that seemed venial alongside those with which he was already likely to be charged.

'Right then,' he said aloud, dropped the keys into his pocket, took a last glance at the black hump of Percy's body and then walked away towards the door in the fence.

Poxy's motorbike had gone. Christian pulled the door closed behind him and then, seeing a padlock on it, snapped it into place. No point risking a premature discovery of Percy's body by inquisitive vandals.

He went back to his car. A man walking his dog stared at him as he passed. He had perhaps seen him coming from the line of hoardings and would remember him later when the police asked for witnesses. It didn't seem to matter.

He drove to the office and parked on the double yellow lines outside it. The whole area, the business section of the town, was deserted.

Having at various times been entrusted with the office key, he selected it easily from the bunch that he'd taken from Percy. It turned in the lock, the door opened and he stepped inside before switching on a light. The premises were fitted with a burglar alarm but, Christian knew, it was an antiquated device that covered only the windows facing on to the street. Percy's faith had been in locks and bars and in the squat, refrigerator-size safe that sat in a corner of his office.

It was to this that Christian was making his way, first through the reception area with its balsawood models and display photographs, then through the offices with their covered drawing-boards and finally to Percy's inner sanctum for which another key would be needed. This time he tried several before getting it right. He went in, switched on the desk light and then carried it over as far as its flex would permit so that it illuminated the door of the safe, which was green with its maker's name in gold

179

across it.

The second key from the bunch that he tried caused the well-oiled mechanism to turn, and the bolts to slide back. Christian pulled open the heavy door, and the contents of the safe, with all Percy's closely-guarded secrets that they might contain, were there defenceless before him.

He scanned the shelves quickly, disappointed to find that so much was instantly recognizable. There were company cheque-books, account books, ledgers, a metal box that was unlocked and contained two hundred or so pounds in cash, three company seals, more accounts, registration documents and then, the only surprise, a half-full bottle of whisky. Christian regarded it in disbelief. Surely Percy, the committed teetotaller, hadn't been a secret tippler? More likely that he'd kept this single supply of the demon drink for those of his clients who would expect it.

On an impulse, Christian unscrewed the cap and took a swig. It was a welcome refreshment which also carried a small thrill of the sacrilegious.

And then back to business. He sorted quickly through the neat piles but found nothing that his first glance hadn't already revealed. Company records, financial accounts and the other paraphernalia of the business world. It would have been fascinating to him at any other time; now it was a bitter disappointment. He closed the safe. There was nothing there that would help him.

Without much hope, he pulled open the drawers of Percy's desk but found only current correspondence, memos, indigestion tablets and paperclips. He thought of the Drawing Room, where the plans were stored, but there were many, including himself, who had keys to that: it would have no secrets to tell.

Accepting that he had drawn a blank, he switched off the light and retraced his steps through the offices, locking doors behind him.

Out in the street, his car was waiting. He got in, started the engine and set out for what he knew was his last hope. His visit to the office had felt less like naked burglary and more like the return of an employee after hours. Now he had no choice but to raid the man's home.

The red, white, and blue floodlights, operated by time-switch, had come on in the garden of 'Beaumont'. Otherwise the bungalow, with its long windows and formidable door, showed no signs of life within or without. Christian drove through the wrought-iron gates and parked in front of it.

Now he was on less familiar ground. Were there burglar-alarms to be negotiated here or was it another locks-and-bolts job? He'd visited the bungalow in the past, of course, but only under sufferance as the unpopular son-in-law when relations between himself and Percy had soured. Certainly he hadn't been shown any alarm system – which might mean that there wasn't one but might also mean that, even then, Percy had distrusted him sufficiently to keep it from him.

He left his car door open, using its pale interior light to help him select the most likely-looking key for the door. Success was immediate. Holding his breath, Christian turned the handle and pushed it open. There was no sound. No bells or klaxons or bleepings. He breathed again, went back and closed the car door, then went into the dead man's bungalow.

More than ever he felt himself to be the common burglar, even finding a small thrill in the act of trespass. He began by switching on only the light in the inner hall, which he calculated couldn't be seen from outside, but then, after he had ventured into the lounge and hit his shins on a low coffee-table, he decided – what the hell – the owner was dead and hardly likely to return and, anyway, his own car was standing outside the front door for all to see; and so he began switching on the lights of each room as he came to it until everywhere was illuminated and he could start his search in earnest.

First the lounge. He lifted each of the brash, modernish paintings to look behind them but found only bare wall. The floral carpet was fitted and showed no sign of ever having been moved. There were bookcases, full of real books, against one wall but these were too heavy to shift.

From there he went into the dining-room, which was oak-panelled. There was a sideboard, which again couldn't be moved, and two pictures of hunting scenes, which hid nothing. The carpets stretched from wall to wall and was firmly secured. As a final check, Christian went round tapping on the oak panels but found them everywhere solid.

The kitchen and scullery displayed all the pristine cleanliness that might have been expected from a fastidious widower backed up by a daily cleaner. It was unpromising territory for Christian's search but, wanting to leave no stone unturned, he had a quick check through the cupboards and even looked inside the refrigerator. There were rows of utensils and piles of crockery, and a few items of carefully chosen food – wholemeal bread, yoghurts, prunes – under the circumstances all a rather sad testimony to Percy's concern for his own state of health.

The bedrooms, of which there were three, were more promising but, as Christian progressed from one to the next, they too seemed to have no secrets to yield. There were rows of clothes – shirts ironed, trousers newly-pressed, jackets dry-cleaned – piles of spare bedding with moth-balls and rows of polished shoes. The paintings on the walls were reproductions of French Impressionists. Christian looked behind each one but found nothing, not even dust or cobwebs.

He was becoming desperate, hurrying, no longer caring about whether he had exactly replaced the things he had moved. His elbow sent a vase in one of the bedrooms spinning to the floor where it shattered. He let the pieces lie and moved on.

The excitement of the voyeur had left him. Not only because of his failure to find what he wanted: overseeing the effects of such a life in which everything was in its place and under tight control was a depressing business. He had nowhere come across the smallest evidence of human fallibility, weakness or self-indulgence. It was like a tour through a gaudy monastery.

With nowhere else to go, he ended up in the bathroom. Here walls were tiled and bowls and mirrors polished; even the bars of soap seemed whole and unused. Without hope but so that his search should be complete, he moved the shaving mirror.

What he saw behind it made him laugh aloud with relief. It was a grey, metal square flush with the wall – the safe for which he'd been searching.

'The old bugger,' he said in admiration of the cunning that had placed it there.

And – his luck coming good at last – there was no combination to defeat him. It was a straightforward lock, for which only the right key would be needed. He fumbled with the bunch he had taken from Percy, able now to eliminate most of the keys on it, and tried first one, then another.

It was the third that opened it. He gave a sigh of relief, pulled open the small door and looked inside.

'Yes!' he said. It was a shout of triumph.

For this wasn't the well-ordered office safe with its deodorized contents fit for public scrutiny. Here were bundles of letters, envelopes, papers of all shapes and sizes, held together by elastic bands. Christian scooped them out and piled them in the wash-basin. His hands were trembling now that the chance of escape, of which he'd so nearly despaired, seemed to be before him again. All depended still on whether he was right in his guess as to what this motley collection of old papers would contain. And whom it would betray.

He sat on the side of the bath and, taking a bundle at random, pulled off the elastic band and stared eagerly at the top paper, which was a letter dated June 2nd 1968, and then at the second, and then, proceeding now with feverish haste, at the rest. As he digested the contents of each one, he let it fall to the floor so that there grew a pile of them around his feet.

'Oh great,' he muttered, weak with relief. 'Bloody marvellous!'

It was just the hidden treasure for which he'd been seeking though, like the Elephants' Graveyard or the Holy Grail, he'd had no real evidence of its existence until now that he held it in his hands.

The more he read the more he realized how damning were the contents of that shaving-mirror safe. There was material here to incriminate politicians, civil servants, public officials, councillors, the high and not-so-high throughout the land. It documented a cesspit of corruption. They were all well-and-truly in it, and Percy had clearly intended that they should never be allowed to climb out of it.

Even on a quick first reading, it was a breathtaking jigsaw that would take time and effort to build into a complete picture but whose individual pieces were damning enough. There were letters bearing the crests of Town Halls, the Ministry of Defence, the Coal Board, various Trades Unions, British Rail, Marylebone Cricket Club; others bore private addresses, and others no addresses at all; while scattered throughout was the distinctive design of House of Commons notepaper.

Generally speaking, the letters were of two types: those expressing gratitude for favours done, and those hinting that further favours would be much appreciated. Christian began to see a pattern emerging: the first, surprised, cautious reaction to a bribe perhaps unexpectedly received; then bolder expressions of gratitude for what had become regular payments; and then, bolder still, blatant demands, mentioning specific sums in return for continued preferential treatment.

The tone was polite, eager and greedy.

'. . . I find your generosity overwhelming and trust, of course, that it can be kept as a confidential matter between us . . .'

'. . . It is true that I have incurred certain expenses and am therefore grateful for your cheque. I will be happy to continue our relationship on this basis . . .'

'. . . Do let me know if I can be of further use. And just one small favour if I may? Could you please ensure that further payments are in my wife's name rather than my own? I am sure you will understand . . .'

'Just to let you know that I received the envelope. Contents much appreciated.'

'. . . I am expecting an appointment in the new Cabinet, one which I am confident will allow me to be of even more help to you than previously. Doubtless you will bear this in mind . . .'

'. . . To put it bluntly, I'm a bit short of cash. I know that I need say no more than this for you to respond with your customary generosity . . .'

'. . . I can probably swing it providing that there's enough money to oil the wheels. I'm sure you know what I mean . . .'

'Dear Percy, Your suggestion will be most acceptable providing (a) the amount is double that which you have suggested, and (b) it comes to me in cash. The Inland Revenue people are already sniffing around . . .'

The growing mound around Christian's feet provided all the evidence of human fallibility and weakness that he'd found so conspicuously absent elsewhere in the bungalow. No wonder Percy had displayed such high-handed confidence. Coming each morning to his shaving-mirror, he would have been daily reminded of the hostages he held. No wonder too that he'd been undismayed by Christian's attempts to shake him on the discovery of the Naughton Point skeletons. These bundles of papers guaranteed him the assistance of men of influence and power whenever he should snap his fingers and call for it. They would only ever escape his clutches through death. As it happened, his death rather than theirs.

Out of the mass of material with its various headings and crests that Christian allowed to float to the floor, there were odd letters that he began to put to one side.

'Dear Percy,' went a typical one, 'With this kind of majority we can do no wrong. Can I take it that payments will be on a sliding scale according to the size of the contracts landed? Best wishes, Bill.'

And more of the same, spanning the nineteen-sixties and seventies and mostly on House of Commons notepaper.

'Percy,' said another. 'I take your point about the Nottingham business. Let me have a word behind the scenes, see if we can't get round the bloody regulations. God knows, this country needs men of vision like you to be allowed to get on with things and not to be held back by petty rules and whatnot. By the way, I enclose a bill for those extensions I had done. Can I leave you to take care of it? Cheers, Bill.'

And one, interestingly, sounding a note of caution:

'. . . Such high office will, of course, only increase my ability to influence things your way. We must remember, however, that not everyone (e.g. bloody Fleet Street) would take a sympathetic view of our relationship, so can we tread carefully, especially now . . .'

Christian realized that his backside was aching and glanced at his watch.

'Christ!' he said, seeing that it was after eleven. He'd already been there for over two hours, poring over this catalogue of greed. He now needed to act. The letters had proved so absorbing as to distract him from his own predicament. It would need only one of the bodies – Janice or Percy – to be discovered and it would be too late. He'd be beyond help and all his labours would have been for nothing.

Most of the letters signed 'Bill' were on House of Commons notepaper but there were two or three, dated in the seventies, which bore a London address and, beneath it, a telephone number. Christian, moving stiffly, took them with him into the main bedroom where a telephone stood beside the bed.

He dialled the number from the letterhead and waited. The ringing at the other end went on for so long that he was about to despair of an answer when the phone was finally picked up and a woman's voice said, 'Yes?'

'Can I speak to Lord Bradshaw please?'

'No, I'm sorry, he's not available.'

'Wait!' said Christian quickly, sensing that the phone was about to descend. 'It's important. Very urgent.'

'I'm sorry,' said the woman icily. 'I've told you. Lord Bradshaw is not available.'

She was probably his wife. So he was probably in bed. Or drunk. Or . . . or anywhere.

'Listen!' said Christian desperately. 'Tell him that Percy Jordan's dead. Right? This is Christian Lewis. He knows me. I'm ringing from Percy's bungalow. He's dead and I've got to speak to Lord Bradshaw within the next five minutes. Otherwise I'll be speaking to the press.'

It was a wild threat but the best he could manage.

There was no response from the other end so Christian said, 'Tell him now. He's got five minutes. I'm at Percy's bungalow.' And he read out the number on the telephone.

'I'll tell him,' said the woman flatly. It suggested that she wasn't promising anything. And she rang off.

Christian sat on the bed and waited, willing the phone to ring. Suppose that Lord Bradshaw never got the message? Or that for some reason he was beyond caring when he did? Was there any other name that he could dig out from all that material on the bathroom floor? It would have to be someone with sufficient clout to take on the police.

The telephone rang. Christian snatched it from its cradle before the first ring was completed.

'Yes?'

'Bradshaw here. I gather you wanted a word.'

Christian's relief at hearing that familiar old voice was so overwhelming that his first response was of effusive gratitude that the man had rung back at all. Then, remembering that he was embarked on something close to blackmail, he came abruptly to the point.

'Percy Jordan's dead. I've got all his papers. And I need your help.'

'I see. What sort of help?'

Christian told him quickly about Janice in the hotel – and, God, how much longer could it be before someone became suspicious and that room was opened? – and about Percy's fall from the tower block. Also about Poxy, whose name he didn't know but whom Lord Bradshaw seemed to recognize anyway.

There was a silence after he'd told his story. Christian's spirits sank. Could anyone, even an ex-Home Secretary, have enough influence to save him from that unholy mess?

Lord Bradshaw finally spoke. 'Just one thing.'

'What?'

186

'You say that you have all Percy's papers?'

'Yes.'

'What exactly do you mean by that?'

'Letters. Going back years. Letters that you've written and other people as well. He'd kept them all. In his bungalow. And now I've got them.'

'I see. And you'll take good care of them, won't you?'

'I'll take very good care of them indeed,' promised Christian fervently, his spirits rising.

'Well then, you'd better give me some more details about this hotel and about where exactly poor old Percy is and, er . . . well, I'll see what I can do.'

20

It was Christmas Eve, time yet for the snow that the weather-forecasts had been predicting but which had tantalizingly refused to arrive. Christian, not feeling like work, had come out for a walk around the bursting shops and now, with a gold bracelet that would be a surprise extra present for Diane in his pocket, he was returning to the office in time for lunch.

A Salvation Army band was playing in the centre square and he stuffed a pound note into a collecting-tin. It was, after all, the season of goodwill and for perhaps the first time in his life he felt completely in tune with it.

'I'm back again,' he sang out as he went through reception.

'Yes, Mr Lewis,' said the girl behind the desk.

The office decorations were restricted to a Christmas tree and some bunches of holly out of respect for the recent and tragic death of the firm's founder but still there was a buzz of anticipation about the place with nobody doing much work. Christian, not caring, went through to the inner sanctum where his own name had replaced that of Percy on the door.

'Anything for me?' he called to Margaret, whom he had inherited as his secretary.

She came to the door. 'There was a call from Doctor Bellish. Can you call him back? It's about the hospice.'

'Is it,' said Christian, not keen. 'See if Mr Randall can talk to him, will you. Tell him I'm tied up.'

Margaret pursed her lips – her usual sign of disapproval – then said, 'Yes, sir,' and went out, closing the door behind her.

Christian smiled. He knew that she regarded him as a poor replacement for Percy, sloppy and easy-going after the other man's punctiliousness, but he'd no intention of seeking to emulate his father-in-law. There'd be time enough for him to prove that he had qualities of his own.

He got to his feet and crossed to the drinks' cabinet – one of his few innovations – and poured himself a sherry. Sipping at it, he thought back over the events of the last few hectic weeks.

Although Percy's Will had yet to be proved, the Chief and Principal Architects of the practice, Messrs Randall and Harper, had early on recognized the reality of the situation and had persuaded Christian – not a difficult task – to anticipate its effects by installing himself immediately in Percy's office. And, indeed, in Percy's shoes. For the Will simply and straightforwardly left everything to Diane, Percy's only child. Which meant that Christian, her husband and an experienced architect, could either ascend the throne in Percy's place or nominate one of the older men to do so in his stead. Once it was obvious to them that he had every intention of taking up the reins on his own behalf, they had bowed to the inevitable and assured him that it would be best for all concerned if he adopted his new role immediately, thus assuring continuity and stability. No one, they urged, would think the worse of him for it. Christian, after a few modest disclaimers, had allowed himself to be persuaded.

Not surprisingly, the circumstances of Percy's untimely death had attracted an amount of ghoulish interest from the public and comment in the press, all of which had been particularly distressing to Diane.

'Why would anyone want to do a thing like that?' she kept on demanding plaintively. 'Why would anyone want to kill him?'

Christian could only shake his head sadly and take her in his arms. She wouldn't, he knew, find it any consolation to be told how things might have turned out much, much worse.

Percy's body had been discovered by workmen the morning after his fall from Meynell Point, leading to some ugly speculation about the possibility of his having committed suicide. The most common theory was that he'd been overcome by remorse on recognizing the shoddy nature of his work, had gone to the top of one of the worst examples of that work, and had jumped off it.

However, even before the day was out, further developments were to suggest otherwise.

Firstly, an inquisitive neighbour, finding the door ajar, had entered a flat in Ramsden House and found the body of a young woman, a Miss Janice Telfer. She'd been strangled and left lying across her bed.

Shortly afterwards, following a flurry of police activity, it was announced that a man was helping with enquiries, a middle-aged man with a pockmarked face who'd been picked up at his house on the Sunningdale Estate. Two hours later a further bulletin stated that he'd been charged with both murders.

As if that weren't enough, the following morning brought another twist to the tale when that same man was discovered dead in his police cell. He'd hanged himself from the window bars using strips of cloth torn from his shirt. Fortunately the police had his statement, made and signed the previous night, in which he admitted both murders. In what would now remain an inexplicable outburst of violence he'd broken into the Ramsden House flat, surprised the defenceless Janice and strangled her. After which he'd gone to Percy Jordan's bungalow – a man by whom he'd apparently been employed in some obscure capacity in the past – and forced Percy at knife-point to accompany him to the top of Meynell Point where there'd been a struggle which had led to Percy's fall. No one, certainly not the coroner, could advance much in the way of motive for such a progress of mindless violence. Though no one could doubt the man's guilt either; his signed statement was produced in court, together with a flick-knife, forensic evidence that indicated that he'd been in contact with the dead woman, and a quantity of heroin taken from the house.

It was an open-and-shut case that certainly made his suicide a good deal easier to understand than his murders.

Percy's funeral was on a grand scale as befitted one of the town's leading citizens. Wreaths and expressions of regret arrived from all over the country, some from prominent figures, well-known politicians even, with whom Percy had had professional dealings. They all paid tribute to his great energy and vision, a self-made man whose legacy of fine buildings would ensure that he wouldn't be forgotten. More than anything else, it was the number and generosity of the tributes that helped Diane through the early stages of her grief.

Christian had chatted about the case with Dennis Joiner,

meeting him one evening in the squash club where he'd gone for a quiet drink.

'I must admit I think there was something fishy about that,' said Dennis, as they sat watching the ladies coming from the courts in their short skirts.

'Really?' enquired Christian.

'He wasn't interviewed by local CID you know, the chap that did it.'

'No?'

'No. They came up from London. Which makes you think, doesn't it?'

Christian waited, knowing there would be more to come.

'What I think,' said Dennis, 'is that there was something in that man's past that doesn't stand investigation.' Then, mindful of Christian's feelings, he added quickly, 'Oh, I don't mean anything to do with your father-in-law or the woman. No, I think they were just unlucky to be in the way when he went berserk. But I mean, what was it in his past that made him do that, eh?'

'I've no idea,' said Christian.

'Some of those SAS people go peculiar as they get older,' said Dennis.

Finishing his sherry in the office, Christian decided that it was time for lunch.

The first pale flakes of snow were floating downwards, saving the reputations of the weather-forecasters and brightening the dirty, winter streets of the town. Christian found himself humming 'Hark the Herald Angels Sing' as he strode through them. Coming along Market Street, he caught up with Bill Croasdale on his way to The Old Ship.

'All right, Bill?' he asked cheerily.

'Yes, thank you,' said Bill formally. Then he pointed ahead of them. 'Well, that's the end of an era anyway.'

'What is?' asked Christian, puzzled.

'Last one gone.'

And he realized that there was indeed a change to the skyline. Meynell Point, then Crag and now Fothergill had gone the way of Naughton Point and been reduced to rubble. Where once their four concrete fingers had pointed the way to a bold, new future for Gowling, there were now only the open Pennines beyond.

The two men parted company and Christian descended to the bowels of The Hermitage.